# WAS IT MURDER?

### The Murder Blog Mysteries #4

## PAMELA FROST DENNIS

## ~ *A Big Thank You to* ~

My dear friends who always
ask me how my current writing
endeavor is going.
Writing is a lonely business
and your support means so much to me.

### My Readers
Your kind comments on Amazon and
Goodreads make it all worthwhile.

### Dr. Dorothy Dink
Your wisdom and humor sustain me.

THIS BOOK IS DEDICATED TO:
My number one fan

# PROLOGUE

"Come, Charlie. Time for our walkie." The woman attached a leash to the corgi's collar and opened the front door.

Front paws planted on the threshold, Charlie sniffed the misty late night air and skittered backwards into the house.

"I know it's unseasonably chilly, dear, but nature's calling, and we must answer." She wrapped a red wool dog coat around the boy, kissed his head, then stepped out onto the slate porch and gently tugged the leash. "Come, sweetheart."

The dog plopped his rear on the floor with a beseeching look that seemed to say, *Must we?*

"The sooner we do this, the sooner we can get tucked in snug and watch our shows." She yanked on Charlie's leash, but he didn't budge. "You're not going to win, you know." She ruffled his russet neck. "If you're a good boy, I promise to give you a biscuit."

The Pembroke Welsh Corgi jumped to his feet, grinning and wagging his tail. Now eager to do his business, he scuttled over the doorstep, shoving his muzzle into the laughing woman's slender legs.

"Oh, now you're in a big rush." While Charlie pranced around the porch like a goofy puppy, she zipped her jacket and adjusted her muffler. "Brrr. It's colder than I thought." She removed fuzzy knit gloves from her pocket and pulled them on. "All right, then, Mommy's ready."

As she set her foot on the first step, Charlie scooted down the next three. She gripped the iron handrail and hauled back on the leash. "Charlie! Slow down! The steps are slippery."

The excited dog dashed to the bottom jerking his mistress forward. Her feet slid on the icy stone, and she lost her grip on the railing, plunging headfirst down the steps.

# WELCOME TO MY BLOG

I can't believe it's been over a year since I started this blog as a way to vent my anger-hostility-betrayal-rage over my divorce from Chad-the-Cad. Those of you who've been following me know that it was my best friend Samantha who encouraged me to start blogging.

Truth be told, I'm sure she was sick of listening to me whine. I can't blame her—I was sick of listening to me, too. There's only so much sympathy a person can have for another before they're fed up. Even when it's your best friend.

*A little story—please bear with me—it does have relevance.*

I used to go to this nail tech, Vanessa, (I thought acrylics would cure my nail-biting), and every time I went she'd gripe nonstop about her boyfriend. Same complaints every time.

The guy was a slob. The guy drank too much. The guy cheated on her. Wah-wah-wah.

And every time, she'd ask me what I'd do if he were my boyfriend. My answer? "Break up. The guy is a jerk."

Two weeks later, I'd be back for a nail fill and have to listen to the same old set of bellyaches, again. Vanessa didn't want advice, she wanted to moan and groan, and I was sick of listening to it. I was actually starting to feel sorry for her loser boyfriend.

Here's the thing: I can be a very sympathetic person and wholeheartedly will listen to someone's problems, and if asked, gladly give advice, but once I realize that the person has no intention of fixing their problems—in other words, they enjoy being the victim—then count me out.

When Samantha suggested I start a blog I thought it was a silly idea until she explained that it would be more like a diary where I could vent my feelings, and no one would have access unless I gave it to them. That's when it dawned on me that I'd become a "Vanessa."

Umpteen blog posts later, I'm still at it. It's become an almost daily ritual, and it sure beats going to a shrink.

*If you're wondering what happened to Vanessa...*

During my final nail appointment, she told me her boyfriend had kicked her new kitten across the room.

I said, "So you broke up with him, right?"

"No. He was really, really sorry, and he promised he'd never do it again."

I reported them to the SPCA and went back to biting my nails.

Oh, what a tangled web we weave,
when first we practice to deceive.
*—Sir Walter Scott*

# CHAPTER ONE

**Wednesday, April 8**
*Posted by Katy McKenna*

My romance with my next-door neighbor, Josh Draper, secretly A.K.A. "the Viking," (if you saw him, you'd get it—he looks like a Nordic god) has been complicated lately, to say the least.

He's a divorced, former narcotics detective. When I asked him what caused his split-up, he told me, "When you take on an assignment like that, you live and breathe it. I was hanging with lowlife scum, and after a while, the lines got blurred and eventually my wife had enough of it. Said she didn't know who I was anymore. Hell, *I* didn't know who I was anymore. After she left me, I realized I had to get out of it, so I quit. I was broken, and it took a long time to heal."

Nicole and Josh have remained good friends. She's still single and works as a paralegal at a law firm in Los Angeles, three-and-a-half hours south.

Recently, when she was diagnosed with stage four colon cancer, the first person she called was Josh, and being the good guy that he is, he immediately offered his help. She's been staying with him while she does chemo, but since her prognosis is pretty bleak, she wants to move into a nursing home. Of course, Josh won't let her do that. The guilt would kill him.

Yesterday, he had called and said we needed to talk. I'd wanted to shout, "Now's not a good time," because I was pretty sure I wouldn't like what he had to say. Instead, I had invited him over.

As a stall tactic, I offered him coffee which neither of us wanted. I took my time setting a filter in the Chemex glass vessel and filling it with dark roast. I drizzled hot water over the grounds, willing myself not to throw up in the process. Finally, I poured two cups and got the half-and-half out of the fridge.

We leaned against the tile counter clutching our warm mugs, staring at each other, waiting to see who would break the silence.

"Okay. I'm ready," I said. "Tell me what you came to say."

"I don't know how to say this without hurting you."

I tucked a tendril of hair that had escaped my ponytail behind my ear and shrugged. "That's not a good start." One of my fingernails found its way into my mouth and I nervously nibbled.

He gently pulled my hand from my mouth and held it. "I'm moving. Temporarily. To Nicole's condo in L.A. to take care of her. It's too damned hard living next door to you and not being with you every possible moment. But knowing she still loves me..." He shook his head looking so forlorn that I wanted to take him in my arms and tell him everything would be all right. "She told me if she weren't dying, she'd beg me to give our marriage another chance."

Barely able to speak, I removed my hand from his and murmured, "Would you want to do that? I mean, if she was healthy?"

"No. But how can I tell her?" He blew out a long sigh, raking his fingers through his blond hair. "Please know I'm not trying to lead her on. But it was my fault our marriage broke up, and I do still care about her. Always will."

"If she beats the cancer, then what?"

"Then we move on. She lives her life, and I live mine. Hopefully with you." Josh put his coffee on the counter, then set my cup next to his and placed my hands against his heart, gripping them tightly like a lifeline. "Katy. I can't ask you to wait for me. This could drag on for a long time, and that's not fair to you."

"I can wait."

He shook his head with a melancholy half smile. "I want you to have fun. Meet other men. With any luck, they'll make you think I'm worth waiting for."

"I already know that," I whispered.

———

Just after sunrise this morning, I hid behind the trumpet vine that drapes across the eaves on my porch and watched Josh load suitcases into his BMW sports coupe. I'm sure he knew I was there, because he paused, gazing at my porch for a long moment.

After they drove away, I spent the next hour sitting on my porch swing crying buckets. My sweet yellow Labrador, Daisy, did her best to soothe me, but to be honest, deep down inside, I was actually feeling a bit relieved—if that makes any sense.

———

My plan for the next day or two or three was to wallow in self-pity and watch weepy old movies. First pick of the day: *The Way We Were*. Robert Redford was about the same age as Josh when the film was made in 1973, and I was struck by how similar they look, although Josh is taller, his hair is shorter, and I think he's better looking.

When my mother called, I was still in my flannel pajamas

moping in the living room with a tub of mint chip ice cream in my lap. Tabitha, my gray tabby, was perched on top of the chair, one paw resting on my shoulder. Francine, my black, tan, and very gray senior dachshund rescue was tucked in next to me, and Daisy was sawing logs in a sun puddle.

I wasn't in the mood for chitchat, but I answered the phone anyway, ready to share my misery with her, but instead she shared hers with me.

"Honey, I have some sad news." Mom sounded stuffed up.

Feeling apprehensive, I set my ice cream on the side table and straightened up. "What's wrong?"

"Aunt Edith has—" She hiccupped a sob. "—passed away."

"When? What happened? She was fine when she was here for Christmas."

"I know. She wasn't sick. She had a bad fall." Mom sighed and blew her nose again. "Could happen to anyone. You just never know."

"Oh, my God. I can't believe this. How can Aunt Edith be…" I could not say "dead." "Gone? Do you want me to come over?"

"No. Your dad and I are at Mom's. She's devastated. This has hit her hard."

The shocking news made my pity-party seem so pathetic and childish. My dear, funny aunt was suddenly gone, and all I could think about was Ruby—my grandmother, and the devastating loss of her big sister. I desperately needed to wrap my arms around her and tell her how much I loved her. So, of course, I went over. How could I not?

———

Ruby is the executor for her sister's estate and will need to go to England to clear out and sell Aunt Edith's home. Mom wanted to go with her, but Pop is scheduled for a knee replacement. Several years ago, he got early retirement from the police force after taking a bullet in the knee. He offered to reschedule the surgery, but he's been putting it off for years and is in constant pain, so Ruby wouldn't hear of it. That means I'm going.

Aunt Edith had always said that under no circumstances would she want a funeral. The last time she visited, she told us that she had arranged to donate her body to forensic science. Edith said it made her happy knowing she would be doing one last good thing after she departed her old carcass, but it troubles me thinking of my great aunt's body being studied as she decomposes. She also promised me that it would be years before that happened. Instead, it had been just months.

# CHAPTER TWO

**Tuesday, April 14**
*Posted by Katy McKenna*

Friday morning I'll take the dogs over to my parents' house. Tabitha is staying home, and Mom will check on her daily.

I'm concerned about leaving Francine so soon after adopting her. When her elderly owner died, no one in the family wanted her so they dumped her in the no-kill facility. How can people do that to old pets? I hope she doesn't think I've abandoned her, too.

Friday afternoon, we fly out of our regional airport here in Santa Lucia to San Francisco, and from there we'll hop a plane for London, landing the next day at 3:50 in the afternoon. From Heathrow, we'll drive to Aunt Edith's cottage in the Cotswolds in south central England. It's about an hour and a half drive to her village—Bridleford.

Sunset is close to eight p.m., so we'll arrive long before dark. I'm the designated driver, and there is no way I'm driving through the English countryside on the wrong side of the road—on the wrong side of the car—after dark. I'll be freaked out enough in broad daylight. The only thing scarier would be my lead-foot granny behind the wheel.

# CHAPTER THREE

**Friday, April 17**

*Posted by Katy McKenna*

*Somewhere over the Atlantic*

It's still Friday for me, but according to the time change, it's Saturday. Anyway, it's late. Or early. Depends on where you are. Ruby's snoring next to me, but I'm wide awake, so time for a blog catch-up.

First off, our connecting flight in San Francisco arrived nearly two hours late due to dense fog in Seattle. That meant we'd land in London close to six p.m. That still gave us plenty of time to get to the cottage before dark, so I wasn't worried. However, I had not, in my wildest dreams, anticipated the next delay.

You may already have seen this on the news since everyone had their cell phones out, but allow me to give you my eyewitness report. An aging hippie with knee-length gray hair boarded the plane with her miniature donkey in tow. He had to weigh at least three-hundred pounds, and his last meal apparently had not agreed with him.

When the flight attendants tried to turn her away, she waved a document in their faces bellowing, "I have the right to travel with my emotional support burro, and I'll sue this airline and everyone on board if you try to stop us."

The woman proceeded to drag the farting animal through the crowded plane yelling, "Outta my way!" at everyone in her path.

In coach, she tethered the donkey to an aisle seat next to a mother traveling with her wailing curly-topped toddler. "Ed loves little kids as long as they don't touch him—then all bets are off," she warned the mother.

The frazzled mom screamed, "Get your donkey away from my baby!"

"Sorry. No can do. This is Ed's assigned seat. You might wanna tell your brat to pipe down. She's scaring Ed." The loony woman marched to business class and plopped in the seat across the aisle from us seemingly unaware of everyone pointing their phones at her.

The poor donkey was not happy, the toddler was terrified, and both were bellowing at the top of their lungs. Finally, security guards escorted the odd couple off the plane.

You can't make this stuff up.

---

The minute we hit cruising altitude we ordered wine and commenced reminiscing about Aunt Edith.

"Remember how excited Edith got at Disneyland when she found out they were building that new Star Wars land?" said Ruby.

"She was so funny. She made us pinky-swear to go with her after it opened."

"It's open now, but she'll never get to see it. You, Marybeth, Emily, and I will keep that promise for her." Ruby removed a tissue from her airline goody bag and dabbed away tears. "Oh, Katy, I miss her so. It's hard to believe my big sis is gone."

We talked, cried, and laughed until an attendant asked us to quiet down. We'd been so caught up in our mini-wake, that we'd tuned out everyone around us and lost track of time. I whispered apologies to those close by that were still awake, and within minutes Ruby conked out. A few minutes later, I felt like I should apologize again—this time for her snoring.

Tomorrow, or rather today, is going to be a long one, so I need to sign off now and read for a while. That always knocks me out.

# CHAPTER FOUR

**Saturday, April 18**
*Posted by Katy McKenna*

The plane landed at Heathrow Airport hours later than we had planned. By the time we got through customs it was dark and raining.

A shuttle bus took us to the rental car agency where we had a choice between a Fiat 500 and a Vauxhall Adam. The Fiat won because it was an automatic.

I settled behind the wheel and took my sweet time adjusting the seat and side mirrors. Truth be told, I was stalling because I terrified about driving on the wrong side of the road.

Back home, I'd downloaded a UK navigation app on my phone and loaded in Aunt Edith's address. I set the phone in the cup holder and fidgeted with it to get the screen facing me just right.

"Geez Louise. Are you ever going to start the car?" asked Ruby.

"Not if I can help it." I pulled a deep breath, then another. And another.

"You can do this," said Grandma, squeezing my arm. "I have faith in you."

"That makes one of us." I started the engine, turned on the headlights, and groped for the windshield wipers. "I can't find the damned wipers."

Ruby leaned over and turned a lever on the steering wheel. "Honey, try to calm down."

I fumbled with the gearshift knob with my clumsy left hand, then reluctantly set the car in motion. My phone told me to proceed to the highlighted route.

"What highlighted route?"

The GPS lady assumed that I could navigate the car out of the rental lot, and intuitively know what direction to turn to get on whatever-the-hell was my highlighted route.

At the parking lot exit, I took a wild guess and made a right turn onto the street, and Ruby shrieked, "You're in the wrong lane!"

"Oh, crap!" I slowed to a crawl and eased across the lane to the other side, coming to a stop at the curb. "This is horrible. I can't go any further."

"Sweetie, we've only traveled about a hundred feet," said Ruby.

"Please proceed to the highlighted route," said the bossy GPS.

"Shut up!" I yelled at the phone.

"Maybe if we go a little further down this road the GPS will tell us what to do," said Ruby.

"I looked at a map back home, and I think we're supposed to get on the M4. Or maybe it was the M40. Crud, I don't know."

Ruby squinted through the windshield. "There it is. See it? M4."

"No." I leaned over the steering wheel, peering through the water cascading over the glass. "Oh, yeah. You're right. There it is."

Holding my breath, I gently accelerated away from the curb. At the end of the block, I turned onto what appeared to be the entrance to the M4. I realized I wasn't yet on the freeway when I saw a sign that said: M4 (W) and Gatwick—with an airplane symbol next to it.

Naturally, I didn't take that turn since it would've taken us back to the airport. I took the M4 (E). By the time the GPS lady realized we weren't heading to our destination—it was too late. There was no way to get off the highway, and we were driving straight into downtown London.

On a Saturday night.

In the dark.

In the rain.

On the wrong side of the road.

"Sweetie. You need to speed up a little."

"I'm going thirty," I muttered through clenched teeth.

"That sign we passed with the red circle said the speed limit is seventy, honey."

*Don't "honey" and "sweetie" me,* I thought. *No way am I going seventy.*

Beads of sweat popped out on my forehead as I pressed the gas pedal and watched the speedometer needle creep up. "There. We're going fast. Are you happy now?"

Ruby leaned over to read the gauge. "Wow. Forty-five."

"If people don't like it, they can use the other lanes."

The GPS bitch kept nagging me to take the next exit and go back, but every exit included a multi-lane roundabout.

"No freaking way am I driving into a roundabout."

"At some point, we may not have a choice."

I ignored her and stayed the course until the road ended in a gigantic roundabout that must've had a hundred lanes with a million exits. Somehow, I wound up in the innermost lane with no clue how to escape.

"No! No! No!" I screamed. "What do I do?"

The GPS zombie had lost its mind and kept telling me to turn here, turn there, go left, go right, make a legal U-turn.

Ruby calmly said, "I think you take the next exit."

"I can't get over. Too much traffic. Oh, God. We're doomed." We zoomed around the multi-laned maze over and over, passing the exit that Ruby kept yelling to take.

I had two choices. Move away from the center of the circle or stay where I was until the car ran out of gas. I checked the gas tank and it was full, so that was not an option. I held my breath, gritted my teeth, and eased my way into the next lane. Ten minutes later, I made it to the outer lane, and Ruby shouted, "Take the next exit."

Big mistake. The exit drew us deeper into downtown London. I crawled through the dense traffic and slow-moving herds of oblivious pedestrians while police blew their whistles at us, yelling, "Move along!"

I inched along, honking the horn at everything in my path and turned into the first quiet side street I saw. The street sign said "No Parking," so I parked on the sidewalk.

"What're you doing? You can't park on the sidewalk."

I rested my forehead against the steering wheel. "I can't go any further. I'm done. D.O.N.E. Done."

"Well, *I* can't drive," said Ruby. "I can't see a damned thing at night, especially in the rain. Besides that, I'm not on the car rental or the insurance."

"I know. But there's no way we're getting to Bridleford tonight." Without lifting my forehead from the steering wheel, I pivoted my head to gaze at her. "Or ever. Because I am never driving again."

"Let's find a hotel. Then we'll have a nice, relaxing dinner." She spoke as if she were talking down a jumper off a skyscraper. "And a nice glass of wine. Won't that be nice? Then a *gooood* night's sleep. How's that sound, lovebug?"

"Pretty good, I guess." I sat up straight, biting my nails and sniveling. "But what hotel?"

A small group had gathered on the pavement to watch the crazy ladies in the tiny car. Ruby opened her window. "We're having a bit of a difficult time."

A twenty-something fellow wearing a beanie leaned his elbows on the sill to talk to us. "American, huh? You should have seen me navigating through Boston last year. Oh, my God. Dreadful."

A stylish brunette pixie joined him. "I didn't think we'd survive, but we did, and so will you, love."

"Can you suggest a decent hotel nearby?" asked Ruby.

"It's Saturday night," he said with a doubtful shrug.

"Yes, but it's not the tourist season yet," said his pretty friend. She scrolled through her phone. "Oh dear, things are looking a bit bleak. Unless you want to spend a bloody fortune. The St. Barnaby has rooms available. It's very posh, and it's close."

"Grammy. I want to spend a bloody fortune. I'll pay."

"Can you point us in the direction?" said Ruby.

The cute guy said, "We can do better than that. We'll lead you there. But you have to turn around. It's only a block away, in the other direction."

"I can't. I just can't," I said.

The woman chuckled. "Jonathan, how many times did you say that in Boston?"

The kind-hearted couple stood in the middle of the narrow lane, ready to stop any oncoming traffic while I did a three-point turn. Then we followed them as they marched down the center of the street to our final destination.

At the hotel, they pointed us to the underground parking while shouting a merry, "Cheers!"

# CHAPTER FIVE

**Sunday, April 19**
*Posted by Katy McKenna*

It was a dazzling blue-sky day, and the scenery was spectacular. Driving took every ounce of my concentration and by the time we arrived in Bridleford, I had a raging migraine.

We drove over a stone bridge, turned right, and a moment later, Ruby smacked the dashboard, pointing at a three-story stone cottage with two dormer windows jutting out of the slate roof. "There it is."

"Wow. It's so charming. Look! There's a plaque on the stone wall: Ivy Cottage. But I don't see any ivy, and I don't see a drive-way, either."

"You can't park on the street, so pull up on the sidewalk while we unload the luggage. Then you'll have to park up there." She pointed to a lane a short block ahead where several cars lined the street. "That's where Edith parked until she got rid of her car."

After wrestling the suitcases out of the vehicle, I left Ruby waiting on the sidewalk while I parked on Church Lane. I returned a few minutes later to find the luggage still sitting on the sidewalk, but no Ruby.

"I'm up here," she called from above.

I followed a gravel path that led to the slate stone staircase to Aunt Edith's front porch, then continued up the gentle slope to another cottage behind. Ruby was sitting midway on the steps looking down in the dumps. I sat next to her and wrapped my arms around her slim shoulders.

She pointed to the bottom of the steps. "When I think of her lying there, dying. All alone. In pain."

"Grammy, I doubt she felt any pain. I know from personal experience that your body's adrenaline suppresses the initial pain from an accident. The pain comes later." Even as I said it, I knew it wasn't helping. Statements like that are on par with telling a grieving person that their dearly departed is in a better place.

"If you survive," she said in a bitter tone.

"Aunt Edith wasn't alone when she died. Her dog stayed faithfully by her side." At that point, I mentally slapped myself for continuing my annoying platitudes.

She sighed. "Yes. Charlie. Such a good boy. I'm thankful the neighbors have given him a home. We should take them out to dinner, to thank them." She stood, brushing the seat of her gray pants. "The solicitor told me the key would be under the doormat. Let's go in first. We can get the luggage later."

"Aren't you worried someone might take it?"

"This is Bridleford, honey, not New York City. Nothing bad happens here."

I unlocked the Dutch door and we stepped inside. Midday sun streamed through the two paned-glass windows illuminating a layer of dust on the wooden furniture in the small living room. A basket of kindling sat by the cast iron fireplace, ready to stoke a fire. Family photos and ceramic figurines lined the deep windowsills. A wooly brown sweater covered in snags was slung over the wooden baluster at the foot of the stairs. A basket full of colorful yarns and knitting needles sat by the couch. *Harry Potter and the Deathly Hallows* lay on the coffee table next to a chipped white mug with half-an-inch of moldy tea, its rim stained with Aunt Edith's signature Revlon Fire and Ice red lipstick.

Ruby slumped into the worn maroon, chenille sofa clutching the cup. "The only person in my life who knew me as a child is gone. God, I feel so old and lonely."

I snuggled next to her. "You know you're not alone, Grammy. You have a bunch of people who love and adore you. Mom, Pop, Emily, me, Ben, your friends."

"I know that, sweetheart. But there's no one in my life now that shares my childhood memories. And...and—I loved her so. You couldn't ask for a better big sister."

Outside, a dog was barking and a feminine voice scolded, "Charlie, slow down."

"That must be the neighbor," I said. "We should say hello. Are you up to it?"

"Not really, but I don't want to be rude."

We went out to the porch and were greeted by a rosy-cheeked, curvy brunette standing at the bottom of the stairs.

"Hello. I'm Diane Morton. I live in the cottage behind you. You must be Edith's sister." She smiled brightly and chuckled. "If not, I'd better call the police!"

"Yes. I'm Edith's sister, Ruby Armstrong. It's nice to finally meet you, Diane. My sister spoke highly of you and your husband. She said she couldn't ask for nicer neighbors. And Charlie. How are you, sweet boy?"

The red and white corgi strained on his leash with a cheerful grin as Ruby stepped down the stone stairs and perched on the bottom step. "You poor baby. I'm so sorry you lost your mama."

I eased around Grandma and extended a hand to Diane. "Hi, I'm Katy. Ruby's granddaughter. Thank you for giving Charlie a home."

"No problem. We love the little fellow to bits."

I squatted to pet him and got a face full of doggy kisses. "Aren't you a little darling?"

"I'm so sorry we have to meet under such sad circumstances," said Diane. "My husband Bill and I would love to have you come to dinner this evening. I know you must be exhausted, so we'll make it an early evening."

———

The Morton's cottage was a light and airy contrast to Aunt Edith's rather dark and dreary home. White walls, beamed ceilings, a long wall of windows, and contemporary furniture, rugs, and accessories. I was drawn to a big stone fireplace with a rough, hewn wood mantel complete with a cooking pot hanging on a chain.

I ran my hand along the wood thinking about all the hands that had touched it through the centuries. "This mantel is beautiful. In fact, the whole place is so lovely it should be in a magazine." I gazed out a window at their fenced backyard. "I love the old wavy lead-paned windows."

"They're original," said Bill. "Over four hundred years old."

I'd say Bill Morton is in his late fifties. Close-cropped silver hair, tan, weathered friendly face with striking blue eyes, horn-rimmed glasses, and a nose that looks like it's been punched a few times. Diane appears a few years younger—her perfectly applied makeup probably helps—so she could be older for all I know. Short, edgy hairstyle, warm brown eyes, flawless creamy skin. They made a good-looking couple.

I got comfortable on an orange leather chair across from Diane and Ruby on the sofa, and Bill handed me a glass of white wine.

"I remembered your aunt telling us you're a vegetarian," said Bill. "So I've made a nut loaf from a recipe I found on the BBC food website."

Actually, I'm a pescatarian so I eat a little fish, but I kept that to myself. Instead, I said, "I hope you didn't go to too much trouble. Everyone always thinks they have to make me something special to replace the meat, but it isn't necessary. I eat everything else."

Diane laughed. "Don't worry about Bill. He loves to cook for company, and he's been wanting to try this recipe for a long time."

"Well, then, I know I'm gonna love it." I sipped my chilled wine. "Ooo. This is good. What is it?"

"It's a blend from Australia," said Diane.

"My wife is the wine expert," said Bill. "I don't drink. It doesn't agree with me."

Diane touched Ruby's arm. "All this talk about meat has made me think about the steak and kidney pie at the Mermaid Café at the other end of the village in the Mermaid Inn. It's delicious. You have to try it."

I had to squelch a shudder. A pie with kidneys in it. That's just not right.

Bill stood. "I better go check on things."

"May I help?" I trailed him to the kitchen. "Wow. Your kitchen is a chef's dream."

"We recently remodeled it."

"You could run a catering business in here." I stood in front of a tall refrigerator with clear glass doors revealing an organized interior, which made me think of the chaos in my fridge.

At the end of the counter, a tall rectangle about three feet wide and reaching almost to the ceiling was cut into the thick wall that backed to Aunt Edith's cottage.

"What're you doing here?" I asked.

"Going to build an inset bookcase for cookbooks and pottery," he said. "We have quite a collection."

A timer jingled and Bill said, "Time for dinner."

———

After the delectable main course, Ruby said to Bill, "I hate to spoil our lovely dinner, but you were the ones who found my sister, and I need to know about her last moments."

Diane reached across the table and squeezed Ruby's hand. "Of course you do, love."

Bill removed his glasses while exhaling a long sigh. "It was around ten-fifteen." He glanced at his wife. "Right?" She nodded. "Diane was in bed watching one of her shows on her tablet, and I was watching the telly."

"In his man cave," she said. "We converted the attic a couple years ago."

Bill continued. "Edith always took Charlie for a late night walk, so hearing her outside at that time was normal. But that night Charlie was barking nonstop. I can't say for how long because I had the volume turned up." He shrugged. "It was a play-off. Anyway, when I finally noticed, I realized he sounded frantic. I thought I'd better go down and check.

I found Edith lying at the bottom of the steps." He stopped, perhaps wondering if his narrative would be too much for my grandmother. She nodded, and he continued. "I ran back here, called an ambulance, then went upstairs to get Diane and—"

She interrupted. "—I had headphones on, so I didn't hear Charlie barking."

"I ran back to Edith and checked her pulse but couldn't find it." He paused, swallowing hard, trying to stay composed. "She was lying facedown, and I was afraid to turn her over and hurt her if she had any broken bones, but I had no choice." He cupped his calloused hand over his mouth and cleared his throat. "Sorry, this is hard. I began CPR. Diane joined me, and we continued until the paramedics arrived." He reached for his water.

Tears rolled down my grandmother's face as Diane took up the narrative. "The paramedics did everything they could to revive her, but she was gone. After they took her...away...we brought Charlie into our house." She reached down and stroked the dog, who lay by her chair. "Poor baby. You knew something terrible had happened to your mum, didn't you?"

"Do you think she suffered?" whispered Ruby.

"No, I don't," said Bill firmly. "I can't tell you how many times I've gone over this in my head. If I'd gone out the minute Charlie started barking, would it have made a difference?"

"You didn't hear him, Bill," said Diane.

"But maybe I shouldn't have taken the time to get you."

"It wouldn't have changed anything," she said.

"At least it was quick if that's any comfort to you," he said.

Ruby stood and went around the table to hug the dear man. "It is, and I'm thankful you both were with her. The thought of her lying there all night long would have made this so much worse. She had dear friends by her side, and I'm sure she knew it."

Charlie broke our somber mood by taking his leash from a basket by the front door and trotting it over to Bill.

"I guess we better not say the word W-A-L-K again." He petted the dog. "Not yet, Charlie."

Ruby returned to her seat, dabbed her eyes with a napkin, and drained her wine.

Diane refilled her glass. "What are your plans for tomorrow?"

"I imagine we'll see the solicitor, then start packing things," said Ruby. "Although I have no idea what we'll do with it all. My sister had planned to get rid of everything and start fresh when she moved to California. Anyway, I don't plan to keep anything, other than some personal mementos."

"There's going to be a jumble sale at the church on Sunday, after services. All proceeds go to the Cotswold's Food Bank."

"How far away is the church?" I asked.

"Just up the road, beyond the car parking area," said Diane. "You follow the lane; it leads to the church. There's a building next to it where they hold social functions. You can't miss it. Later this week, I can introduce you to the ladies in charge."

"I have a truck, and I'd be happy to haul things over," said Bill.

"You two are lifesavers," said Grandma. "What would we do without you?"

"I'm sure you'd manage, but we're happy to help," said Bill. "It feels good to be useful."

The talk turned to Edith's house and what we planned to do with it.

"There's an estate agency here in the village," said Bill.

"Actually, it's the only estate agency in town," said Diane.

"An estate agency? It's only a two-bedroom cottage, not a castle," said Ruby.

Diane chuckled. "It's the same thing as a real estate agency."

"We watch your *House Hunters* show," said Bill. "We're always amazed at the prices in Los Angeles and San Francisco."

"So are we," said Ruby.

Bill popped up from the table and returned with a business card for Ruby. "I had this in the desk."

"Thank you, Bill." She glanced at it. "Harrington Estate Agency. Nigel Harrington."

"I'm sure you're eager to get this all sorted. I can't begin to imagine how hard this must be for you—losing your sister, and then having to deal with all the legalities in a foreign country," he said.

"He sold us this cottage," said Diane. "He's a bit stuffy and la-de-da, but it's a business transaction not a friendship. If you don't like him, there are other agencies over in Downshampton."

"We don't have to be best friends. I'm sure he'll be fine."

"We have leftover boxes from our move here, stored out in our shed," said Bill. "I knew they'd come in handy one of these days. I'll set them by your door in the morning." He shoved away from the table and stood. "May I serve you ladies some dessert now? Apple pie with custard sauce."

"Geez, Bill. Are you trying to kill us?" I said laughing.

He grinned devilishly. "That's the plan."

# CHAPTER SIX

**Monday, April 20**
*Posted by Katy McKenna*

After a quick shower and makeup, I found some coffee in a kitchen cupboard but no coffeemaker, so I settled for a cup of tea and a couple of stale cookies.

After my "breakfast," I peeked in on Grandma. She was still sawing logs, so I donned one of Edith's warm jacket and ventured out for a stroll to see where the church hall was located. It was a chilly, foggy morning and my hands were freezing so I slipped them into the jacket pockets and discovered a half roll of butter rum Lifesavers—Edith's favorite. Filled with sweet nostalgia, I sucked on one as I passed by the church hall and continued on to the graveyard.

Most of the headstones in the cemetery were unreadable, the inscriptions worn away eons ago, but I was able to decipher a few. "1607? Why does that sound like it should mean something to me?" I dug my phone out of my pocket and googled the year. It was the year that Jamestown, Virginia was founded.

Whistling "The Star Spangled Banner," I meandered through a rickety gate that opened into a wild English garden. Beyond that I discovered a country manor surrounded by acres of emerald green grass. Not seeing a "No Trespassing" sign, I crossed the lawn to the same river that flows through the village and stood under a tree marveling at the enormous mansion.

I didn't dare venture closer since I probably was trespassing, so I returned to the cottage and found Ruby sitting on the couch watching a talk show. She held up a mug. "There's coffee on the stove. Help yourself."

"How'd you make it? I couldn't find a coffeemaker."

She followed me into the kitchen and pointed at a glass pot on the stove. "This, my child, is an old Pyrex percolator. It belonged to my parents and it makes great coffee; however, it helps to have good coffee to start with, which Edith did not since she made coffee only for company after Albert died. But beggars can't be choosers."

I checked the coffee can's expiration date. Four years ago. "Company she didn't like, it seems."

"I found some evaporated milk in the cabinet for you."

I'd never tasted percolated coffee before, and I gotta say, it wasn't bad. Can't wait to see how it is with good coffee. While I doctored my mug with milk and sugar, Ruby recited the day's agenda.

"We need to start packing. Meet with the attorneys—I mean, *solicitors*—this afternoon and then, depending on what they say..." Ruby held up the business card Diane had given her. "Call this realtor." She sighed, looking misty. "Do you remember the wild idea that Edith got while we were staying in that vacation home rental near Disneyland?"

———

*Last December*

Mom, Emily, Ruby, Aunt Edith, and I were recuperating in the living room after our first full day at Disneyland.

"Before I left Bridleford," said Edith. "I told my neighbors that I was planning to sell the cottage when I got back. They told me they would love to buy it and turn it into a bed and breakfast. Bill is retired from the military and his wife, Diane, works out of the house as a virtual bookkeeper. This would be their retirement career. Not my idea of retirement, but they're very excited about the idea. They asked if I would consider being the banker for the loan. They're lovely, reliable people, and I said I thought we could work something out. It would be nice to have a steady income flow after I move to California, and it might save me some money on taxes rather than selling it outright. The house would remain in my name until they paid it off."

"So you think the time has finally come to leave jolly old England?" said Ruby.

"I do. This fun vacation with my favorite people and the glorious weather has clinched the deal. It was bitter cold when I left home. My joints ache year-round now. It's arthritis, and it's getting difficult to give Charlie his nighttime walkies. Especially in the winter. And most days my hands hurt too much to knit." She flexed her hands. "No arthritis in sunny California. And look at me now. I'm wearing a sleeveless top. In December." She raised her arm and waggled her upper-under arm. "Although, I probably shouldn't."

Ruby lifted her arm and they compared bat wings. Aunt Edith won.

"But now, I'm having second thoughts about selling the cottage, which I know will be a big disappointment for Diane and Bill. Before I left, they showed me a brochure that Diane has been working on for the B and B."

"Why're you having second thoughts?" asked Mom.

Edith glanced around the spacious living room. "Staying here has given me an inspiration. I could turn my home into a vacation rental. Everyone is doing it these days. That way, I wouldn't be completely severing my ties to England, and I'd have that income flow I was talking about."

"And when you want to go back to visit your friends, you'll have a place to stay," I said.

"Or you could use it, you know, for a honeymoon?" she said, arching an eyebrow.

"Been there and done that," I said.

My baby sister, Emily, cleared her throat. "Hello? What about me? Maybe I'll get hitched and need a honeymoon getaway."

"Oh, honey. I'm sorry," said Edith. "I wasn't thinking. Of course you might. Are you dating anyone special?"

"No, well, I mean kind of. Or I was. It's complicated."

*At the time of this conversation, Emily had broken it off with her girl-friend, Dana. Now they're happily living together in Los Angeles and both work at Roxy Studios.*

Mom jumped in before Aunt Edith could bombard Emily with more questions. "Tell us more about your vacation rental idea."

"The cottage is paid off, so other than a few expenses, it would be positive income. And I wouldn't have to worry about what happens if my neighbors miss a payment."

"It's a wonderful idea. And you can live with me." Ruby threw her arms around her big sister. "Wouldn't it be fun?"

"Ruby, you know I adore you, but we would drive each other nuts. You're very tidy, and I'm rather sloppy. And you have your delightful boyfriend, Ben." She took her sister's hands. "What I want you to do is let me know when a suitable house comes available in your senior complex."

"I'll get right on it," said Ruby. "This is going to be so much fun. And when you're ready to move, I'll fly over and help you pack."

"Most of it we'll get rid of. It'll be new furniture and dishes, linens, everything—for my new easy, breezy life. I'm going to reinvent myself. Maybe even get blonde highlights like my little sister—and a cute boyfriend, too. I'm so excited, I don't think I'll get a wink of sleep tonight."

———

*Back to the present*

Ruby sighed. "If only I'd said, 'I'll fly back to England *with you* and help you pack.' Then Edie never would've fallen down those damned steps."

"Still so hard to believe she fell like that," I said.

"For the last couple years she'd complained quite a bit about arthritis. Maybe that's why she fell." Ruby slowly shook her head, her lips pressed tight. "Ain't no fun getting old, kiddo."

———

I set a cardboard box on the kitchen floor and opened a lower cupboard. "It was thoughtful of Bill to bring over all these boxes. Funny they didn't mention wanting to buy the house for their bed and breakfast retirement dream," I said.

"No doubt they gave up on that idea when Edith told them about turning the house into a vacation rental." Her voice quivered and she swiped a tear onto her sleeve.

"Do you think we should ask them if they still want to do the B and B thing?" I asked.

"That might seem pushy, and I don't want to deal with that, anyway." She opened a cabinet full of canned food and removed a can of Heinz Baked Beans. "Edie loved eating these on toast."

"I guess that could be good," I said. "We could try it for dinner one night, if we had some bread. We need to go to the store."

"We'll need to get beans, too. These expired three years ago."

————

We got most of the kitchen packed up, except for Aunt Edith's vintage glass percolator, which I'd like to take home if I can fit it into my suitcase, and a few mismatched dishes for our use, that we could toss when we leave.

Next, we tackled the living room. There were several colorful landscapes and still lifes on the walls that I hadn't taken time yet to closely inspect. The painter's signature surprised me. "I just realized that Aunt Edith painted these. They're very good, you know."

Ruby was wrapping a green glass vase in newspaper. "She took up painting after she retired. We'll have to ship those home. But we should give the one of Charlie to the Mortons."

————

The solicitor, a tall, big-boned redheaded woman told us that Aunt Edith's will is up-to-date with everything going to Ruby. They had a brother, but Ted died a while back—it's a long, painful story that I blogged about at the time. Bottom line—the man was pond-scum who caused a lot of pain for our family, and the world is a better place without him in it.

When the legal matters were taken care of, we decided to saunter around the shops for a while to look at stuff we don't need. After that, we popped into a Marks and Spencer Grocery store for a few things to tide us over.

————

I unscrewed the bottle of red wine that I'd purchased at the store. A full-bodied, fruity Merlot from Spain that needed to breathe. I wanted to show Ruby the grand estate I'd discovered, so I suggested a walk before dinner.

Beyond the cemetery, I opened the gate that led to the expansive lawn. "I don't know if we're allowed out here, but I really want you to see this place. It's like something out of a novel."

"Oh, we're fine. That big house is a hotel and restaurant now. The Bridleford Manor. Come on, I'll buy ya a drink in the bar."

For such a stately manor, the front entrance was a letdown. Earlier, I'd imagined a grand, sweeping marble staircase. Maybe a pool and fountain on the ground level. But it was just an old wood door.

The bar, however, did not disappoint. It were as if we'd stepped into an Agatha Christie mystery. Dark wood paneling. Warm, cozy lighting. Leather wingback chairs. We settled near the massive stone fireplace and gazed for a while at the mesmerizing flames.

I glanced around at the other patrons wondering which one could be the murderer in my Christie novel. Was it the elderly woman with the tight perm? Or the dashing playboy leaning his elbow on the long, mahogany bar? Okay, he wasn't that dashing—more like nerdy. Could it be the young couple snuggling in the corner? Perhaps it was the handsome bartender with the slicked-back black pompadour and manicured beard.

A quivery female voice coming from behind us interrupted my musings. "There's so few places where you can get a decent martini these days." Her nasal accent was very proper, like a queen on steroids. "Oh, there are still a few bars in London, but even there it's difficult. Now it's all about those froufrou drinks that they call martinis. They get this from the Americans, don't you know." She cackled derisively. "You know. The Hollywood set."

I twisted in my seat to see who was talking, but the woman's winged back chair was sideways to me so I couldn't see her face, but I got a glimpse of white hair as her head bobbed back and forth. She wore a classic black and white tweed suit and sensible shoes. Her veiny, delicate hand that held a martini sported a substantial diamond ring. I couldn't see who was in the other chairs.

"Quit gawking. It's rude," whispered Granny. "Now tell me what you saw."

I leaned close to describe the Grande Dame.

"Shush," said Ruby. "She's talking again."

"But a classic, well-made martini is impossible to find these days. All the great bartenders died years ago." She sighed as if all the world's problems rested on her shoulders.

"Ow!" said a screechy voice in a Cockney accent. "Did ya know that James Bond likes his martinis shaken, not stirred?"

"Daphne, you know I don't watch movies. Where was I? Oh yes. Gerard, the bartender here—even though he's quite young—does make a passable martini." She paused to slurp her cocktail. "When he comes by, be a good boy, and order Mummy another, won't you, dear?"

"Perhaps you've had enough, Mother," said a peeved upper-crust male voice—answering the question of who was sitting in the third chair.

Gerard approached us for our drink order. "What would you ladies like?"

Ruby gestured him close and whispered, "We'll have two white wines, but play along with us for a moment, just for fun." She pointed behind her hand at the martini snob. "Ask us again, only louder, please."

With a grin, he said, "What may I get you ladies?"

"I'm absolutely dying for a martini," said Ruby, in a bad southern accent. "I ain't had one since we left Hollywood."

"Oh? Are you in the movie business?" Gerard sounded as if he were reading a script—badly.

"Perhaps you've seen the *Mission Impossible* movies? Right now —" she lowered her voice to a level that anyone in the bar could hear—"we're scoutin' locations." She looked at me. "Do you think Tommy would like stayin' here?"

"Yup." I pressed my lips tight to squelch the giggle that was bubbling up.

"So, that martini," said Ruby. "I simply adore them with lots of maraschino cherries. And can you make it slushy? Perhaps a big glop of whipped cream?"

"Oh, my God," sputtered Martini Lady. "Americans."

# CHAPTER SEVEN

**Tuesday, April 21**

*Posted by Katy McKenna*

I never checked my messages yesterday. I'm afraid to. I keep imagining Josh sending me a text that says he's going to remarry Nicole to make her happy. Guilt can make people do crazy things.

Turns out I had several vital messages when I checked this morning.

- My prescription is ready at CVS.
- Verizon told me I'm almost out of storage. I'm always almost out of storage.
- Samantha sent a cute photo of Casey covered in mud.
- Josh: *Miss you.*

"Yeah, me, too." Now I feel like throwing up. Wish I hadn't checked my messages.

———

We spent a good part of the day packing. Books, knickknacks—all the stuff a person collects over a lifetime. It isn't fun dumping a loved one's belongings into cardboard boxes to be sold to strangers for pennies on the dollar, but it helps knowing that Aunt Edith had planned on chucking most of it before moving to California.

"What're we going to do with the furniture?" I said.

"Oh crud, I hadn't thought about that. Maybe there's a used furniture store that will come get it."

I was researching that idea online when Diane Morton dropped by.

"How's the packing going?" she asked.

"We're doing pretty good," I said. "But we've hit a stumbling block. We have no idea what to do with the furniture."

"Have you talked to the estate agent yet? He might have some thoughts."

"Oh, my God, Katy!" said Ruby. "We completely forgot to call yesterday. Thank you for reminding me, Diane."

While she made the call, I chatted with our neighbor. "At least Edith didn't have a car that we have to get rid of."

"Oh, that reminds me. She has," she paused, casting her eyes to the floor, "I mean had…" She flicked a tear from her cheek. "Edith had a bike that she rode around the village. It's in our garden shed. Want to see it?"

I followed her to the far end of their property to a ramshackle wooden shed half hidden under a blanket of ivy. On the way, she asked why I call Ruby by her given name rather than grandmother.

"I always have, although I often call her Grandma. My mother calls her Ruby half the time, too. I guess it just suits her."

"She is quite a delightful character," said Diane. She pressed a code into the padlock and swung open the double doors revealing a shiny red three-wheeler tricked out with a big shopping basket in the front, a brass horn, and a dog carrier in the back.

"Anytime you want to ride it, the code is two-four-six," she said. "I know you won't have any trouble selling the bike, so when you're ready, say the word, and I'll spread it."

We stepped out of the shed, and she locked the door. "Oh! Did you hear that someone broke into Rose Cottage last night? Perhaps broke into isn't the right term. More like, walked in. Most people around here don't lock their doors at night. Mr. Collins is an elderly man with creaky hips, so he sleeps on the sofa rather than climb the stairs to his bedroom. And he always keeps his hunting rifle close at hand, ever since the night a bear woke him up."

"There are bears here?" I shuddered, remembering that Granny and I had walked home in the dark from Bridleford Manor.

"A few years ago, a little black bear escaped from the Wildlife Refuge and walked through Mr. Collins' open back door and gave him a terrible fright, although I'm sure that cranky old man gave the poor bear a worse fright. Collins chased her out the door and shot the poor thing in the arse."

"Oh, my God. Did the bear survive?"

"She did. In fact, Edith was her veterinarian." She laughed. "What a fright Collins must have given those sneak thieves last night. You must've heard the shots."

"I was dead to the world. Did he hurt anyone?"

"No. He told Bill he chased them out and shot into the air to scare them away."

I said goodbye at her doorstep and returned to our cottage to begin the depressing task of weeding through Aunt Edith's clothes. I found Ruby upstairs standing in front of her sister's open pine wardrobes staring at the contents hanging inside. I leaned against the doorframe and watched her a moment. She sat on the bed, pulled a tissue from her sleeve, and blew her nose.

"Hey, Ruby. Doing okay?"

"I'll survive. The realtor said he'd come over within the hour so I don't know how far we'll get on this today."

We laid all the hanging clothes on her bed. One pile for the church jumble sale, one for charity, and another for the trash bin. I caught a whiff of Edith's signature perfume, Chanel No°5.

Ruby sniffed. "It's too soon for me to be doing this. When your grandpa passed, I waited over a year before clearing out his clothes; and even then, it was too soon."

I hugged her. "Why don't you go downstairs and leave this to me."

"No. That's not fair to you. Let's get it done."

After we finished with the clothes, Ruby picked up the wooden jewelry box sitting on the dresser. "Let's have a cup of coffee and go through this downstairs." She paused in the doorway, then set the box back on the dresser. "I've done enough for now. Still could go for a cup of coffee, though."

I slapped my forehead. "Darn it. I meant to get some coffee at that little market in the village."

In the kitchen, Ruby spooned the stale Tesco coffee into the filter, and set it inside the glass pot. "When it comes to a boil, we'll turn down the heat and wait until the coffee gets strong enough. About eight or nine minutes. Then let it sit a minute before we pour it."

"Are you kidding? This sure seems like a lot of work for a cup of coffee."

"And yet, you're willing to get in your car and drive three miles to Starbucks, then stand in line and wait for who-knows-how-long to order a cup of coffee."

Ten long minutes later, I filled our mugs. Just as we sat down at the dining table, someone knocked on the door.

"That's got to be the realtor. I mean *estate agent*. Nigel Harrington," said Ruby. "I need to tinkle, so will you let him in?"

I invited the silver-haired, well-dressed gent inside. "My grandmother's upstairs. I'd offer you a cup of coffee, but it's pretty bad. Would you like tea?"

"No, thank you, I'm fine." He glanced around the living room. "I'm very fond of these old stone cottages."

"Hold on a sec." I went to the foot of the stairs. "RUBY!"

"Coming," she answered.

We heard the pipes rattle as the toilet flushed.

The man removed papers from a leather satchel and spread them on the dining table. "I did a little research and found Ivy Cottage's floor plan online. Two bedrooms, semi-detached, one bathroom upstairs. The lounge area is an adequate size."

"What lounge?" I asked.

"We call it the living room," said Ruby from the foot of the stairs.

After they introduced themselves, Harrington continued with the floor plan. "The kitchen is quite small but presents well."

I glanced at the plan. Total square feet: 738 or 68.6 square meters.

"What do you think the market value is for a house like this?" asked Ruby.

"I think we can get 255,000 pounds."

"How much is that in dollars?"

"I knew you'd ask." Harrington picked up a paper and read aloud. "It's $323,467 and fifty cents at today's exchange." He eyed Ruby with an arched brow. "A tidy little sum, wouldn't you agree?"

Ruby crossed her arms. "I was thinking of selling it furnished. You know, turnkey. But I doubt anyone would want this old stuff."

"Oh, no! It's a definite plus. Yes, let's do include the furnishings. We'll call them eclectic midcentury period pieces."

I silently chuckled. *Talk about a positive spin. He must be a former used car salesman.*

He gathered his papers, shuffled them into a neat pile, and stuffed them back into his satchel. "I know you have a lot to do, but I do hope you have some time to mix some pleasure with your business." Harrington withdrew a brochure and two tickets from the side pocket of his bag. "I took the liberty of getting complimentary tickets for you, courtesy of the Harrington Estate Agency. I thought you might enjoy this. Not too many tourists know about it."

Ruby glanced at the pamphlet and the tickets, looking dubious. "A coal mine tour?"

"Yes. It's really quite fascinating. Coal mining is a big part of our history. Down the road from the mine is a delightful teashop. Have you ever had a ploughman's sandwich? If not, you must try one. It's an English tradition, and the teashop is famous for them. The date on the tickets is for tomorrow, but if that doesn't work for you…"

"This sounds fun. Let's take a break tomorrow and go do this." Ruby handed the brochure to me. "You know what they say—all work and no play makes Jack a dull boy."

"Sounds super fun," I said. *Not.*

Harrington glanced at the stack of cardboard boxes near the door.

"We're donating that stuff to the church jumble sale," I said.

"Would you ladies like some help transporting those boxes over to the church?"

I started to answer no, but Ruby beat me to it. "Yes, we'd love some help."

After a couple trips to the church hall, the agent left, and I suggested dinner at the Mermaid Café. "But first, I want to walk to that little store and get some decent coffee for breakfast. Want to come with?"

Ruby stifled a yawn. "I think I'll take a snooze, or I'll never make it to dinner." She went to the foot of the stairs and stopped. "You know, I feel like I've met Mr. Harrington before. Something about him…"

"I got that same feeling, too. But I can't imagine where."

She shrugged. "Oh well, doesn't matter. It's probably all those English shows we watch, like *Midsomer Murders*. See you when you get back."

The fresh air and soft breeze revived me as I sauntered along, stopping to admire the front yards of the cottages along the way. Just before I turned to cross over the stone bridge to the store, I noticed a cottage in desperate need of TLC. A rusty placard on the gate said, "Rose Cottage," but there was nary a rose in sight. The weeds looked healthy though. I wondered why anyone would bother breaking into a cottage that looked so run-down.

In the market—a combination of a café, gift shop, and deli—I ran into Diane in the wine section.

"Small world," I said. "I'm here to buy some coffee. Any suggestions? I like a dark roast."

She steered me to the coffee section and pointed at a bag on the top shelf. "Bill and I like this one."

"Fuzzy Buzzy," I said. "Sounds good."

"If you need something sweet, I suggest the Bakewell Tarts."

I grinned. "When do I *not* need something sweet?"

Diane led me to the counter glass display. "The owner of the shop makes them, and they are to die for."

"Would you like one, miss? They're still warm." The middle-aged woman behind the counter spoke with a lovely Jamaican accent.

"Tamila, this is Edith Halsey's grandniece," said Diane.

Her warm smile faded into sad concern. "Your aunt was a dear woman. Everyone loved her. She will be missed for many years to come." The woman shoveled several baked items into a box. "My treat."

"Well, I for one, am not going to miss your aunt," snarled a tall, bulky woman standing near the window. "She slaughtered my dear Annie during childbirth. Literally butchered her alive."

Without thinking, I moved toward the woman. Diane stepped in front of me acting like a human shield. "Margaret! How dare you!" she snapped. "You know she did everything humanly possible to save your cow. Even sprained her wrist trying to turn the calf around."

"How dare I?" She moved into Diane's personal space,

snorting a nasty laugh into her face. "We spent our life's savings on breeding Annie with a champion steer. We were planning to retire and move to Spain after we sold the calf. Instead we lost everything. Everything!" Her ruddy rosacea cheeks flushed a deeper red. "And then my husband left me, as you well know." She turned away from Diane and focused her hate-filled eyes on me, sending chills down my spine. "And that's on your aunt! All of it!"

Diane crossed her arms. "Well, it was a pretty stupid retirement plan if you ask me."

Margaret glared at her. "You of all people should be the last person to say anything."

"Margaret?" Tamila leaned her elbows on the counter. "Now you know Dr. Edith told you that Annie was too old to breed—yet you chose to risk her life."

"So shame on you," I blurted without thinking.

Margaret's bushy brows knit into an ugly scowl. I took a step back as she moved toward me, looking like she might throw a punch.

Diane grabbed my arm and ushered me out the door. "Margaret is a miserable woman. Always has been, always will be, and that's why her husband, Mark, left her. He'd had enough." We strode briskly home as she continued her story. "She's one of those people who always has to blame everyone else for her problems. She needs to see a therapist, but she never will because then she'd have to admit that she is her own worst enemy. I had an older sister just like her. Always thought we were all out to get her. Blamed everyone for her problems. Her teenaged son finally convinced her to see a psychologist, and she was diagnosed with a personality disorder."

"Did she get better then? You know, with medication or a support group?"

"No. She got mad at the doctor and never went back. She wound up committing suicide." Diane shook her head. "A sad, wasted, miserable life."

We walked in silence for a while.

As we drew near to the cottage, Diane said, "I wouldn't be at all surprised if Margaret does the same thing one day. She's all alone. No friends, no family. Another very sad, miserable life."

————

Everything on the Mermaid Café menu sounded like a gourmet's delight. I finally settled on the goat cheese and red onion tart. Ruby ordered the duck breast with a chunky orange sauce.

While we ate, I told her about my ugly confrontation with Margaret Sullivan.

She gave my hand an affectionate squeeze. "I know this isn't any fun for you. Heck of a way to spend your first visit to England."

"Don't worry about it. I'm not here to have fun. I'm here to help you."

"I feel bad that we had no time to sightsee in London. Westminster Abbey is absolutely amazing. Did you know that it has been the coronation church since one thousand-something? And the present-day church was started by Henry the Eighth?"

"No." *How would I know that?*

"Oh well. You're young, so I'm sure you'll be back someday." Ruby shoveled a forkful of braised cabbage into her mouth and chewed a few moments. "By the way. You need to call your mother tomorrow. She texted both of us that your father got through the operation fine. Didn't you see it?"

"No. I forgot to charge my phone, plus the time difference is so confusing."

"I'm the ancient one here. I'm the one who's supposed to be confused. I've earned the right. But you're still young and have most of your brain cells."

"What else did Mom say?"

"He goes home in a couple of days, and that's when the real fun begins."

"I feel bad that we're not there to help her," I said.

"Me, too. Speaking of fun, I'd like to go on that coal mine tour that Mr. Harrington told us about," said Ruby. "Just think, I'll be the only one in Shady Acres who can say they've done that."

"Yeah. Talk about making all your friends super jealous." I got my hand smacked for that.

After dinner, we were walking through the hotel lobby, and guess who was staffing the check-in desk? Nasty Margaret Sullivan. Luckily, I saw her before she saw me, and I yanked Ruby behind a pillar. "See that woman at the desk?"

She sneaked a peek around the pillar. "The one who looks like a Russian weightlifter having a bad hair day?"

"Yeah. She's the one that blames Aunt Edith for her cow's death. I don't want to have another go-round with her, so when you see her looking the other way, let's get out of here."

Ruby peeked again. "Too late. She's heading this way."

With no way out, I stepped into the open to meet the enemy. "Hello, Margaret." I threw back my shoulders. "Fancy meeting you here."

She poked me in the sternum. "I saw you hiding from me."

"Touch my granddaughter again, you old battle-ax, and you'll wish you hadn't," said my petite granny, puffing up her perky 36-Bs.

"You mean this?" Margaret jabbed me again.

I swatted her beefy hand away. "Cut it out, Margaret."

Ruby stepped between us. "Back off!"

I set my hands on Grammy's shoulders and tried to guide her away before she got punched in the nose, but she shook me off.

"My granddaughter told me what you said to her. How dare you accuse my sister of killing your cow. I remember when it happened because Edith called me. Long distance. On a landline. The call must've cost a fortune. She was heartbroken because she loved your cow—and she was also very concerned about your financial loss. And yet you blame her for all your bad decisions. How dare you?"

My turn. "It was your heartless cruelty that forced my aunt to retire long before she'd planned."

Margaret looked shaken and replied softly. "Oh, my God. I-I didn't realize."

———

I talked to Mom. Pop is hurting big time and being ornery. He's refusing to take enough pain meds to get the pain under control. Says he doesn't want to get hooked on opioids.

The orthopedic surgeon had a long talk with him about how a good recovery depends on his ability to rehab. That means controlling the pain so he can do what he is supposed to do.

I've never seen him drink more than three beers, so I don't know why he's so paranoid.

# CHAPTER EIGHT

**Thursday, April 23**
*Posted by Katy McKenna*

*Today is going to be a quiet day of R and R, because yesterday darn near killed us.*

Wednesday
*Part One*

While we were eating breakfast, Nigel Harrington called with good news. He said he might already have a buyer for the cottage. The person is a London bachelor who wants a weekend home in the Cotswolds.

After Ruby finished the call, I glanced around the dreary living room. "I can't imagine a London bachelor wanting to live here."

"Just because he's a bachelor doesn't mean he's a sexy young playboy like Hugh Grant. He could be a doddering old man."

"Hugh Grant is old enough to be my father, you know."

"Oh, whatever. Maybe the guy is looking for a cottage to flip, and that would be fine by me. I just want to be done with it as soon as possible." Ruby checked her watch. "Time to get going. Our coal mine tour is at eleven, and we don't want to be late."

*Yeah, we sure wouldn't want that.*

———

*10:45 a.m.*

In the dingy Wakeham Coal Mine office, Ruby smacked the antique bell on the counter. A moment later a trim, blond, and balding man clad in faded overalls came out from the back room. "Hello. You must be my eleven o'clock party."

"Yes. I'm Ruby Armstrong, and this is my granddaughter, Katy McKenna. We're a little early, so please don't let us rush you."

"No worries. I'm Quentin Wakeham, and I have to apologize to you." He flashed us a rueful smile. "Mathew, my cousin, accidentally took the key home last night."

"The key?" Ruby asked.

"The key to the coal mine. We keep the entry gate padlocked at all times. Can't risk any curious children going into the mine and getting lost."

I could understand that, but I had to ask the obvious question. "You only have one key?"

"It's a very old padlock, and if there ever was another key, it was lost years ago." Quentin looked chagrined. "Normally, it's not a problem, but I guess I should buy a new padlock with several keys."

"Or you could get one with a combination lock," I said. "Then you'll never lose a key."

He thumped his head. "Why didn't I think of that? A few years ago, I inherited the mine from my father, and I still haven't gotten around to changing much of anything. Usually, Mathew does the tours and I run the office so the key is the last thing on my mind." The good-looking forty-something man sighed, and I felt his frustration.

"But Mathew isn't feeling well today. I suspect his sudden illness —" he finger-quoted the word illness—"has something to do with the darts tournament at the pub last night. I played a lot back in the day but finally learned the hangover isn't worth it. The good news is, at least for me, is I'll be your guide today." Quentin glanced out the window. "There he is now. I guess we won't be running late after all."

*Oh, yay.*

His red-eyed, brown-haired cousin strolled through the door. "Hello, ladies. I hope I haven't kept you waiting (massive belch)— excuse me—long." Mathew set a rusty skeleton key and a brown lunch bag on the counter. "I was picking up a ploughman's sandwich at Helen's Tea Room when you called. Since you're doing my tour, I thought you should have it. Least I could do."

"Thanks, but what about you? This is your lunch," said Quentin.

"I'll go back and get another. Or I'll go home and take a nap." He pondered that idea a moment, stifled another burp, and nodded. "Nap, it is."

Quentin opened the bag, pulled out a delicious-looking sandwich on a crusty wheat roll, and sank his teeth into it, chewed a moment, and cocked his head, pursing his mouth. "Tastes different. They must've changed the pickle brand. Doesn't taste like Cranston's."

Mathew shrugged. "Hey, if you don't want it..."

"No, no. It's okay. Just different. They need to go back to Cranston's."

Mathew stretched, and his t-shirt rode up, revealing a white six-pack and a frizzle of tummy hair. "I'll get these lovely ladies kitted out while you finish your lunch, mate."

I wanted to abort this crazy adventure but didn't want to disappoint Ruby, so I followed Mathew to the back room. He removed two scuffed yellow helmets with headlights from a shelf and adjusted them to fit snug on our heads.

"And now the battery pack. You wear it like a purse."

We slung the pack straps crosswise over our chests with the battery hanging in back. Mathew connected the batteries to the helmets and checked the lights.

"Are you sure the battery will last the entire tour?" I asked.

"No worries. We keep them freshly charged so the LED lights will last ten–twelve hours or more."

"Is that how long the tour is?"

He chuckled at my ridiculous question. "More like an hour, an hour and a half at the most. Depends on how chatty Quentin gets. He hasn't done a tour in a while so he'll probably be very chatty." He gave us each a water bottle on a strap to hang around our necks and took two sets of kneepads from a shelf. "You'll need these, too."

"Knee pads?" I said.

"You'll do a bit of crawling."

"Crawling? You're kidding, right?" I said.

"No." He shook his shaggy head. "Not kidding. I don't want you to ruin your pants."

"Not with what jeans cost these days." Ruby slipped on the brown kneepads acting like it was no big deal. "Buck up, kid. This is gonna be a hoot."

*Oh, yeah. A hoot.* I curled my lip and shot her my long perfected fourteen-year-old eye-roll.

"There's my little darlin'." She chucked me under the chin. "I haven't seen that look in a while."

"You'll want to leave your purses here, and you won't get any cellular service in the mine so if you need to text or ring anyone, do it now," said Mathew. "You can store your things in one of the lockers under the window. But keep your sweaters. The coal mine is twelve degrees, year-round."

"Twelve?" I yelped.

"That's Celsius. Sorry about that. Fifty-six degrees Fahrenheit."

Whenever the temperature dips into the fifties in Santa Lucia, you'll see people bundled up in down parkas and mufflers. Ruby and I were going to freeze to death in the coal mine.

"We'll be fine, honey," said Ruby. "The helmets will help keep us warm."

We returned to the front office just as Quentin hurled his crumpled lunch bag into the garbage can. After he grabbed his gear, we left the building and trudged along a dirt trail to the mine. The path gradually dipped down into dug-out earth that was held in place with stacked stone walls, covered in ivy. Up ahead, a medieval-looking wrought iron gate welcomed us with a weathered, hand-painted "Keep Out – Danger" sign hung on it.

Ruby sensed my growing trepidation and poked me in the back. "Sweetie, if it were dangerous, they wouldn't do this."

Quentin inserted the skeleton key into a large rusty padlock that had probably done dungeon duty back in the day. A squeaky turn of the key and he yanked open the lock. Once we were inside the cave of doom, he relocked the padlock, slipped the key into his quilted vest pocket, and flipped on a string of lights that cast a gloomy glow down one of the four passages.

To perk up my sour mood, he said, "Your helmets can withstand tons of impact per square inch. An anvil could land on your head and your helmet will not crack. The LED lamp has two power settings. One press for main lighting and two for emergencies."

"And, uh, exactly what would be an emergency?" I said.

He snickered. "There won't be any, because we're no longer a working mine. Turn on your helmet lights now and let's get going."

Our bright LEDs should have boosted my spirits, but seeing the rough walls lined with timbers did the opposite. We followed Quentin down the damp trail, sliding our hands along a rusty pipe handrail. I didn't pay much attention to the "scenery" as we turned down one passageway and then another until my helmet clunked against the rocky ceiling and I had to bend at the waist.

Onward we marched and soon I was bent at a ninety-degree angle at the waist. It wasn't long before I was bending my knees too.

Being five-foot-ten, it wasn't my idea of fun, but since my seventy-five-year-old grandmother was cheerfully chattering with our guide, I kept my lips zipped.

When we reached the point where we were crawling on all fours, Quentin said, "How're you holding up?"

My lower lumbar and knees were screaming for a handful of ibuprofens and an ice pack, but I grinned like the trooper I'm not and gave him a thumbs-up. "Doing great, but how much further are we going? This has got to be getting difficult for my grandmother."

Ruby was probably doing fine because she religiously does yoga, Pilates, Zumba, and pole dancing for sassy seniors.

"I'm doing all right for the moment," she said. "Although crawling is not something I can keep up for very long on these bony old knees of mine. Even with kneepads."

"Neither can I," said Quentin in a congenial tone. "Just a little further. I know it seems like we've been walking for a long time, but it's been less than fifteen minutes."

*Fifteen miserable minutes out of my life that I'll never get back.*

Shortly after, he stopped and told us to get comfortable. Usually in a place like that, I would have laughed at his statement, but once I was sitting cross-legged against the jagged wall, the burning pain in my lower lumbar let up, and I actually felt pretty good. Quentin shimmied up a low ledge a few feet away and turned around to face us. Lying on the shelf were a pickaxe, a hammer, a wedge, and a bucket that once contained blasting powder.

He tapped the rock surface and held out a shard for us to inspect. "Coal, or as we like to call it, fuel." Quentin offered his hammer and wedge. "Would you like to take a turn, Katy?"

"Age before beauty." Ruby grabbed the tool, hunkered down, and took a hard whack at the wall. A small chip dropped to the ground. She picked it up and held out her hand proudly. "Not bad for my first try, eh?"

Quentin peered at it. "It'd be even better if it was coal."

"Oh, fiddlesticks. Let me try again." Ruby went back to hammering the rocks.

"Have either of you ever experienced total darkness?" asked our guide.

"Sure," I said. "Camping in the woods on a moonless night. Boy is that dark."

He laughed. "In other words, no. Now, turn off your head-lamps and prepare for complete and utter absence of all light."

We all pressed our buttons and Quentin turned off the lights lining the shaft, pitching us into an inky, black void of nothingness.

"Oh my God," I gasped.

"This is what darkness truly is," he said.

"Okey-dokey," said Ruby. "Time to turn the lights back on."

We pressed our helmet buttons, and the sudden flare of the bright LED lights was almost blinding. Quentin reached to flip on the shaft lights, but they didn't respond. He flicked the switch several times. "That's odd. There must be a short. That's never happened before. Oh, well. No worries. Our headlampth will see uth thafely home." He looked perplexed. "My tongue feelth thwollen."

"Do you feel okay?" I asked, pointing my light at his face. "You don't look so good."

"Huh?"

Ruby aimed her light at Quentin, too. "Katy asked if you feel all right."

"My tongue ith numb. I'm thorry, but we better go back." He slid off the ledge, and we crawled up the trail with our guide in the lead.

After the first turn, we were able to stand on our feet, walking ape-style. Quentin stumbled, lost his footing, and grabbed for the handrail, missed it, and fell to the ground. He rolled up to a sitting position clutching his chest, his eyes squeezed shut. "Woo. That hurts."

Ruby and I squatted next to him. "What's wrong?"

He opened his eyes, his gray face contorted in pain. "I dunno. Maybe heartburn. Maybe..." He gestured me away, but before I could move, I caught a spew of hot vomit on my thighs.

"That's pretty intense for heartburn." Ruby leaned over him feeling his forehead. Her headlamp illuminated his ashen face. "You look terrible."

"Do you think it's a heart attack?" I whispered in her ear.

"I don't know," she answered. "Could be."

"Quentin, do you want some water?" I asked.

"Yeth." He exhaled a huff and blinked at me. "You're all blurry."

I held my water bottle to his lips, and his body started jerking. I screamed, spilling most of the water on his vest.

Ruby shouted, "Move out of the way. He's having a seizure."

"Oh, my God. What do we do?"

"There's nothing we can do. Just give him room."

This was my first experience with a convulsion, and I thought he was dying. It was hard to watch him writhing and do nothing to help. When it finally subsided, Quentin lay still, eyes closed.

"Wake up," shouted Ruby, shaking his limp shoulders. "Come on! Wake up." She felt his neck for a pulse, moving her fingers several times before she said, "There's a pulse, but it's weak."

"Should you do CPR?"

For several years now, my grandmother has taken a yearly refresher CPR course at the senior center. The catalyst for this was watching a friend die from a heart attack at a bingo game.

"He's breathing, so no." She glanced at me, her face grave. "Katy, I don't know what to do."

"We need to get help."

She pulled her cell phone out of her back pocket and glanced at the screen.

"You brought your phone? I thought you left it in the locker."

"I was going to take pictures. Unfortunately, Mathew was right. There's no reception down here." She slipped it back in her pocket. "One of us needs to stay with him." Ruby reached for my hand, squeezing it. "Honey. I have to be the one who stays. In case his heart stops. Plus, you have a better chance of finding your way out of here than I do. Do you think you can do it?"

"I can't leave you behind, Grandma. What if I take a wrong turn and get lost? Then no one will know you're down here with him."

"That's not going to happen. And even if you do get lost, it won't be long before someone starts wondering where Quentin is. Plus, our car is in the parking lot so Mathew will come looking for us."

"But he went home. He wasn't feeling good, remember?"

She sighed. "Okay, worst-case scenario, we're stuck here until tomorrow."

"What if they're both sick with the same thing?" I said. "You know, like maybe this is a really intense killer flu. Mathew could be unconscious, too. Then no one will be looking for us."

"Mathew has a hangover. That's all." She aimed her helmet light at our guide's comatose face. "You need to get going, Katy."

I knew she was right, but I was terrified. One—to be alone in the coal mine, and two—to leave her alone.

She read my mind. "Sweetheart, I know you're scared. Who wouldn't be? But all you have to do is follow the railing. It'll take you straight to the mine entrance, so there's no possible way you can get lost."

"You're right." I kissed her cheek. "I love you."

"And I love you, too." She patted my cheek. "Next thing you know, we'll be enjoying one of those ploughman's sandwiches and a cup of coffee at that tea room, right?"

"Right."

"No, make that a beer for me. Coffee for you since you're the designated driver." She gave me an impish grin that was meant to buoy my flat-lined spirits.

I stood up to a ninety-degree bend at the waist under the low rock ceiling and aimed my nose forward. The bright beam from my LED hardhat lit the tunnel ahead. I placed my hand on the pipe rail, inhaled a deep breath of dusty, dank air, and started marching. After counting fifty steps, I glanced back.

"Keep going, sweetheart. I'm fine," Ruby called. "You can do this! You're a tough, resilient woman whom I'm proud to call my granddaughter."

# CHAPTER NINE

**Thursday, April 23**
*Posted by Katy McKenna*

Wednesday
*Part Two*

Once I was out of Ruby's view, I hunkered down to do some yoga breathing and chew on my nails. It's a good thing I never took up smoking—I'd probably be a chain smoker. I was totally freaked out and hoped a good dose of oxygen would help me get a grip.

"Why couldn't we have gone to a damned castle like normal people? Or a museum. Anything but a coal mine. Who does that? Okay, breathe, Katy. Just breathe." I inhaled one more long breath, pulling it deep into my lungs, then slowly exhaled and didn't feel one bit calmer.

I set my hand on the railing and resumed my journey. Minutes later, my feet skidded on loose rocks, and I pitched forward, slamming my chin into the ground, shredding my palms, knocking off my helmet, and scaring the you-know-what out of me. I rolled over into a sitting position and took stock of the damages. My scraped chin and bloody hands were stinging like crazy, but nothing was broken.

I strapped the helmet back on and continued at a snail's pace, aiming my light beam in front of my feet to avoid further spills. Gripping the rail with my sore hand was difficult, but no way was I letting go.

There was an open area at the end of the passage, and the ceiling was high enough that I could stand erect. After stretching the kinks out of my back, I surveyed my surroundings. There were four tunnels now. Three had handrails, and not one had an exit sign. Who doesn't put an exit sign in a coal mine?

"Oh God, which tunnel do I take?" I went to the closest one and peered inside. Rocky walls supported by heavy timbers. Ditto for numbers two and three. There had to be something that would indicate which passage to take. I turned in a slow circle. "Wait! The tunnel will lead up, not down."

I entered the nearest one and about twenty feet in it began to descend. "Okay, not this one. Let's try tunnel number two."

I got lucky. The trail headed uphill. I felt confident that I would soon be outside in the fresh air. About a hundred steps further, my headlamp was dimmed.

"Oh, hell no. Are you kidding me?" Afraid to touch the on-off button, I knocked on the helmet, hoping that would joggle any loose connections. It did not. "No, no, no. You cannot go out." I upped my pace knowing I had to beat the dying light. "I thought he said the battery pack would last for at least ten hours. It's only been like two or three hours at the most. Probably way less. Maybe the bulb is burning out. No! It's an LED. They're supposed to last forever."

I pressed the button once, to the high emergency level, but the light continued fading like a candle slowly burning down. My hand clinging to the rusty railing for dear life, I tried to hasten my pace, but it was impossible to see more than a few feet ahead in the feeble glow.

Minutes later, the light went dead. I stood rooted to the spot, terrified to take another step. My claustrophobia kicked in, and I felt faint. I slinked down, wrapped my arms around my knees, and squeezed my eyes shut. I wanted my mommy. My daddy. My sweet Daisy. But at that moment, most of all, I wanted Josh to save me. But he was thousands of miles away saving his ex-wife. My despair bottomed out and I sobbed, rocking on my heels. And then a weird thing happened. Trapped in the black bowels of the earth, I finally acknowledged my rage at Josh for leaving me—something I could not do in the cold light of day—because it was selfish. He was doing the right thing, and how dare I fault him for that? But in that moment, I hated him for that.

My sudden fury ignited my adrenaline. I jumped to my feet, turned to face the wall, and ran my fingers up and down searching for the rail. Had I got turned around without realizing it? With arms flailing, I took baby steps searching for the other side of the tunnel.

"Oh, God! Where's the damned wall?" I thought I'd been walking straight from one wall to the other, but maybe I was moving at an angle. I inched along, and finally my hands slapped against craggy, damp rocks. I worked my fingers down and connected with the cold, crusty metal rail.

It was time to start moving again. But which way? "Up. I need to be going up." I reached up and felt the craggy ceiling inches from my head. I took a few tentative steps, but it was impossible to tell if I was going up or down.

I remembered it hadn't been steep when walking down the shaft, more like a long gradual downhill trek. After several steps, it dawned on me that when I was walking into the shaft, my right hand had been on the railing; therefore, walking out, my left hand should be on the railing. Feeling brilliant, I clutched the bar as I turned around and grabbed it with my left hand.

Keeping my right hand outstretched, I slid one foot forward, then the other, always maintaining contact with the ground. At this sloth-pace, the sun would be long gone before I made it to the entrance. The only sounds I heard were the scuffle of my shoes dragging over the rocky floor and the echo of dripping water. Eventually, I felt a soft wisp of fresh air kiss my face. Gazing ahead, I could perceive a lighter shade of dark.

# CHAPTER TEN

**Thursday, April 23**
*Posted by Katy McKenna*

*Tired of typing but want to get it all down while it's still fresh in my mind.*

Wednesday
*Part Three*

Guess what I'd forgotten? The key to the gate—safely tucked away in Quentin's vest pocket.

I flung my helmet to the ground and sank to my knees, gripping the gate rails, unable to hold back the waterworks. Now what was I going to do?

If this had been a movie, I would've plucked the one bobby pin securing my sexy up-do, releasing my silky auburn locks into cascading waves down my back, and with a sassy toss of my head, reached through the railing and picked the lock open in three seconds. But I don't own a bobby pin, and the last time I picked a lock, I had a kitchen full of gadgets to try, and it still took over an hour and several YouTube how-to videos to do it.

I rattled the gate rails while screaming a steady stream of "Help!" After several minutes, I was hoarse, and my screams were pretty feeble.

Then I got an idea. I could break the padlock with a rock. I found a good candidate, and slipped my hand through the rails, leveraging myself into a position to commence hammering. One good, hard whack and the rock cracked in half.

No other brilliant ideas were popping into my head, so I grabbed another stone and went back to banging on the lock until it felt like my hand would fall off.

"Meow."

An orange tabby cat jumped down from the stacked stone wall outside the mine entrance, and meandered to the gate like she or he had all the time in the world. I slipped my hands through to pet her. "Hey, kiddo. How're you doing?"

She purred and shoved her head against my hands.

"Hey, sweet kitty. Why can't you be Lassie and go tell someone that Katy is trapped in the mine?" I stood and stretched my sore body. "I need to get back to work, so you better scoot out of the way. You don't need me dropping a rock on your head."

Lassie didn't mind me and continued nuzzling the rusty gate while I pummeled the lock. After several blows, the cat moved a safe distance and watched me work. About a hundred whacks later, I'd managed to knock off the little metal flap that covered the keyhole, but it didn't look like the stubborn old relic would break apart anytime soon.

It was time for a new plan of attack. I held the lock with my left hand while I pounded the rock on the spot where the shackle connected into the padlock body. More often than not, I wound up hitting my fingers.

"Ouch. Ooh. Ouch." That's not really what I was yelling, but I need to keep the expletives to a minimum because my mother reads my blog.

Finally, I felt the lock give way a fraction. "Okay, Lassie. I'm going for it. Bloody fingers be damned!"

I yelled, "One!" And gave it a hard whack. "Two! OW! Three! Oh, that really hurts. Four! I can't keep doing this! Five! Holy crap! Six! I'm dying here!"

Lassie took pity on me and returned to the gate, mewling sympathetic kitty words.

I squatted to eye-level and petted her. "You're a nice cat, aren't you?"

"LOLA? LOLA? Where are you, you naughty kitten?" called a feminine voice from somewhere beyond a dense grove of fir trees. "Time for tea, love."

I cupped Lassie's chin. "Is that your mama?" Whether it was or wasn't, that woman was going to be my salvation. "Lola's over here!" I hollered. "At the coal mine gate!"

"Lo-laaaa!" The woman was moving further away. "Looo-laaaa."

The cat started up the path heading toward the trees.

"No, no. Come back, Lola," I cried. "*Pleeaase?* Come on, nice kitty, kitty, kitty."

She glanced back as if to say, *Sorry, love, but it's my tea time.* And with that, the bitch bolted.

I hollered, "Help" several more times, but my feline salvation was long gone. Resting my head against the bars, I wondered how Ruby and Quentin were faring. I knew I wasn't going to die there, nor was Ruby, but I wasn't so sure about Quentin. He needed medical help, and I was the only one who could make that happen.

"This is such a stupid, stupid day. Stupid England. Stupid coal mine tour. Stupid Ruby for wanting to do this, and stupid me for agreeing. Everything is just plain stupid."

And that made me think of Samantha's little boy Casey. Whenever I say the "stupid" word (which is often), he always solemnly says, "Aunt Katy. Stupid is a bad word."

And I say, "No, it's not, Casey. It's only a bad word if you're calling someone stupid. But sometimes we do stupid things. And sometimes the only word that can describe what we did is the word stupid."

The last time we had this little conversation, Casey solemnly ended it with, "Shit is a bad word, too."

That sweet memory boosted my spirits, and I was ready to get back to work. I slid my hands through the bars, grabbed the wretched padlock, and gave it a good, hard shake. And it popped open. Not kidding. It was just like that.

Fearing I might accidentally re-lock it, I oh-so-carefully lifted the lock off the gate latch, flung it aside and pushed the gate. It didn't budge. I leaned my shoulder against it and gave it a mighty shove, and it creaked forward about two inches.

"What the hell? This day keeps getting better and better."

I planted my feet and rammed my back into the gate with all my might, and it gave up about three inches. When I pulled away, it swung back at me, opening wide with a pissed-off screech.

Talk about feeling stupid.

———

Of course, the coal mine office door was locked. I sprinted to the back of the building and found another locked door. Back at the front porch, I tried opening the sash window with no luck. I was about to hurl a rock through it when I became aware of cars zipping by on the two-lane street.

I dashed to the road and waved at passing vehicles yelling, "Help!"

When the umpteenth car zooming toward me actually acceler- ated, I screamed at the jerk, "Are you kidding me? What part of

HELP do you not understand?" The driver's answer was to flip me the bird.

I returned to the office and pitched a rock through the window. The glass fell away in large shards—obviously not safety glass. I used another stone to scrape away the remaining fragments from the frame, then dragged a porch bench to the opening and climbed through.

An old-school black phone sat on the oak desk behind the counter. I picked up the heavy receiver, heard a dial tone, stuck my index finger in the "zero" hole on the dial, spun it around to the metal finger-stop—and got nothing.

"How can zero not get you an operator? Isn't zero like the international number for the operator?" I dialed 9-1-1 with no luck, then tried several random numbers thinking something would go through to somebody out there, but no. I pumped the little buttons in the receiver cradle like people do in old movies. They always yell, "Operator? Operator? Get me the police!" But no operator answered.

My purse was in a locker for safekeeping, and Ruby had the key. I figured there must be a backup key, so I rummaged through the desk drawers, and while I didn't find locker keys, I did find a key for the old truck parked outside.

I climbed into the dusty, green little Morris Minor sinking low on the broken, ripped leather seat, and jammed the key into the ignition, turned it, and nothing happened. I tried again and then realized it was a manual transmission.

Ruby drives a stick; I do not. She tried to teach me when I was a teenager, and after one lesson, gave up on me. She feared I would strip the gears on her red 1964 Triumph Spitfire. I reached into my hazy memory bank trying to recall what she'd taught me.

"It has to be in neutral." I fluttered the gearshift, and it felt neutral to me. "And I have to pull the choke thingie out." I pulled out the black knob, and turned the key. Nothing happened. "The battery must be dead." I noticed another black knob with an "S" on it. I pulled it, and the engine started.

"Something about that other pedal—the clutch pedal. I'm supposed to press it down when I shift gears."

After several fails, I screeched the truck into first gear and lurched out of the parking lot. On the road now, I was still in first, and the engine was begging me to shift.

The poor motor shrieked in agony as I drove as fast as I could to the teashop. In the parking area, I slammed on the brake to avoid a car backing out and killed the engine. I left the truck where it died and ran into the restaurant yelling, "I need help."

A pale, sweet-looking teenager behind the counter backed up against the wall looking like she thought I was an ax murderer. I glanced around at several wide-eyed patrons gawking at me.

"I said I need help! My grandmother's trapped in the coal mine." Even I realized how absurd that sounded.

The swinging door near the counter squeaked open and a young woman poked her curly head out. "Everything all right, Tessa?"

"No. Everything is not all right," I snapped.

As soon as I said that I caught sight of myself in the gilded mirror hanging on the wall behind her. Dirty, sweaty face; bleeding chin; hair in a tangled, dusty mess; bloody hands, filthy clothes. No wonder everyone was acting like I was an escapee from the loony bin.

The kitchen girl stepped to Tessa's side, looking ready to take me down if I didn't quiet down.

I attempted a serene NPR tone. "Tessa. I need help. Our coal mine tour guide, Quentin, got sick while we were on a tour and…"

"Quentin Wakeham?" said Tessa. "He never leads tours. That's Mathew's job."

"Well, today he led the tour, and he's very sick. My grandma's with him down in the mine."

"You're an American, right?" hollered a whiskery old geezer at a back table. "Americans are always so bloody excited. Everything's an emergency. Hurry, hurry, hurry."

An ample-figured woman in a yellow dress stood up, holding a cell phone. "Never mind Angus. He doesn't like women."

"Bollocks," he growled. "I liked Margaret Thatcher."

"I'm calling the police," she said. "They'll alert the fire department."

After she made the call, she came to my side. "I'll take you back and wait with you. Shouldn't be long." The motherly woman turned to the plump girl standing next to Tessa. "Wendy, give..." she paused. "What's your name, dear?"

"Katy."

"Give Katy a takeaway cup of tea. Lots of sugar, I think. Lemon or milk?"

I didn't want tea, but I said, "Milk."

"And a few biscuits."

"I don't have any money. My purse is locked up in the coal mine office."

"Never mind about that, love. I own the shop. My name is Helen. Tessa is my daughter."

"Thank you, Helen. You're the first bright spot in this perfectly awful day."

"Give your key to Tessa," said Helen. "She'll park the truck for you."

"The key's still in it. It's a stick shift."

"Not a problem," said the girl, looking less sure than her statement.

"Thank you, Tessa. I'm sorry I yelled at you."

Tears welled in her big, brown eyes. "It's okay. I'll pray for Quentin and your grandmother."

Wendy handed me the tea and a bag of biscuits, and Helen took my arm and guided me to her little blue car. Just as we were leaving the lot, a police car, an ambulance, and a fire engine whizzed by, sirens screaming and lights flashing.

In the Wakeham parking lot, Helen stayed by my side while I spoke with the fire captain. After about a zillion questions, I lost my cool. "Captain Taylor, we're wasting time. Quentin could be dying."

The burly captain ignored me and asked the firefighters and paramedics if anyone had ever been in the mine.

An older man said, "About ten years ago before you were here, we did a rescue training in there, sir. I'm the only one left that did it. There's a lot of mine shafts..."

The captain turned to me. "We need to get this Mathew you spoke of out here to lead us in there."

I wanted to stamp my foot and scream like a toddler, but I kept my cool. "I already told you he went home sick."

"Do you know his last name?"

Lips pressed tightly, I shook my head.

A fire fighter spoke up. "I do. He's a friend of a friend. Mathew Miller."

"Call your friend and get this guy's number."

"Calling him now." A pause. "Sorry, sir. It's gone to voicemail."

"You don't need him," I muttered through gritted teeth. "I can lead you to them right now."

"We can't risk endangering you, ma'am."

"Somehow I managed to get out of the mine with no light. Not even a key to unlock the padlock." I displayed my shredded hand for emphasis. "So going back in with all of you will be pretty darn safe, I think."

"Sorry, ma'am," said the captain. "I don't know how you do it in the States, but this is how we do it here."

"If you're worried about a lawsuit, I promise I won't sue. But I'm not standing here doing nothing." I started marching toward the mine entrance, yelling over my shoulder, "Anybody got a flashlight I can use?"

"Make that two flashlights." Helen scurried to catch up with me. "I'm going too. Since you're all so intent on doing nothing, why don't you go have a nice cup of tea at my shop down the road? My treat."

That seemed to light a fire under the captain. "All right, people. Let's move."

At the open gate, Helen took my hand. "Katy, now that you have proper escorts, I think I'll wait for you here. I've managed not to set foot in this coal mine my entire life, and I'd rather keep it that way."

I hugged the dear lady. "Thank you. You've been a godsend."

Inside the mine, the captain said, "We'll take it from here. Ms. McKenna, show us which shaft to follow and then go outside and wait with your friend."

I shook my head. "Unh, uh. I'm worried about my grand-mother, so I'm going."

He crossed his beefy arms, looking surly. "Which. Shaft. Is. It?"

I crossed my scrawny arms and scowled back at him. "Not telling you until I have a flashlight and a helmet."

Taylor looked like he wanted to strangle me, but instead he turned his back on me and barked at his crew, "Somebody get this woman a helmet and a flashlight."

When I was ready to go, I pointed to the correct shaft and was immediately sent to the rear of the line. It annoyed me, but at least I wasn't kicked out. We trudged along until we arrived in the vast open chamber with the four shafts leading off in different directions.

"Now where, Ms. McKenna?" snapped the captain.

Rather than answer, I edged my way to the front of the group and led them into the correct tunnel.

When we got to the point where we were crawling on all fours, the captain, who was nipping at my heels, growled, "Miss McKenna. Are you sure this is the right shaft?"

"Positive, and I think we're very close now." I glanced ahead. "Look! There's a faint glow of light." I cupped my hands and hollered, "Ruby! Ruby!"

"Well it's about damned time!" echoed back at us.

We found her sitting cross-legged, her face illuminated by her cell phone. The paramedics went into rescue mode with Quentin.

"Pretty sure he's dead," Ruby said grimly as they checked his vital signs.

"He was breathing when I left you," I said.

"That was nearly three hours ago. Where the hell have you been?"

"I went for a nice cuppa tea." I peeked at the phone screen. "You're playing solitaire?"

"I thought it was appropriate given the circumstance."

# CHAPTER ELEVEN

**Thursday, April 23**

*Guest Posted by Ruby Armstrong*

*Katy asked me to write about what happened after she left her poor, old decrepit grandmother alone in the mineshaft with Quentin. This will be short because my carpal tunnel is killing me.*

Wednesday
*Part Four*

Watching my granddaughter walk away into the dark tunnel was awful. By staying behind with Quentin, I felt like I was abandoning her. But how could I leave him?

Quentin hadn't moved since his seizure, and his breathing was so shallow it was nearly impossible to detect. I tried to rouse him several times but yelling and shaking him did nothing. About thirty minutes after Katy left, he gasped and I nearly jumped out of my skin. His eyelids fluttered as he exhaled a long shuddering breath, and then nothing. He stopped breathing and I couldn't find a pulse. I immediately went into aggressive resuscitation mode and administered CPR. I've only done this on practice dummies, but I knew that every second counted.

It wasn't long before my right shoulder and arm started killing me. A bad mix of arthritis, carpal tunnel, and old age. I continued CPR until the pain was unbearable and I could not push anymore. Clearly, the poor man had died when he expelled that last gasp, and no amount of chest compressions would bring him back from the other side.

I said to Quentin, "I'm so sorry, but I have to accept the fact that you're gone and my continuing to do this to your body is probably annoying you. So, my friend, it's time to fly with the angels." I closed his eyes, and when they popped open again, I gently turned his face away from me.

I set his helmet on the ground facing down the shaft. A beacon of light in the darkness for my rescuers. I turned mine off to save the battery and settled my aching bones against the rocky wall.

It had been at least two hours since Katy left and I was terrified that she could be lying somewhere, injured or unconscious. I wondered if I should continue to wait or leave. After deliberating the pros and cons, I was about to venture forth, when I heard Katy calling, "Ruby! Ruby!"

I didn't want her to know how terrified I'd been, so I yelled, "Well, it's about damned time," and quickly snatched up my cell phone and pretended to play solitaire.

# CHAPTER TWELVE

**April 23**
*Posted by Katy McKenna*

Wednesday
*Part Five*

After going through the chain of events with the police at the coal mine, Ruby and I were allowed to leave. However, we were told that we might be needed for more questioning, which I took to mean, *don't leave town.*

We won't know the cause of Quentin's death until after an autopsy has been performed. Unless it makes front page news, that means Ruby and I will never know. Up until he collapsed, Quentin seemed healthy, so I think it had to be a heart attack. A few years ago, one of Samantha's cousins died while running a 10K. Just keeled over. Heart attack at age twenty-six. The guy was in the Coast Guard and a health fanatic. No dairy, no gluten, no caffeine, no sugar, no salt, no fun. Never smoked, didn't drink. Worked out daily. Makes you think.

———

My plan for the evening was to take a long, hot shower and then zone out on the sofa watching mindless telly drivel with a glass of wine and a bag of taco chips. My plans changed abruptly when we arrived and found the front door ajar.

"That's odd. I know I locked it." Ruby stood on the threshold and pushed open the door. "Oh, my God!"

"What's wrong?" I eased her aside and peeked in.

The cottage had been trashed. But what terrified me the most was the cryptic warning that had been spray painted on a wall: *Go home or you'll be sorry*.

Diane and Bill came running down the gravel path. "We heard you screaming. What's wrong?"

Ruby pointed a shaky finger through the doorway. "Someone vandalized the house."

Diane was the first one up the steps. When she peered inside, she gasped. "Who would do something like this?"

"Whoever did this could be hiding in there, waiting for us." I stepped aside so Bill could have a look.

"What the bloody hell? Come on. Let's go." He took my grandmother's arm and gently guided her down the steps with Diane and me in the rear. We were silent until we were inside their home. Bill led Ruby to the sofa, but she declined to sit.

"We're too filthy. We had some trouble on the coal mine tour."

"I was wondering," said Diane. "That's a nasty scrape you have on your chin."

I was about to explain when Ruby wobbled and grabbed my arm. I held her steady. "Are you all right?"

"I've been better. Feeling my age, that's for damned sure."

Diane spread a fleece throw on the couch. "Sit before you collapse. The blanket is washable."

Bill left the room and returned carrying a cricket bat. "Diane, ring the police."

"What're you going to do?" I asked.

"Going to do a little housecleaning." He smacked the bat against his palm. "If they're still in your house, they'll wish they weren't."

Diane set her hand on his arm. "Bill, please be careful."

"No need to worry about me, love. It's the other bloke you should be worrying about." He pecked her cheek and left.

"Diane, please stop him," I said.

"We don't want your husband risking his life for a bunch of stuff," said Ruby. "It's not worth it."

"Don't worry about Bill. He fought in the Falklands and the Gulf War. If anyone's still in your house, I feel sorry for them."

While Diane rang the police, I stood at their open front door in case Bill yelled for help. After the call, she said, "I told them you're visiting Americans and would be waiting in our house. They said they'd try to get someone over here tonight, but it's more likely to be tomorrow or the next."

"Are you kidding me?" yelped Ruby. "We could all be dead by then."

"There've been massive budget cuts, and all of the constabularies are understaffed." Diane shrugged with a rueful smile. "The fact that you're not locals may make them respond quicker. That's why I made a point of saying you're Americans."

"Hopefully, that won't work against us," muttered Ruby.

"Wow. That's crazy. I'll never complain about our police department again." I thought of my friend, Police Chief Angela Yaeger. "Actually, I don't think I've ever complained."

"I'm sure that if Bill catches the vandals, the police will try to get here quickly," said Diane.

A few minutes later, Bill returned. "Whoever it was is gone.

What a bloody mess. First the break-in at Rose cottage and now this."

"Did you hear any noises earlier?" I asked.

"No. But we were both watching the telly." Diane shook her head. "Maybe if we'd been in the kitchen…"

Bill set the dinged-up bat by the door. "I'd like to get my hands on the blokes who did this."

"Go home or else." Ruby ran her fingers through her limp blond weave. "That's exactly what I want to do. Right now." Her voice caught on a sob. "Why did Edie have to die? I just don't get it. Why wasn't she wearing her damned ice cleats? If she had, then none of this would be happening."

Diane slipped an arm around her shoulders. "We'll make you both a nice hot cuppa. Bill baked fresh scones this morning."

While they busied themselves in the kitchen, I huddled next to Grandma and held her delicate hand, noticing the blue veins and age spots. I never think of her as growing old, but she is, and I need to cherish every moment with her.

Bill set the tea and scones on the coffee table. "I wish I could offer you a glass of wine, but…"

"We need to be clear-headed to talk to the cops who probably won't get here until next week," I said.

Ruby nearly spilled her tea in her lap as she lifted her delicate china teacup. Diane noticed her shakes and tucked a throw around her.

"Try a scone," said Diane.

"Diane made the jam," said Bill. "Blackberry."

I was so overwrought I didn't think I could swallow even a morsel of food without vomiting. But to be polite, I slathered a scone with clotted cream and jam and sampled it. The delicious combination of flavors zinged through my depleted body, bringing me back to life. "Grandma, you have to try this."

She shook her head. "I'm sorry, I'm too upset to eat."

"Just one little bite. Please? For me?"

If looks could kill, I would've melted like the wicked witch in *The Wizard of Oz*, but she broke down and took a nibble, then stole my scone.

––––––

*9:35 p.m.*

I cautiously peeked out between the front window curtains hoping it was the Mortons knocking on our door, but fearing it could be our vandals back to finish us off. Instead, I saw a rumpled middle-aged man with baggy puppy dog eyes. Standing next to him was a trim, prim younger woman. They saw me looking at them and held up police badges and I opened the door.

"I'm Detective Chief Inspector Jonathan Nelson, and this is Sergeant Anne Caldwell. We have a report of a break-in. Are you..." He checked his tablet. "Ruby Armstrong?"

"No, that's my grandmother. She's upstairs getting ready for bed. I'm Katy McKenna."

"I'm sorry this happened to you," said Nelson, with a kind smile.

Caldwell's scarlet lips pressed into a prissy frown as her suspicious eyes darted about.

I stepped aside. "Come in. I'll go get Ruby."

I dashed upstairs praying she wasn't already asleep and found her in the bathroom brushing her teeth.

"They're here? Now?" She rinsed her mouth and peered in the mirror. "Geez. I look like ninety-nine miles of bad road. Give me a sec to put on a little lipstick."

We went downstairs and I introduced her to the cops.

Nelson said, "*Go home or else*. Does that mean anything to you?"

"Other than the obvious?" said Ruby, sounding snippy.

"The obvious?" he asked.

"The obvious being—go home, or someone is going to do something to us that probably won't be pleasant," I said.

Nelson ignored my snarky tone and studied his tablet a moment. "I see that earlier today you were at the Wakeham Coal Mine and a man died. Your tour guide."

"Things have not been going well, to say the least. Including the fact that the reason we're in England is that my grandmother's sister died."

"I'm sorry for your loss," said Nelson.

Caldwell echoed his words with zero compassion, as though it were something she said ten times a day.

"The door was open when we got home but I am positive that I locked it when we left this morning," said Ruby. "So how did they get in?"

Caldwell inspected the door handle. "It's a spring lock. Ridiculously easy to open. Probably used a credit card."

"Did you have anything of value in the house?" asked Nelson.

Ruby's eyes bulged. "My sister's jewelry box."

We followed her upstairs to the bedroom on the second floor. "Oh, thank goodness. It's still here."

Just as she was about to open the box on the bureau, I said, "Wait. Don't you have to dust it for prints?"

"Generally, we don't dust for prints," said Inspector Nelson.

"You're kidding. Why not?" I said.

"For prints to yield any positive results, there has to be someone in the system to compare the print with," he said.

"If we've had a string of burglaries that might be related, we'll dust a few areas with the hope of comparing the prints from other scenes," said Caldwell.

"There was a recent break-in down the way at Rose Cottage," I said. "There, now you have a string. Two break-ins in the same area."

Inspector Nelson scrolled through his tablet, shaking his head. "Looks like no one reported it."

Sergeant Caldwell smoothed back a nonexistent stray hair from her tight blond bun that would've given me a migraine. "Most burglaries that get solved are ones in which the perpetrators get caught in the act or the stolen items are tracked down."

"I bet that means most burglaries don't get solved," I said.

"Unfortunately, over ninety percent," said the inspector.

"And murders?"

"Nine out of ten," said Caldwell flatly.

"Are solved?" said Ruby.

Nelson looked miserable. "No."

"I read that about one-third go unsolved in the US," said Ruby. "So we don't have anything to brag about, either."

"We'll follow up on the Rose Cottage, and we'll go ahead and dust a few items here just in case," said the inspector.

Obviously, he was trying to appease us, and I appreciated that.

"After you look in the jewelry box, Sergeant Caldwell will dust the exterior. Don't touch the bureau, either. She will also dust the point of entry." He sighed, looking road weary. "But don't get your hopes up."

Caldwell snapped on a pair of latex gloves and opened the velvet-lined box.

"May I touch the jewelry?" asked Ruby.

Caldwell nodded.

Grandma inspected the jumbled contents of the jewelry box.

"My laptop!" I yelled. "Oh crap. I bet they took it." I dashed upstairs to my bedroom on the third level and checked under the bed. It was still there. I rejoined them in Grandma's room. "They didn't take it. Thank goodness. I write a blog." As soon as I said that I felt like an idiot. Woo-hoo, I'm a blogger.

"My wife's a blogger, too." The inspector's somber demeanor lit up. "*The Joy of Kookies* spelled with a K is the name of her blog, and the reason I keep gaining weight." He patted his cookie belly with a grin. "She has over two million followers now and has been a judge on *The Great British Baking Show*."

"Whoa. I'm impressed. I love that show. Mine's really more of an online diary than a blog, and only a few family members and friends have access."

I was about to elaborate on why I started my blog-diary when Nelson said to Ruby, "Anything missing?"

"At first glance, I don't think so. It's hard to say. Here's her good watch and her old Timex. And her antique gold locket." She dangled a pearl necklace. "Her cultured pearls. Arthur, he was her husband, gave it to her on their fifteenth anniversary which annoyed her because pearls are for your thirtieth."

I noticed the sudden frantic look on her face as she pawed through the jewelry box. "Is something missing?"

"I don't see her diamond necklace. Another anniversary gift from Arthur—in the wrong year—again. Diamonds are for the sixtieth, and he gave it to her on their fiftieth. A gorgeous pear-shaped diamond pendant necklace."

"Are you sure it's not in there?" I asked.

Sounding peeved, she said, "I don't see it. You look."

The jewelry was a chaotic pile of bracelets and necklaces and what-have-you, so it was hard to tell what was in there. "We need to get everything out," I said. "May we take it to the dining table?"

"After I dust it for prints, I'll carry it down for you," said Caldwell.

A few minutes later, she set the box on the dining table. We immediately dived in, pawing through the trinkets until I decided to be more methodical and laid out everything in groups on the table. Earrings, necklaces, bracelets, rings, watches. Most of it was good quality costume jewelry. The diamond necklace was not in the box.

"I bet she locked it up somewhere," I said. "You know, like in a safety deposit box."

Ruby was still going through the jewelry. "I can't find our mother's wedding ring, either. Edith wore it for years on her right hand until she put on the menopause weight and her fingers got too pudgy. She was planning on giving it to your mother. It should be in here."

"Did you hear what I said about a safety deposit box?"

"Yes. She would have told me if she had one. Besides, she always said that jewelry was for wearing and enjoying."

Inspector Nelson said, "Did she have the pieces listed with her insurance company, along with photos?"

"Not likely," said Ruby.

I shook my head. "It seems like whoever did this is going to get away with it."

"Give Sergeant Caldwell a description of the missing items, as best as you can recall," said Nelson. "Tomorrow, call the insurance company just in case she did list the jewelry. And look through her photos. Perhaps you'll find a picture."

Ruby groaned. "I can't think about tomorrow. I need to go to bed before I collapse."

On cue, Diane poked her head in the open front doorway, "Would you two like to spend the night in our guest room? Then I could help you tidy up tomorrow."

"Oh, no. We can't impose on you." The truth was, I preferred to sleep in the mess because I didn't have enough energy left to be friendly.

"Are you a neighbor?" asked Nelson.

"Yes, my husband and I live in the back cottage."

"We'd like to speak to both of you when we're done here," said Nelson.

Diane's sunny smile faded. "Shall I get my husband?"

"No, we'll come to your place in a few minutes."

After Caldwell finished checking for useable prints, she concluded that the burglar had worn gloves. As they were leaving, Inspector Nelson gave me his card and said to call if we found anything else missing or located photos of the missing jewelry.

I locked the useless door lock and turned to Ruby. "Well, that's that. A fine conclusion to a perfectly horrible day. At least we're alive. That's something to be thankful for."

"You're right," said Ruby. "I need a glass of wine. How about you?"

"One glass. Then I'm off to bed. Although I doubt I'll get any sleep."

"Me too. I'm just sick about the jewelry. Especially my mother's wedding ring. That cannot be replaced."

After I swept up the broken dishes on the kitchen floor, I poured us each a glass of water in the only glasses left in the house —our toothbrush glasses. I handed a glass to Ruby and flopped next to her on the sofa. "Sorry. No wine. They took it."

"Well, of course they did. Oh well, it wasn't that good anyway." She patted my thigh. "I'm sorry about dragging you on that damned coal mine tour. I don't know what I was thinking. If we'd been home, this..." She swept her hand toward the ominous warning on the wall. "Probably wouldn't have happened."

"Hindsight is twenty-twenty, as they say. And who knows— maybe if we'd been home, whoever did this might have hurt us. Or worse. So maybe being in the coal mine wasn't that bad." I sipped my water a moment. "I still can't believe what happened. I wonder if Quentin was married or had kids."

"I hope not." Ruby stuffed a throw pillow behind her back with a groan. "All things considered, losing a couple pieces of jewelry is nothing compared to what that nice young man lost."

"He seemed way too young to have a heart attack, and he looked like he was in good shape."

"We're *assuming* it was a heart attack, you know," said Ruby.

"What else could it have been?"

She shrugged. "Who knows."

# CHAPTER THIRTEEN

**Friday, April 24**
*Posted by Katy McKenna*

The Harrington Estate Agency has a charming exterior. Potted topiary plants, striped black and white awning, hanging flower baskets brimming with red ivy geraniums. One window displays local house listings. I scanned the photos to see if ours was there, but it wasn't. Guess it was too soon.

The outside carried into the interior with a cheerful mix of white, black, red, and yellow. Past the cozy reception area were several tidy desks with side chairs for clients, and a coffee and tea counter. The only thing missing was people.

"Maybe they're all out on caravan," said Ruby.

"What's that?"

"It's a house tour for agents so they can see what's new on the market," she replied.

"You'd think there'd at least be a receptionist on duty."

She shrugged. "You would think. Maybe everyone's in a meeting." She cupped her mouth and shouted, "*Helloooo!* Anyone here?"

A door opened down the hall, and Mr. Harrington stepped out. "Ladies. How lovely to see you. How may I help you?"

I waved a hand at the empty desks. "Where's everyone?"

"Out looking at new listings."

Ruby elbowed me. "See? Told ya."

"I'm sure you'd like to talk about your house. Please step into my office and have a seat."

We sat on delicate brocade chairs fronting his massive desk. Mr. Harrington settled into his king size leather chair behind his desk and folded his manicured hands on the blotter.

Not wasting breath on niceties, Ruby said, "How goes it with our interested buyer?"

The man twiddled his silver mustache, looking distraught. "Unfortunately, he found something in Bourton-on-the-Water."

"Well, that's disappointing," said Ruby.

Harrington continued. "I feel confident we'll have another buyer in no time."

Ruby scooted forward in her chair, setting her hands on the glass-topped desk. "Did you hear about our burglary yesterday?"

His eyes widened and he cleared his throat. "No. What happened?"

"Someone vandalized the house and stole my sister's diamond necklace and our mother's wedding ring while we were on the coal mine tour that *you* recommended."

"That's dreadful. How much damage did they do to the cottage?"

"Nothing that can't be easily fixed."

"That's a relief. Did you enjoy the tour?" he said.

"That's a story for another day. Look, all I want is to get my sister's affairs in order and go home as quickly as possible."

"Perhaps you may want to consider a price reduction to speed things along."

"If you think best," said Ruby. "It was my sister's home, not mine."

Harrington glanced at his gold Rolex and stood abruptly. "Let me go over some numbers and recent sales and see what I can come up with. Although the cottage really isn't suitable for a modern family these days. Families tend to want more open space now so they can keep an eye on their little ones at all times, although I cannot fathom why they'd want to do that. But I know there are people in London, Liverpool, Bristol—even up in Scotland, who'd love having a quaint, historic country getaway."

He opened the office door and was about to give us the boot, but a voluptuous thirty-something blond bombshell was blocking our exit. "Hello," she said coyly, giving us a quick once-over.

I immediately knew that she had to be his trophy wife. But I couldn't fathom what this gorgeous woman saw in Mr. Old-Stuffed-Shirt. Other than his money, that is.

"Daphne, darling." He pecked her airbrushed cheek, and said to us, "Thank you for coming in, ladies."

"Blimey! Aren't yew gonna introduce me to your friends?" She flashed a blindingly white, pearly veneered smile.

And that's when I realized where I'd heard Harrington's voice before. At the manor house. With Martini Lady—his mother! I glanced at Ruby and she gave me a little half-smile. Luckily, he did not seem to realize we were the obnoxious American "talent scouts."

"Ladies, this is my wife, Daphne. Daphne, this is Ruby, uh…"

"Ruby Armstrong." She shook Daphne's thin, blue nailed hand.

"I'm Katy McKenna. Granddaughter."

"Ow, you mus' be da Americans from California."

"Let's not hold up these charming ladies, dear," said Mr. Harrington. "I'm sure they have things to do."

"No. Not really," said Ruby with a casual shrug. "Daphne, did you know my sister—Edith Halsey—the village veterinarian?"

"I met 'er at a few fundraisers at the country club, but we don't 'ave any pets. Nigel 'as a deviated septum an' animal 'air sets off 'is allergies, so..." Her voice trailed off. "But I'm terribly sorry for your loss."

Listening to Daphne's colorful Cockney slang was like listening to Eliza Doolittle.

Nigel took his young wife's hand. "Unfortunately, dear, we are in a bit of a rush. We have a reservation for lunch, and we don't want to be late."

"Would ya like to join us?" said his wife. "It's not often I get a chance to talk to anyone from California. Do ya know any movie stars?"

"Dear," said Nigel, "our reservation is for two. You know how crowded it gets at The Country House."

"Oh, that's okay," I said. "But thanks for asking. As far as movie stars go, the answer is no. But my sister, Emily, works at Roxy Studios, and she's shared some juicy stories with me."

Daphne's brown eyes grew wide. "Like?"

I leaned toward her, dropping my voice. "Hugh Jackman and—"

"Ow, I love 'im," she said. "He's gorgeous."

"Daphne!" Nigel tapped his watch. "We're running late."

———

After we buckled into our rental car, Ruby said, "What about Hugh Jackman?"

"Who knows? I was making it up to annoy Nigel."

"What would you have said if he hadn't interrupted?"

"I dunno. Maybe...he's having an affair with Meryl Streep?"

"No! Really? Oh, my God. Emily told you that?"

"Granny! Seriously?"

"You know, I'm suddenly hungry." She flipped down the visor

and checked her makeup. "Why don't you put that restaurant they were going to in your phone's GPS."

"Do you remember the name?"

"The Country something."

"House. The Country House." I scrolled on my phone for the address while she touched up her lipstick. "It's not far. Four stars. That famous T.V. chef Jordan Halsey owns it, so we probably won't have a chance of getting a table."

---

*The Country House*

Contrary to what Nigel said, the restaurant was not crowded. While we waited to be seated, I scanned the dining room and spotted our quarry sitting by a window overlooking a grassy meadow.

A young guy dressed in jeans, black vest, and a white button-down approached us. "How many in your party?"

"Just us," I said. "I thought for sure you wouldn't have any tables available."

"We only recently started opening for lunch and word hasn't spread yet. But it's still early."

"Do you mind if we sit at that table next to the window? It's such a lovely view," said Ruby. "Or is it reserved?"

"We don't take reservations for lunch." He led us to it and said our server would be over soon. "Would either of you care for water?"

"Yes, we both would."

"Sparkling, mineral, still, or tap?"

"Tap is fine," I said. *And free.*

"Lemon? Cucumber? Mint?"

I shook my head. "Nope. Just plain old water."

"Katy?" called Daphne from their table. "Wha' a lovely surprise. Look, Nigel. It's Ruby an' Katy."

He turned in his seat wearing a toothy grin, bringing to mind the Joker. "This is indeed a surprise."

Daphne waved us over. "Do join us. I'm absolu'ely dyin' to 'ear about Hugh Jackman."

I lifted my brows, grinning at Nigel. "We don't want to intrude."

He stood and moved his chair to make room. "Yes, by all means, do join us."

A server rushed over to help us settle at their table. "I'll be right back with the menus."

"And a double scotch on the rocks for me," Harrington snapped. "Ladies?"

"I'll 'ave a champagne cocktail." Daphne leaned forward on her elbows, and I feared her boobs would spill out of her low-cut dress. "Usually, I never drink before five, bu' I feel like celebra'in. This is so fun."

The waiter was eyeballing Daphne and with obvious reluctance turned his attention to us.

"Oh, maybe a glass of your house white," said Ruby.

"And you, miss?"

"I'm fine with my water." I hate being the designated driver. "Daphne, did Nigel tell you that our cottage was vandalized?"

"No, he didn'. 'Ow dreadful for you. Did they take anything?"

I opened my mouth to reply and was interrupted by her husband. "Good God. What's taking them so long to bring our menus? That's the trouble with these celebrity restaurants."

I started to answer Daphne again and was interrupted by Ruby. "What do you mean?"

"They think they can get by on their fame and the hell with service," he grumbled.

"Our waiter is young and probably inexperienced," she said. "We should try to have a little patience with him."

Daphne giggled. "Patience is no' one of Nigel's virtues."

The unwitting waiter returned with our drinks and menus. Nigel downed his double and ordered another while the young man told us about the lunch specials.

We opened our leather-bound menus, and I cringed at the exorbitant prices. "What're you having, Ruby?"

She quickly scanned the menu. "Hmmm. Maybe just a little salad. As it turns out, I'm not that hungry. What're you going to have?"

"The same."

We placed our orders and settled into polite chitchat.

Ruby sipped her wine. "This is very good. You want a little taste, Katy?"

"No. Better not. I might get drunk and crash the car."

"Sorry, love." Daphne slurped half her champagne in one gulp. "Katy? 'Ave you spent any time in London?"

I sipped my ice water and set it down. "We came straight here. No time for fun on this trip."

She gave me a pouty face. "Aw. That's too bad. Nigel's mum lives in Kensington. Lots of movie stars live there." She sighed, looking star struck. "I adore Kensington. I wish we could live there. Or Chelsea. It's so bloody borin' 'ere."

Nigel shot her a disapproving glance. "My business is here, Daphne."

"I know," she said. "Nigel wants 'is mum to sell 'er place an' move in with us. She had a bad fall recently, and well, you know 'ow these things go. Next thing you know, you get pneumonia an' die."

"How's she doing?" I said.

"Healthy as a horse," said Nigel, glaring at his innocent-idiot wife. "Although she needs a walker to get around. As a matter of fact, she's visiting us right now."

"How fun it will be for you to have your mother-in-law living with you full time, Daphne," said Ruby. "I certainly cherished the many, many, many years that my husband's mother lived with us. She was about eighty when she moved in. She lived to the ripe old age of one-hundred-and-three. She was *healthy as a horse,* and we had twenty-three fun years together."

Never happened, but you should have seen Daphne's face.

Nigel cleared his throat. "Good God. What does it take to get a bloody drink here?" He stood, tossing his cloth napkin on his seat. "I guess I have to get my own damned drink."

Daphne watched him stomp away, then leaned toward us speaking in a confidential tone. "You'll 'ave to excuse 'im. Business is in a bit of a slump. That's why 'e wants 'is mother to sell 'er apartment an' move 'ere."

"Why would that help?" I asked.

"Her place is worth a bloody fortune."

"How much do you think?"

She shrugged her bony shoulders. "Ten million quid, at least. I guess with that much money in our pockets, I can stand living with me mother-in-law." Daphne drained her cocktail, then rested her chin on her hand. "Now tell us abou' Hugh."

"Yes," said Ruby. "Do tell."

———

We spent the remainder of the afternoon cleaning up the vandalism mess at the cottage. I was in the middle of griping to Grammy that we'd have to buy paint to cover the warning on the wall when our knight-in-shining-armor neighbor dropped by and kindly offered to do the job for us.

"I have some white paint that's close to the color of the other walls. I'll paint the whole wall, and no one will ever notice."

"But you've done so much already," said Ruby.

"We haven't done any more than what any good neighbor would do. When we moved in, Edith was a tremendous help to us.

Lovely woman. If the new owner is half as nice, we'll consider ourselves lucky."

After he painted the wall, he suggested painting the front door. "They say a cheery entrance will entice more prospective buyers. I have some red paint left over from our door that would brighten it up."

"We'd love that, right, Ruby?"

"On one condition," she said, looking stern. "We take you and Diane out for a nice dinner before we leave."

"I accept your terms." He crossed his arms and laughed. "To tell you the truth, I've wanted to paint that faded door for a long time. Now we'll have matching entries."

While he cheered up the front door, we shoved the furniture back into place, rehung the drapes, and vacuumed and dusted.

A little while later, I noticed Bill was scraping the front window trim, so I popped my head out to see what he was doing.

"I noticed the paint is flaking and peeling," he said, "so I'm going to paint it, too."

"Bill, you're doing too much." I stepped outside and admired the shiny red door.

He grinned slyly. "I have an ulterior motive."

"Oh? What would that be?"

"Your cottage faces the street and the better it looks, the better it is for our property value."

"Are you thinking of selling?"

"No, but who knows what tomorrow may bring?"

# CHAPTER FOURTEEN

**Sunday, April 26**

*Posted by Katy McKenna*

*Church Jumble Sale*

We still had one more load to drop off, so we dashed to the church hall early this morning and found the wood-paneled multiuse room buzzing with activity. Volunteers were arranging folding tables loaded with dishes, pottery, clothes, lamps, knickknacks, and what-have-you. A big silver coffee urn was percolating on a table laden with tantalizing homemade scones, cookies, and pastries.

"Hello, ladies," said a stout, cheerful woman at the entrance. "Have a few more things to donate, I see."

"Yes," said Ruby. "Towels. Some nearly-new sheets, and a few odds and ends. Where should we set the boxes?"

She pointed to a table at the other end of the hall. "That's our linen department. Joyce will help you."

We said hi to Joyce, set the boxes on the floor, and turned to leave.

"Wait!" she snapped, sweeping her wispy gray bangs off her sweaty forehead. "I'm desperate for help. Everyone's leaving boxes, but no one will stay to sort it all, and the sale starts right after the morning church service. Would you help me fold these sheets and organize them by size? Then we can add your things in." She glanced around the noisy room and checked her watch. "Diane should've been here forty-five minutes ago."

"Would that be Diane Morton?" I said.

"Yes."

"She's the one who told us about the jumble sale."

"You must be Edith's American relatives."

"I'm her sister, and Katy is my granddaughter," said Ruby.

Joyce took Ruby's hand. "I'm so sorry for your loss, dear. Edith was a lovely woman. Warm-hearted and generous. When she retired the village lost a wonderful veterinarian." She glanced past Ruby's shoulder. "Finally. Here comes Diane."

"Hello, ladies. Sorry I'm late."

"What kept you?" asked Joyce, sounding snippy again. "You're usually so prompt."

"I got caught up in the sermon and forgot the time." She turned her attention to me. "I didn't expect to see you two this morning."

I pointed at our cardboard boxes. "We had a few more things to drop off."

Ruby was attempting to fold a queen-sized fitted sheet. "I've watched Martha's video countless times, and still can't get the hang of it."

"That's why I don't bother." Actually, I don't bother because I only have one set of sheets.

Diane held out her hands. "Let me help you."

"Where's that diamond necklace that your husband gave you

for your birthday, Diane?" asked Joyce. "You've worn it constantly since you got it."

*I haven't seen a diamond necklace on Diane.*

Our neighbor didn't make eye contact with Joyce. "I didn't think it was appropriate for the church. A bit too showy, don't you think?"

"Yes, I do. But then who am I to say? I've never owned a diamond necklace. My husband doesn't make that kind of money."

"You know we're not rich, Joyce. Far from it." Diane returned her attention to Ruby. "The trick to folding a fitted sheet is to drape one corner over your hand and then set another corner over that and then—"

"And then let you finish it," said Ruby in a chirpy voice. "Because this old gal is a lost cause."

Diane laid the perfectly folded sheet on the table and picked up another to fold.

"Speaking of diamond necklaces," I said. "When our cottage was vandalized, they stole my aunt's diamond necklace and my great-grandmother's wedding ring."

"Oh, that's bloody awful," said Joyce. "I don't recall ever seeing Edith wearing the necklace."

"Her husband gave it to her on their fiftieth anniversary," said Ruby.

"You know, Grandma," I said. "We're assuming those things were stolen on Wednesday. But maybe they've been gone for a while."

"I suppose it's possible. However, I would think that Inspector Nelson would have said so."

"*If* they were reported stolen," I said. "I doubt Aunt Edith wore the necklace very often, especially since Uncle Arthur passed, so it's possible she wouldn't have noticed that it was gone—given how crammed and unorganized her jewelry box is."

"No matter what, hopefully, the police will recover the jewelry," said Diane, squeezing Ruby's arm.

There was an awkward moment of silence while we each tried to conjure up something to say, and then Joyce said, "Have you two done any sightseeing yet?"

"Just the Wakeham Coal Mine, if you can count that as sightseeing," said Ruby. "You know what I always say. Seen one coal mine, seen 'em all."

"I'm glad you haven't lost your sense of humor," said Diane. "Bloody awful experience."

"What happened at the coal mine?" said Joyce.

"I'll tell you later," said Diane. "You two need to see a castle. Highclere is very close."

"Highclere! Also known as Downton Abbey. My grandmother happens to be close friends with the owner. The duke."

"She is?" Joyce gazed at me like I was deranged.

"Yes, as a matter of fact, I am." Ruby took on a snooty air. "He used to be my driver."

Diane looked skeptical. "Your driver? You're saying our duke was your driver. In America."

We both nodded.

"You're joking, right?" said Joyce. "It's always hard to tell with you Americans. Your humor is so different from ours. Diane, have you ever watched that American comedy, Seenfield?"

I felt obliged to interrupt. "You mean *Seinfeld*. That show is a timeless classic. It started before I was born, and it's hilarious."

"If you say so. I just didn't get it. I could never figure out what it was about."

I opened my mouth to explain, and Grammy wisely set her hand on my arm to shut me up. Diane took that as her cue to change the subject. "I want to hear more about the duke being your driver." It was clear by the look on her face that she wasn't buying our story.

"He was in our town driving a senior bus for about—how long was it, Grandma?" I said.

"About six–eight months. It was part of his journey to learn about how other people live around the world. Katy was supposed to go out with him, but she kept putting him off. And then he returned to jolly old England to run the family estate."

"You put off the most eligible royal bachelor in England?" said Diane. "Who does that?"

"I started dating someone else."

"Who?" said Joyce.

"My neighbor. Josh."

Joyce looked pointedly at my ringless left hand. "How's that going for you?"

"Not so well," said Ruby. "Anyhoo, Duke said—"

"You mean Ian Herbert," said Joyce. "Duke of—"

"Yes, yes. But we all called him plain old Duke. Of course, at the time, we had no idea he was a real duke. We thought it was his name."

"Wait a sec," I said. "You just said he was the most eligible bachelor. Is he married?"

"Yes. A few weeks ago," said Diane. "They had a big wedding at the castle. Prince William and Princess Kate were there."

"You mean the Duchess of Cambridge," said Joyce.

"I stand corrected. The Duke and Duchess of Sussex were there, too."

"Who's that?" I asked.

"Prince Harry and Meghan Markle," said Diane.

I was feeling betrayed by a man I'd never met. How dare he marry someone else before meeting me? "Is Duke's wife pretty?"

"I wouldn't say she's pretty," said Diane.

*Ha!*

"More like beautiful," said Joyce.

*Oh.*

"Big brown eyes, auburn hair. A little like you, only different."

*As in she's beautiful, and I'm not so much. Thanks.*

My needy feelings must have been written all over my face because she quickly added, "You're much prettier."

"Oh, thank you, but I doubt that."

"She's a movie actor from Hollywood, like Meghan," said Diane. "Does or rather did, those awful slasher horror films. Not my cup of tea. Give me a good ghost story, not a bloodbath. Anyway, they met a couple of years ago while doing work for Habitat for Humanity in Haiti. According to the tabloids, they dated for a while and then it fizzled out. They met again recently at a movie premiere in London, and that was that. The fizzle turned to sizzle."

"I bet there's a baby on the way and that's why they got married so fast," said sour-puss Joyce.

"And they lived happily ever after." Ruby shot me a disgusted look that said *Could have been you.* "Do you want to visit the castle, Katy? Duke said to come see him if we were ever in the area. It might be fun."

"Oh, he's not there now," said Diane. "He's still on his honeymoon."

"Oh, poo. Are there any other castles around here?" asked Ruby.

"I think you'd enjoy Warwick. It's not too far."

On our way out of the jumble sale, we purchased a couple of mugs, plates, and glasses. So ridiculous. We were supposed to be getting rid of things, not buying more.

———

Mom called with an update on Pop. He's getting released from the hospital tomorrow and she's a nervous wreck.

- She's worried he'll trip over the throw rugs and break his neck, so she's removed them.
- She's worried about Daisy knocking him over and he'll break his neck.

- She's worried that he will trip over Francine and hurt her back, and break his neck.

When she stopped to catch her breath, I said, "Won't he be using a walker?"

"Yes."

"Then I don't think you need to worry. But to be safe, how about confining the dogs in your bedroom, and then after Pop is sitting in his recliner, you can let them out."

"That's a good idea. Hey! You'll never guess what happened last night."

"What?"

"It rained. It was a real downpour. The weatherman this morning said we got over half an inch. Can you believe it? I can't remember the last time it rained. Everything smells so good. There are even some puddles."

"That's wonderful. Fingers crossed, we'll get some more. The last time I drove by the reservoir, it was almost empty."

"Oh, I forgot to tell you. Your sister's coming up for a couple days to help. I didn't expect that, what with her new job at Roxy Studios."

"How's that going?"

"She's having the time of her life meeting TV and movie stars. She said her girlfriend can get us a personal tour of the studio if we ever want it. Wouldn't that be fun?"

"Count me in. Ooo, I wonder if she could get us tickets to *Pop Idol*."

"Who knows? But that's your thing, not mine."

"Grammy watches it."

"Then you two can go. It would be completely wasted on me. I'll relax by the pool."

———

*Last thought*

Warwick Castle did not disappoint. From the dungeons to the turrets, it was magical.

# CHAPTER FIFTEEN

**Monday, April 27**
*Posted by Katy McKenna*

I was on my second cup of Fuzzy Buzzy when Ruby trudged down the stairs this morning looking like roadkill.

"Whoa. You don't look like you got much sleep last night. Let me pour you a cup of coffee." From the kitchen, I said, "You were right about percolated coffee. It's worth the bother. Thank goodness those thugs didn't break the pot."

I handed her a mug and she sank into the sofa with a grunt. "I was up half the night fretting about that damned necklace and ring. If only Edith had listed the jewelry with her insurance. Then at least we could claim them."

"Maybe we can find a photo of the jewelry. Then give it to the police; you know, in case anyone tries to pawn them."

"I doubt she took any."

"I meant a photograph of Aunt Edith wearing the jewelry. Did she keep photo albums?"

"Yes. I already packed them, but we can open the box." She stood, suddenly energetic. "Are you ready to take a little stroll down memory lane?"

———

"This photo of you and Aunt Edith is darling. Love the matching poodle skirts."

"That, my dear, was me about to go on my first date. Mom said I had to double date with Edith. It was so embarrassing. Edie thought it was funny."

"How old were you?"

"Fifteen, so my sister was seventeen-and-a-half. We went to a school sock hop. My geeky date, Carl Raney, reeked of garlic so every time it was a slow dance, I begged off. I sure didn't need a chaperone, let me tell you."

"Well, at least you had a date. I didn't get asked out until I was pushing seventeen, ya know."

"I know for a fact that it was because you were so darn pretty that it scared off the boys."

"Spoken like a totally impartial grandmother." I plucked a more recent photo from my pile. "Here's one of Uncle Albert and Aunt Edith all dressed up. He sure looked like an English lord, didn't he?" I glanced at the picture again. "Look! She's wearing a necklace. Is that it?"

Ruby put on her cheaters and squinted at the photo. "I remember this. They were going to a fancy fundraiser at the country club." She took the album to the window. "Yup. That's the necklace. Too bad it's not a close-up."

"Yeah, there's no way you could make an identification with that picture. Let's keep looking."

"Yoo-hoo! Knock, knock," called Diane from the porch.

"Geez, Louise. I look like hell," whispered Ruby. "Don't even have my makeup on yet."

"The curtains are open so she knows we're sitting here."

"Come in," she yelled.

Diane opened the door and stepped inside. "I thought I'd pop by to tell you what a huge success the jumble sale was. All your donations sold. And to give you these." She held out her hand to Ruby. "I'm sure you didn't mean for these to wind up in the sale. Harriet Poole found them in the pocket of a jacket she was trying on."

"What is it?" I asked.

"Edie's pearl earrings," said Ruby. "She wore them almost every day. I completely forgot about these."

Diane smiled. "I don't remember ever seeing her without them. What a shame if you hadn't got them back."

Ruby put the earrings on. "Thank you for bringing me these, and please thank Natalie. It's nice to know there are still honest people in this world."

"I don't know about the rest of the world, but you can trust the citizens of Bridleford."

*And yet, we've been vandalized.*

Diane frowned. "You know, now that I think about it, there've been several burglaries this past year in other nearby villages. I'm sure that whoever broke into your cottage was not a Bridleford citizen." She shrugged. "Anyway, best to keep your door locked. Wouldn't want anything to happen to you."

"We're from California. We always keep our doors locked," I said. "Although that didn't do much good the other day. Maybe we should get a deadbolt."

"Well, I wouldn't worry about it. There's no reason for those vandals to return. I'm sure they've moved on to other villages. Greener pastures, as they say."

After Diane left, Ruby said, "You know, I thought I checked every pocket before we packed up those clothes. Now I don't know what to think."

"If you're thinking the wedding ring and necklace might have been in Aunt Edith's pockets—please don't."

"You're right. That's crazy."

To help Grandma feel reassured that we hadn't somehow overlooked the missing jewelry, we spent the next hour searching the cottage. When we were satisfied that the jewelry was not in the house, Ruby suggested an early dinner at the Bridleford Manor House.

———

The friendly bartender from the other night was cutting limes when we walked in. "How's the location scouting going?"

After we had a good laugh, he nodded to a pair of wingback chairs facing the windows overlooking the patio. "Your favorite lady is here with her son."

Gerard set down his knife and dumped the limes into a bin. "She's actually a very nice lady, just not a happy one."

Ruby shrugged off her pink cardigan and draped it over her shoulders. "Getting old ain't easy. No matter how much money you have, although it's sure gotta help."

"Do you have a reservation for dinner?" he asked.

"No," I said. "May we eat in the bar again?"

He glanced around the room. "Go ahead and seat yourself. I'll bring you a menu and get your drink order in a moment."

"We'll have two white wines." I grabbed a newspaper from the end of the bar and followed Ruby to the vacant seats backing up to Martini Lady and Nigel's chairs, where we commenced our new hobby— eavesdropping.

"Dear, you really shouldn't have." Sniff, sniff. "It's too much."

"I know how unhappy you've been, Mummy, and I thought it would cheer you up."

Mummy Harrington continued, "I'm fine. Really. You need to stop fretting about me."

"I know you don't want to leave London, but you can't manage on your own anymore. You need someone to—"

"Caretake me?" she scoffed. "I may be eighty-five today, but I am not an invalid. I've been alone for over fifteen years since your dear father died, and I've done just fine."

"Yes, that's true, old girl."

Eyes bulging, I mouthed at Ruby, *Old girl?*

The darling son continued, "Until recently, that is. But you've had two falls this past year. The last one could have killed you. If your friend hadn't come around to check on you, who knows?"

"But she did, and I'm fine."

"Your walker says otherwise, Mummy. I promise we will do our very best to make you comfortable in our home. You know Daphne adores you."

"That silly girl barely tolerates me."

"That's not true. She was terribly disappointed to not be able to have dinner with us this evening, but you know how it is."

"Oh, yes. I know. It's her time of the month. Aunt Flow seems to visit that girl several times a month. If you were with someone in your own generation that would not be an *issue*, as they say these days." She snorted unladylike. "Oh, Nigel, do stop fidgeting with your mustache. What is taking Gerard so long? I want my martini."

I eyeballed Grammy with a wicked grin and mouthed *Here we go*.

"I'll go to the bar. Perhaps he forgot," said her son.

"No. No. I don't want to be a bother. And this necklace. It's too much, Nigel. Wherever did you find it?"

"In an estate jewelry shop in London. When I came to see you in hospital after your hip replacement surgery, I was passing by the shop and saw it in the window. I thought it looked familiar so I went in to have a closer look. You can imagine my utter astonishment when I realized it was the one you lost. Look at the engraving on the clasp, Mummy. A heart and the number fifty."

Ruby gasped simultaneously with Mummy.

"It truly is my necklace," she said. "Your dear father gave this to me on my fiftieth birthday."

"I remember," said Nigel.

Ruby gestured me close. "You're not going to believe this, but I think he's given her Edith's necklace. Hers had the exact same engraving. A heart and a fifty for their fiftieth anniversary. What are the odds of two necklaces having the same engraving?"

"Oh dear!" said the old girl. "The insurance money. Eight thousand pounds. Will I have to return it?"

"Don't fret about it," said Nigel. "It's been several years since you lost it. Besides, the insurance company will never know you have it back. Remember, it's not as if we found it under the sofa or something. I paid for it."

"Yes, I suppose you're right."

"It was the least I could do considering you invested the insurance money in my new business at the time. And look how well I've done."

"Your estate agency is truly doing well?"

"Yes, indeed it is. We have several very productive agents and the money is literally pouring in. So stop fretting, dear girl, and enjoy this gift from your devoted son. Here, let me put it on you."

When Nigel stood, we slinked down in our seats hiding behind the newspaper. I peeked out and saw Gerard passing by carrying the grand dame's martini on a tray.

"What a beautiful necklace," said the bartender. "Special occasion?"

"A gift from my dear son. It's my eighty-fifth birthday."

"You wear your years well, Mrs. Harrington. I would not have guessed you're a day over seventy."

"You are a sweet boy. If I'd had a grandson, he'd be about your age. Unfortunately, I have no grandchildren."

"I see the maître d' waving to us," said Gerard. "Your table is ready."

"I have got to see that necklace," whispered Ruby.

"What're you going to do?" I asked.

"Shhh." She scurried to a column near the bar entrance and stood behind it.

I held up the newspaper and peered over the top to observe Mrs. Harrington toddle by, slowly pushing her red walker. Then I turned my attention to Grandma, waiting to see her reaction when she got a glimpse of the necklace.

The trundling pair had their eyes set on the dining room on the other side of the vast hall and didn't notice Ruby skulking behind the pillar. As soon as they were out in the hall, she rushed back to her seat, her mouth pressed tight, face flushed, fists clenched.

"You look like you're about to have a stroke." I handed her wine glass to her. "Here. Take a sip. Or a gulp."

She chugged the glass and slammed it on the table. "I don't know how that necklace wound up in a jewelry shop in London, but it's definitely Edith's. No doubt about it."

# CHAPTER SIXTEEN

**Tuesday, April 28**
*Posted by Katy McKenna*

I checked in with Mom last night. She said that Pop is in a world of pain, but he's being good about doing his rehab exercises. She said the dogs are behaving and are a welcome distraction for both of them. Francine has commandeered Pop's lap. Daisy was a little jealous the first few days, but she's over it now. Mom has been checking in on Tabitha and says she's fine but definitely lonely.

She also mentioned she's having problems with heartburn—something she has not had since she was pregnant. Of course, I teased her about it, but she says it's stress, not a pregnancy. She's perimenopausal, so it still could happen. Boy, wouldn't that be something?

I called Sam and brought her up to speed on everything. She told me she could use a break from the crazy chaos at home, so tomorrow she'll go over and watch a movie with Tabitha. What a good friend.

Midmorning, we took Charlie for a long walk through the village. As we passed by the Mermaid Inn, we decided to continue up the lane beyond. Ruby said she needed to walk off her rage about the necklace.

While Charlie inspected a telephone pole, I told Ruby I had a theory about the necklace. "What if Harrington didn't buy it at a shop in London? What if…" I stopped. "Okay, I need to backtrack a bit. Please bear with me."

"I'm listening," she muttered.

"Remember Daphne said she met Aunt Edith at a fundraiser?"

"Yes. What about it?"

"Well, that would have been a dressy event, which means Aunt Edith probably would have been wearing the necklace. What if Mr. Harrington saw the necklace and realized that it looked like the one that was stolen from his mother? I bet he would have asked her about it, and when he found out about the engraving on the clasp, that confirmed it for him. And then recently, with his mother's birthday coming up, maybe he asked if she would consider selling it to him."

"Yes. Maybe. However…"

"Let me finish my thought before I lose it."

"You're too young to forget what you're saying. That's my department."

"If you don't let me finish, I'll forget." I paused. "Crap, where was I?"

"Asked her if she would sell it to him."

"Oh, yeah. I know you said that Aunt Edith would never sell it in a million years, but what if…"

Ruby was regarding me with a sour look.

"…After hearing Harrington's sad story about the necklace being a birthday gift to his mother from his father, she decided that it should go back to her?"

She crossed her arms and gazed up at the passing clouds.

I continued, "Aunt Edith was a kind soul, and I think she would have sold it to him. I truly do."

Ruby bent to ruffle Charlie's ears. Finally, she cupped his face and said, "You know what Charlie? It's the only thing that makes any sense." She straightened and nodded at me. "I agree. I think she would've sold it to him. I just hope she got fair market value."

"Aunt Edith was a kind person, but..."

Ruby laughed. "But she wasn't stupid." She gave Charlie a good scratching under his leather collar. "I feel much better now."

We returned to the village and stopped at the pub for lunch. We sat outside at a picnic table and Ruby ordered fish and chips; I went for the ploughman's sandwich. The ingredients included the Cranston Pickle that Quentin had talked about, and I was curious about it. Before our meal arrived, Ruby received a call from Nigel Harrington.

"Hold on. Let me put you on speaker." She fiddled with her phone. "Dammit. How do I put this thing on speaker?"

"Give it to your techie-wizard granddaughter." I pressed the icon and handed it back.

"Well, at least you're good for something." Then she screamed at her phone, "Okay. Go ahead. What were you saying?"

In his cultured, British-upper-crust accent, he repeated, "I said we have another offer on your sister's cottage."

"That's wonderful. How much?"

I placed a hand on her arm and whispered, "You don't have to shout."

"Sorry," she shouted at her phone. "How much is the offer?"

"It's a bit lower than we had hoped for, but the good news is they're offering cash."

"How much?"

Harrington cleared his throat. "150,000 pounds."

"Geez Louise. I know I said to lower the price, but wow, that's a pretty big drop from 255,000 pounds."

Charlie barked at a squirrel rummaging for crumbs under the tables, so I scooted him away. I returned when I saw her dump the phone in her purse.

"What happened?"

She waited to answer while a server set our lunch on the table.

"I'll be right back with your pints," said the perky waitress.

"I told him to counter at two-thirty-five," said Ruby. "I mean, really! Who makes an offer that's over one hundred thousand below the asking price? I can understand if you're selling a house priced in the millions, but this is ridiculous."

"I agree, that was an insulting offer, but I doubt they'll go for your counteroffer."

"Hopefully we can meet somewhere in the middle."

The waitress set down our beers with a friendly, "Cheers!" and scurried off before I could ask for napkins.

I went inside and returned with a fistful of paper napkins.

"Oh, honey," said Ruby. "Could you get me some ketchup and malt vinegar?"

As I was pushing through the door, she hollered, "Get some mayo, too."

After I had fulfilled Ruby's condiment requirements, I bit into my sandwich and washed it down with a swig of amber beer. "This is really good." I opened the sandwich to inspect the contents. "The Cranston Pickle is kind of like a chutney. I'll definitely be making these sandwiches at home. Hope I can find this pickle stuff somewhere."

"You can always order it online," said Ruby. "Or something similar."

Her last three words stopped me in mid-bite. "Oh, my God." I dropped the sandwich in the paper-lined basket. "I think I know what killed Quentin."

"Where did that come from?" asked Ruby.

I pointed at my sandwich. "He ate one of these before we went into the mine. Remember what he said about the pickle relish on it?"

"No."

"He said, 'Tastes like they changed the pickle brand.'"

"So?" She dunked a fry in the ketchup, mumbling, "Wish I had some hot sauce."

"So, I'm thinkin' maybe the sandwich was *poisoned*."

Apparently, what I was saying was not earth-shattering because she said, "Did they have any hot sauce? You know how I like to mix it with the ketchup."

"I don't know." I tried not to sound exasperated. "Would you like me to go see?"

"Oh, honey. Would you?"

As I was stomping toward the pub door, she called, "Get some salt, too."

I returned and plunked several more condiments on the picnic table. "Here's the salt. And it's a *no* on the hot sauce. But here's some mustard, some Worcestershire, and something called brown sauce. Anything else before I sit down?"

"Maybe some water for Charlie?"

He gave me a big old grin of encouragement, and I trudged back inside and returned with a bowl of water, a dog biscuit, and a bag of shortbread cookies.

"I didn't ask for cookies," said Grandma.

*Not yet.* "I thought you might like one."

"See? This is why you're my favorite." She chomped into a crunchy piece of cod dripping with malt vinegar. "You were talking about how the tea shop had changed their pickle brand. I'm sure there are lots of pickle brands, so what's the big deal?"

"The big deal is, Quentin said it tasted *different*—remember?"

"So because of that, you think the tea shop poisoned Quentin?"

"Well, no. Probably not. But maybe it was Mathew. He bought

the sandwich. He could've put poison in it before he gave it to Quentin, and that's why Quentin said it tasted different."

"But why would Mathew want to kill him? Weren't they cousins?"

"Are you forgetting that my cousin left me for dead in my attic not too long ago?"

"I see your point. So the question is, what would Mathew have to gain from Quentin's death?"

I thought about that as I dug through my purse for the inspector's business card. "I have no idea, but I'm going to call Inspector Nelson. He needs to know about this."

I pulled out my phone and Ruby grabbed my hand before I could dial. "Why don't you ask him to meet you here later today? Or tonight—when he's off duty. Tell him you've thought of something, but you'd rather talk in person."

"Why?"

"You're suggesting someone murdered Quentin. I don't think that's a phone conversation."

———

*Late afternoon*

I had brewed a pot of coffee (it was either that or take a nap) and was filling two cups when Ruby got a call from Mr. Harrington. The potential buyer had countered her two-thirty-five price with 195,000.

"Mr. Harrington," said Ruby. "Do you think this is their best offer? Or are they bluffing?"

I whispered, "Put it on speaker."

Harrington said, "Yes, I do believe they are firm on this price. And it's still a cash offer. With no inspection and no contingencies."

I couldn't keep my mouth shut. "Mr. Harrington. Katy here. Are you representing both parties?"

"Ooo. Good question, Katy," Ruby whispered.

He cleared his throat. "Yes, but that's quite common. Of course, my first priority is to get you a fair price."

"Give me a day or two to think about it," said Ruby.

"My advice is not to wait too long. There are a lot of houses on the market right now so who knows when another qualified buyer will come along."

She hung up and sighed. "I feel like I don't have a choice."

"It's been on the market for less than a week. This isn't like Los Angeles where people have insane bidding wars." I handed her a cup of coffee and a shortbread cookie. "We don't have to stay here and wait for the house to sell, you know."

"But what if it just sits? Then what?"

"Then you'll wish you'd sold it."

―――――

*Meeting with Chief Inspector Nelson*

We stood inside the pub entrance and scanned the warmly lit room a few times before recognizing Nelson chatting with a pretty woman behind the bar. He was dressed casually in a plaid shirt and jeans. When we approached him, he pecked the woman's cheek, then led us to a table by the fireplace and pulled out chairs for us.

Ruby slung her purse over the chair-back. "The woman at the bar. Is she your girlfriend?"

"No," he chuckled, holding up his left hand and wiggling his ring finger. "Remember, I'm married? That was my little sister, Heather. She and her husband own this pub. What would you ladies like to drink?"

"Fosters will be fine for me." I've read that it's the most popular beer in England. Don't know if it's true or not, but it tastes pretty good to me.

"I'll have a glass of white wine," said Ruby. "Beer makes me burp."

"I'll be right back," he said.

"Beer makes you burp? Since when?"

"Actually, it gives me gas," said Ruby. "I had that beer at lunch, so I'm over my quota now. Trust me, you don't want me drinking more beer."

Nelson returned with a bowl of warm, buttery popcorn. "Drinks are on the way." He angled his chair away from the table and stretched his legs. "Ahhh. Long day."

A barmaid set our beverages on the small, round table. "Can I get you anything else?"

The inspector glanced at us. "Ladies?"

"No, we're good," I said.

He hoisted his stout beer. "Cheers."

Grandma raised her wine glass. "As you slide down the banisters of life, may the splinters never point the wrong way."

They looked at me, expectantly. "Uh... Over the lips, and past the gums, look out tummy, here it comes."

After a couple of swigs, we got down to business.

"I called you because I had no idea who else to call." I leaned forward and lowered my voice as if anyone in the noisy pub could have overheard me. "I think Quentin Wakeham was murdered."

He cocked his head. "Why?"

"Because young men don't just die like that. He seemed perfectly fine when we started out. And then all of a sudden he wasn't."

"And if you're right, how was he murdered?"

I glanced around, and whispered, "Poison."

"What?" He leaned close, touching his ear. "I couldn't hear you."

"She thinks he was poisoned," said Ruby at full volume.

Nelson's eyes narrowed. "Okay. How?"

I told him about my poison pickle theory, and then waited for him to get excited and holler, "Oh my God! You're a genius. I have to investigate this new clue immediately."

Instead, he leaned back and tossed a handful of popcorn into his mouth.

"Well? What do you think?" I asked.

"Your information would have been very helpful if he had, indeed, been poisoned. But, the autopsy confirmed that the poor bloke had a fatal heart attack."

"But he seemed fine."

"Heart attacks can happen to anyone. That's probably why it's the number one killer of men and women."

"But…"

"Katy," said Ruby. "Up until you ate the sandwich today, you had assumed it was a heart attack. And you were right. And I for one, am relieved it wasn't murder."

———

When we got home, Ruby called Nigel Harrington and left a voice mail. She countered the 195,000 with 225,000. We'll see what happens. Not holding my breath.

# CHAPTER SEVENTEEN

**Wednesday, April 29**
*Posted by Katy McKenna*

First words out of Ruby's mouth this morning: "Maybe I should call Mr. Harrington and accept the damned offer."

I stopped brushing my teeth and gazed at her reflection in the mirror. "But it's absurdly low. We need to wait and see how your counter-offer goes."

"I just want to be done and go home." She paused. "No, that's not what I want. I want..." She drew a shaky breath. "I want my big sister back."

"Hold on." I spat, rinsed, and wrapped my arms around her.

"I was so looking forward to her moving to Santa Lucia. You know Edith wasn't just my big sister. She was my best friend, too." Ruby sighed a long, sad sigh. "Losing a sibling is weird, Katy. It makes you feel so...so mortal." She pulled back and swiped a tear away. "I'm really feeling my age."

That was the second time she'd said that recently and it

worried me. She's always been so vivacious, so energetic. So young. But at that moment she sounded so old.

"If you want to accept the offer, then you should do it," I said. "But before you do, let's do some house cleaning. You know you always say that cleaning helps you to make better decisions."

———

Cleaning doesn't boost my mental process, but since it was my suggestion, I couldn't just sit on my tush and watch. While Ruby dusted, I vacuumed the living room, slowly working my way over to the wood stove that provides the cottage's heat. I dragged out a basket of wood pellets that was stowed in a small, low alcove under the stairs and knelt, using the hose attachment to suck up pellet debris on the floor. Leaning my left hand against the back wall of the three-foot-high nook for stability, I twisted down to suck up a thick web draped across the low ceiling. When I pulled my hand away, the wooden wall popped open revealing a crawlspace under the stairs.

"Hey, Ruby. Come look at what I just found."

She crouched, peering over my shoulder. "We need to get those boxes out of there."

The word, "we," meaning, "me," I scrunched low, reached inside, and dragged out a dusty cardboard file box. To get to the other two, I had to lie down and stretch my arm as far as I could into the space, praying nothing would chomp off my hand.

I set the boxes on the dining table and wiped my dusty hands on my jeans. "Wouldn't it be something if we found..."

"A box of rare gold coins like you did in your attic?"

"Or Microsoft shares? Apple? Google? Amazon?"

"With our luck, it'll be Enron stock or DeLorean."

"What's DeLorean?"

"I'll explain later." Ruby lifted the lid from the first box. "Sorry, kiddo. No treasure. Looks like a bunch of old files." She shuffled through the papers. "I think we can toss these. Everything in here looks to be at least twenty years old or more." She pulled all the papers out and set them on the table. "Just want to make sure there are no pictures or legal documents like birth certificates. Things like that."

When she was satisfied that there was nothing worth keeping, she dumped it all back in the box and set it by the front door.

"Now, for box number two." I rubbed my hands together. "Come on, baby. Show me the money."

No money. More old papers.

"These are even older." Ruby glanced heavenward. "Edith— you saved a plumber's bill from 1973?"

"We found all her recent papers in that file drawer in her desk. In fact, I was impressed with her orderliness." I reached into the box, lifted out the pile and plopped it on the table. "She just must've forgotten about these boxes."

Midway through the paper jumble was a small manila envelope with a little bulge. Ruby undid the clasp and peered inside. "Oh, for Pete's sake."

"What is it?"

"Mother's wedding ring set." She tipped the envelope, and a plastic snack bag containing the rings tumbled onto the table. "Boy, this really frosts my pumpkin. I thought the vandals had stolen these. Sure glad I was wrong."

I opened the bag to admire the lovely antique set. "Why would Aunt Edith stash the rings under the stairs instead of in her jewelry box?"

"Probably because she wasn't wearing them and she didn't have a safe. We've been here for over a week and only now found that cubby."

I slipped the rings on my left hand and held it out for Ruby to admire.

"Don't get too attached. They're going to your mother."

"Aunt Edith must've put the ring in that box when the villages around here started having break-ins," I said.

"Don't let me forget to call the police tomorrow to tell them I found the rings."

"And the necklace?"

"I found that, too. Wrapped around Martini Lady's scrawny neck."

# CHAPTER EIGHTEEN

**Thursday, April 30**

*Posted by Katy McKenna*

Today we attended Quentin's funeral. Being that we were the last people to see him alive, we felt we should pay our respects. After the service, we ran into the Mortons.

"Fancy meeting you here," said Ruby. "Did you know Quentin?"

"I knew his father," said Bill. "We served together in the Gulf War. Good man."

"You staying for the buffet?" asked Diane.

"We hadn't planned to, but if you're staying, then we will too," said Ruby.

After filling our plates with sandwiches, potato chips, and pasta salad, we settled at a corner table in the room where the jumble sale had been held a few days before.

I bit into a tuna sandwich on whole wheat and glanced around the crowded room. Mathew Miller was leaning against a wall drinking a beer. The poor guy looked like hell. Probably blaming himself for his cousin's death.

"How is it going with the house sale?" said Bill. "Any interested buyers?"

"We do have one. A cash offer," said Ruby.

"That was fast. Our real estate market has been rather sluggish, lately. Most homes in the area sit on the market for months without an offer."

"Are you going to take it?" said Diane.

"I'm still debating," said Ruby. "The offer is extremely low. I probably should accept it, but I'm also considering getting a different realtor, I mean estate agent. I just don't like Nigel Harrington. There's something about him that I find very off-putting."

"This has been a very trying time for you, to say the least," said Bill. "Wouldn't you rather be done with it?"

*Yes, we want to be done with it. I wanna go home*, I thought.

Diane shook her head, her brown eyes brimming with compassion. "Losing your dear sister has been a heartbreaking shock for you. I know how close you two were."

I saw Ruby's chin tremble.

"And then, instead of having time to mourn, you had to travel thousands of miles to clear up her estate."

Ruby dapped a napkin on the corner of her eye.

"Add to that your dreadful ordeal in the coal mine, and then returning to find the cottage vandalized. The warning on the wall was so frightening. I would not be as calm as you are, would I, Bill?"

He chuckled softly. "If it had been our house, we'd be out of the country by now."

"Preferably in Barcelona." Diane drew the front of her black cardigan together. "Warm, sunny beaches—like California." Her gaze shifted to the window. "Oh, look. It's raining again."

"Are you thinking of moving to Spain?" I asked.

"Maybe retire there someday," said Diane. "It would be nice not to be wearing turtleneck sweaters in the spring. But that's a long way off."

Ruby blew her nose. "I suppose you're right. I need to be done with it and get on with my life."

Diane nudged my arm. "Don't look now, but Margaret Sullivan is standing by the piano."

I glanced over my shoulder. "Really do not want to have another run-in with her. Maybe we should leave now."

"I'd like to finish my food first," Ruby said. "Our backs are to her so it's not likely she'll notice us."

After lunch, we were on our way to the door when Helen and her daughter stopped us. Tessa looked miserable, but I chalked it up to being at a funeral.

"This certainly is a sad day," said Helen.

Tessa told her mother she was going to get a drink. While we made small talk with Helen, I watched the girl fill a paper cup with soda at the beverage table and walk over to Mathew. The expression on his face told me he was not glad to see her. She touched his arm and he jerked away. A moment later, Wendy—the plain and plump girl from the café—scurried up to Tessa, looking protective.

"How old is Tessa?" I asked.

"She'll be seventeen next month."

"She's a lovely girl. She has your gorgeous red hair." I was still keeping an eye on the heated Mathew-Tessa exchange across the room. Wendy had taken Tessa's arm and was trying to coax her away.

"And my freckles, poor thing."

"Does she have a boyfriend?"

"You know how teenagers are," said Helen—totally unaware of the drama that was unfolding behind her. "She doesn't confide in me much these days, but she's been unusually sulky lately and barely speaks to me. I'm pretty sure it has to do with a boy."

"Sounds like a teenager," said Ruby.

Tessa yanked away from Wendy and flung her soda at Mathew, screaming, "It was your bloody baby, you bloody twat. I didn't want to abort it. I hate you! It should've been you that died."

That got her mother's attention and gave us an excuse to get out of there.

At the door, Margaret blocked our exit. "I'd like to have a word with you."

"You've already made it abundantly clear how you felt about my sister. I have no desire to hear more." Ruby slipped on her raincoat. "So if you don't mind, please step aside so we can leave."

She moved away from the doorway, then followed us as we scurried through the rain to our car. "I only wanted to say that I'm sorry."

That stopped us in our tracks.

"You are?" I said. "Really? Why?"

She nodded, looking wretched. "I've thought a lot about what you said to me when I confronted you at the Mermaid Inn." A tear trickled down her plump, ruddy cheek. "I want you to know how sorry I am. For everything I've done."

Ruby stepped toward Margaret with raised arms, causing her to flinch like a dog that's been beaten too many times. "Oh, for God's sake. I'm not going to hit you. I'm going to hug you. It takes a big person to admit when they're wrong. Thank you."

As they embraced, Margaret whimpered, "I've made some bloody awful choices, and my life is a shambles. But now I see how wrong I was to blame Dr. Edith. If only I could go back in time and apologize to her instead of what I did."

# CHAPTER NINETEEN

**Friday, May 1**
*Posted by Katy McKenna*

*Last night*

Got an email from Josh. His cousin, a student at the University of Santa Lucia, is going to stay in his home while he's down south taking care of Nicole. At least he isn't selling his house. So that's a good thing.

I was dozing off when I remembered what Tessa had yelled at the funeral luncheon. *"It was your bloody baby, you bloody twat. I didn't want to abort it. I hate you! It should've been you that died."*

I'm so thankful I never had to deal with an unwanted pregnancy in my teen years. Of course, you actually have to be having sex for that to happen, but still, I am thankful. I could be the mother of a teenager right now.

I have an app on my phone with sleep stories that are supposed to lull you into a comatose state. I plugged in my earbuds and got a boring tale going. Just as I was zoning out, Tessa's last line zinged me awake again.

*"I hate you! It should've been you that died."*

I sat up. Was she talking about the baby, or was she talking about Quentin? I pondered the question a moment and got a sick feeling. Did Tessa kill Quentin?

———

*This morning*

A rude sunbeam glared at me through a slit in the curtains. I adjusted my sleep mask and beckoned sweet slumber to return, but in the next moment, the Tessa memory roused me like a double shot of espresso. I slipped on a cardigan and went downstairs to find Ruby already dressed, made up, and lounging on the couch with her morning coffee and a crossword magazine.

"Hey, sleepyhead. It's about time you got up. Wanna cup of coffee?"

"Ya think?" I poured a cup, dumped four teaspoons of sugar in with a chaser of cream and flopped down beside her with a groan. "I barely got a wink of sleep."

"Talk about not getting any sleep. I'm a wreck."

Ruby-the-wreck looked like she stepped out of a Chico's catalog, while I could have been mistaken for a member of the Walking Dead.

"Anyhoo, I just got a call from our dear Mr. Harrington. He said the buyers have countered at 199,000 pounds. Final offer. And they want an answer by Monday. He insinuated that I was nuts if I don't accept."

"You know, maybe it isn't such a bad offer when you consider what a house inspection might reveal that could wind up costing thousands to repair. So, what'd you say?"

"What could I say? I said okay."

"You accepted the counter-offer? Just like that?" *Oh, yay!*

"No, I said, 'Okay, I'll have an answer on Monday.'"

*Achhhh!*

"And what do you think it will be?"

"I have no idea."

*Oh. My. God. Shoot me now.*

# CHAPTER TWENTY

·**Saturday, May 2**
*Posted by Katy McKenna*

*In the wee hours of the morning*

I awakened from an annoying reoccurring dream where all my teeth crumble and fall out. After running my tongue over my still-intact choppers with relief, I checked my phone. 3:38. I huddled under the covers ready to slumber a few more hours when my nose detected something not quite right.

*Is it smoke? Must be someone's fireplace. Is the window open?* I sniffed the air. *It must be.*

The smoky smell was bugging me, so I got up to close the window in my third floor bedroom and discovered it was shut. I sniffed the air again. "That's odd. I must be super-sensitive."

Back in bed, I pulled the sheet over my nose and tried to focus on a sexy dream scenario. *Who should be my leading man? Bradley Cooper? Chris Pine? Zack Efron?* Chris Pine won and soon he was gazing deep into my eyes, running his fingers down my cheek, and...

Someone was beating on the front door.

I threw back the blankets and rushed down the stairs to Ruby's room on the second floor. "You awake?"

She was sitting up, clutching the blanket to her chest. "Yeah. We locked the door, right?"

"Yeah. Pretty sure. Oh, God. I can't remember. We usually do."

Below the bedroom window, Bill shouted, "Wake up! The house is on fire!"

I went to the stairs and peered down into a dense smoky haze in the living room.

Outside, Diane screamed, "Bill! We can't wait for the firemen. We have to break down the door."

I rushed back to Ruby's bedroom and yanked the blankets off her bed. "Wrap this around you." I ran to the hall bathroom and soaked two washcloths. "Hold this over your nose."

She looked panicked. "Maybe we should try getting out the window."

"We're on the second floor so before we break our necks doing that, let me go downstairs and see how bad it is."

Ruby gripped my arm. "Katy, I can't let you do that. You've got your whole life ahead of you. I'm going."

"I promise, if it's too bad, I'll come right back and we'll go through the window."

Clutching a blanket around my shoulders and holding the dripping cloth over my nose and mouth, I descended a few steps and peeked into the living room. The smoke was thick, but I didn't see an actual fire.

I called to Ruby, "I think we can make it. I don't see any flames."

"I'm still for jumping out the window," she said from the top of the staircase.

"Come on. Let's go, before it's too late."

Diane yelled, "Do it now, Bill!"

I heard glass shattering in the Dutch-style front door.

"We're okay!" I screamed. "We're coming out!"

I led Ruby down the narrow double-back stairs. The ground floor air was a heavy cloud of smoke. Moonlight streamed eerily through the windows giving us enough light to find our way to the open front door.

The Mortons helped us down the stone steps to the sidewalk where we leaned against the retaining wall fronting the house and sucked up big gulps of fresh, cool air.

"I called the fire department," said Diane. "Are you all right?"

Through a coughing spasm, Grandma sputtered, "I will be."

"I don't know where the smoke is coming from," I said. "I didn't see any flames."

"I'm going to take a look. Maybe I can put it out," said Bill.

"Bill. No!" said Diane. "It's too dangerous."

"I don't want their cottage to burn down. Or ours." He sprinted up the steps two at a time.

"Bill! Wait for the fire department to get here," I yelled.

He waved from the door. "No worries, I'll be fine."

I turned to Diane. "First, he goes in the other day when there might have been someone with a gun, and now this. How can you be so calm?"

"Years of this. I learned to get tough when he was in the military." She gestured at our smoky cottage. "This is nothing."

———

*Cause of the fire*

This is really bizarre.

One of the candles in the arrangement on the coffee table had fallen on the couch. A seat cushion had been smoldering for a while. In a few more minutes it would have burst into flames, according to the fire department. From there, things would have moved swiftly. The weird thing is, we have no memory of lighting the candle.

———

All the windows are open to air out the place. We took down the drapes and will get them dry-cleaned. Also we doused the carpets with Febreze. The firefighters had dragged the couch out of the house, and now we have to figure out how to get rid of it.

A friend of Bill's is coming to replace the broken window today. Sure wish I had neighbors like the Mortons.

Unfortunately, this delays our England exit. But you know what? I'm not going to complain. Last night could have been our final exit. So, today I'm counting my many blessings.

———

After dropping the drapes off at the cleaners, we went to the Mermaid Café for a late lunch.

"I'm treating myself to something delicious, and calories be damned," said Ruby. "Like the filet with chips, asparagus, and béarnaise sauce. I can't decide if I want an eight-ounce or a ten-ounce. Mmmm-mmm. Decisions, decisions."

*Sometimes I really hate being a pescatarian.*

"I guess I'll get the ten-ounce. I can take the leftovers home. I think I'll start off with a strawberry and basil mojito. After almost dying in a fiery inferno, I feel like celebrating."

I scanned the wine list. "Since we're celebrating, I'll have a glass of Bulari Brut sparkling wine."

She leveled disapproving eyes on me. "You're driving, you know."

"Geez, Ruby. We're only like a quarter mile from the house."

She crossed her arms looking like a stern schoolmarm. "If you want to risk it, then be my guest."

"Fine. I'll have iced tea."

"Sweetie, I'm kiddin' ya. Have a glass of wine. Have two. It's not like there are any cops in the town to arrest you, anyway."

We placed our order, and a few minutes later our lavender-haired waitress delivered our drinks.

"To a long life," said Ruby.

"L'chaim." We clinked glasses.

When the waitress returned with our food, Ruby asked if Margaret was working today.

She frowned, shaking her head. "No. She's missed the last couple of days."

"Oh? Is she sick?" I asked.

"I have no idea. She's not rang, and she's not answering her phone." The woman glanced across the room. "I have to take care of those people coming in. Enjoy your lunch."

After a bite of Welsh rarebit—which is basically cheese sauce on toast, I said, "That's odd about Margaret."

"Yes, it is." She dragged a juicy piece of medium rare filet mignon through the creamy béarnaise sauce, popped it in her mouth and rolled her eyes. "Oh, that is *sooo* good. How's yours?"

"Fine."

"I bet it is." With an annoying smirk, she sipped her mojito. "Hey! Would it be crazy if we went by Margaret's house to check on her?"

"Considering how she slandered your sister, yes, it would be crazy."

"For some reason, I want to. I guess after what could have happened to us last night, I'm feeling full of brotherly-sisterly love."

After dessert and two cups of coffee, I googled *Margaret Sullivan in Bridleford*. "It looks like her place is just a couple miles from here."

Ruby shoved back her chair. "Let's do it before we come to our senses and change our minds."

The couple miles became more like five since the GPS lady must have decided to take us the scenic route. Finally she announced, "You have arrived at your destination."

"We have? Where?" said Ruby. "I don't see a house."

"Look. There's a For Sale sign by that road leading up the hill."

"Harrington Estate Agency," muttered Ruby. "Figures."

"I think the road is actually a driveway, but I don't want to drive up it. Seems too presumptuous. Let's leave the car here."

As we trudged up the hill, I paused to scoop up a handful of gravel. "I don't think I've ever seen gravel this color before. It almost looks like crushed asphalt."

"Neither have I. Maybe they don't sell it in our area. I like it."

Arriving at the crest of the driveway, we stopped to gaze at the bucolic scene. A pretty stone cottage with cornflower blue shutters sat on the left end of an expansive yard. To the far right was a large, ramshackle barn. Bordering the entire area was a lush fenced pasture of green grass and wildflowers. A dusty, old, brown Toyota Corolla with faded black bumpers was parked near the house.

"That must be her car, so that means she's here," I said. "Let's go knock on the door. I'll let you do the talking since this was your idea."

"I wouldn't have pictured Margaret owning such a charming home," said Ruby.

"The witch in *Hansel and Gretel* had a charming cottage, too, you know," I said. "Now that we're here, I feel pretty silly. I mean, what business is it of ours whether she goes to work or not?"

"We're Americans. We're nosy. It's what we do."

"Stick our nose into other people's business?"

"Yes. Because we care. Don't forget that she apologized. That has to count for something. The woman seems to have a boatload of troubles."

"Yeah. Of her own doing." I banged the cast iron knocker on

the blue door a few times. A calico cat slinked around the corner, and curled through our legs, acting needy. "I think it's hungry."

"Margaret!" Ruby called. "Are you here? It's Ruby Armstrong and Katy McKenna. We just had lunch at the Mermaid. Everyone there is worried about you, so since we were driving by, we thought we'd check on you."

"The waitress didn't seem worried," I whispered.

"Maybe she's in the barn."

Without waiting for my response, she headed toward the old building that hadn't seen a lick of paint in years. I remained at the door feeling more uncomfortable by the second.

I cupped my hands and hollered, "Hey, Ruby!"

She turned toward me. "What?"

"I'm going back to the car."

"Suit yourself. I'll be along after I check the barn."

I scurried down the drive. Just as I was buckling up, Ruby opened the passenger door and slid in.

"That was quick," I said.

"You were right. It's none of our business."

I grinned. "In other words, you chickened out, right?"

"Yup."

# CHAPTER TWENTY-ONE

**Sunday, May 3**
*Posted by Katy McKenna*

We were lingering over our morning coffee watching a home renovation show when Ruby put it on pause. "Oh crap. Guess what I forgot to do yesterday? I was supposed to give Mr. Harrington an answer. Didn't he say the people wanted an answer by Saturday?"

"I think it was Monday, but it doesn't matter anyway since you're not accepting it."

"Oh, you're right. It *was* Monday. Anyhoo, I gave it some more thought last night, and call me crazy, but I'm going to accept the offer."

"It certainly would simplify things, that's for sure. What changed your mind?"

"The fire. We can keep second-guessing this for months to come, or we can be done with it. I'd rather not have this hanging over my head when we go home. It's Sunday so I doubt *Sir* Harrington will be in the office, but I'm calling anyway." She stood and glanced around the room. "Now, where'd I put my phone?"

"I'll ring it."

A moment later, her phone "choo-chooed" upstairs.

"Oh, that's right. I talked to Ben last night."

"I'll get it for you." I sprinted up the stairs and returned with her cell, praying she hadn't changed her mind in my thirty-seconds absence. "Here ya go."

I topped off my coffee, and then sat on the floor cross-legged, propped against her chair.

Ruby dialed. "It's going to voicemail." She listened, then said, "One." She waited. "It's playing 'God, Save the Queen.' Ha! It's the same tune as..." She burst into song, "My country 'tis of thee, sweet land of liberty, of thee I sing. Land where..." She stopped singing. "Mr. Harrington? This is Ruby Armstrong. I'm ready to accept the offer. Talk to you soon." She set her phone on the coffee table. "Now we wait and see."

"Should we tell him about the fire?" I asked.

"Other than the couch, nothing was damaged."

"It still smells smoky in here, and no doubt everyone in town knows about it, anyway. I'll open all the windows again." As I was doing that, her phone rang.

She glanced at the screen. "It's him. That was fast. Here goes nothin'. Hello, Mr. Harrington. I assume you listened to my message." She paused a moment. "Oh, you heard about that, huh? ...It was nothing. The only casualty was the ratty old sofa. No great loss. Everything else is fine...No. No damage at all. There were no flames and...Would you like to drop by and see for yourself?...Yes, I understand that you are obligated to disclose the...As I said, it wasn't really a fire. A few hours more, and it might've been, but luckily that didn't happen. All we have is a bit of a smoky smell that will dissipate in a day or two...All right. I'll wait to hear back from you." She hung up.

"I'm guessing that didn't go so well," I said.

She sighed. "You got that right. How that man can even dare to give me any grief is beyond me."

"Is he coming over?"

"No. He said, *(she mimicked his accent)* 'I am morally, ethically, and legally bound to disclose the fire to the potential buyers. Not doing so could lead to a lawsuit. There could be damaged wiring. Smoldering behind the walls. Irreparable damage to the heating system.' Blah, blah, blah."

"That's crazy. How could there be smoldering behind the walls if the so-called fire was just a smoldering sofa?"

"To listen to him, you'd think he doesn't want to sell the damned house. Clearly, he's on the side of the purchaser, not the seller."

"Which makes absolutely no sense since the selling price affects his commission."

Ruby glanced at the ceiling. "Edith! Why'd did you have to go and die on me?"

We decided to take a walk while waiting to hear back from Harrington. Halfway down the stone steps, Ruby said, "It's a lovely day. How about we see if we can take Charlie with us?"

When we tapped on the Morton's cheery red door, we could hear Bill's voice through the nearby open kitchen window. He called to us, "I'm on the telephone. Be right there."

"It's okay," I said. "We'll see you later."

"No, no. I'm coming." Then, "Ring me later, and let me know how it goes." The door opened. He was grinning like a kid with a new puppy. "Hello, ladies. I hope your day is going as well as mine."

"We were wondering if we can take Charlie for a walk," I said. "But I'm thinking he's not here since he's not giving us the royal greeting."

"Diane took him to our local elder care home for a visit."

"Oh, that's so nice," I said.

"She's just continuing what Edith did with Charlie. She also takes him to visit the kids in the hospital."

"I remember Edith doing that through the years with all her dogs," said Ruby. "It's wonderful that you're continuing the tradition."

"Any news on the sale?" asked Bill.

"I've decided to accept the offer and be done with it," said Ruby.

"When Diane's mother died we took the first offer that came along so we could put it behind us. Maybe we weren't thinking too clearly at the time, and perhaps we could have got more money if we'd waited, but we've never regretted what we did."

"It helps to hear that. Unfortunately, Mr. Harrington has to tell the buyer about our so-called fire. He's acting like it was a big deal, but we all know it wasn't. So now we're waiting to hear back. Fingers crossed we'll have an agreement."

"Let's not keep Bill any longer, Ruby," I said. "Give Diane a hug for us."

"Will do." He gave us a jaunty salute and shut the door.

We headed down the walkway to the street. I suggested we cross the road and walk along the grassy banks of the lazy river. We strolled for a few minutes, then stopped to watch two graceful swans float by.

Stretching my arms overhead, I inhaled a deep lungful of fresh air and released it slowly. "It's so lovely here. Like a picture post-card from fairytale land."

Ruby's phone rang in her pocket. She showed me the phone screen. It was Harrington. "Hello." As she listened, her face became gloomy.

*Oh, this can't be good*, I thought.

"You say they've countered?...One-twenty-five?" she squeaked. "Are you kidding? Because of the fire?" Her face flushed beet-red. "But I told you it wasn't really a fire. It was a smoking sofa. That's all." She paused, tapping a foot. "They want an answer today?"

She glanced at her watch. "It's just after two. Give me a few hours to think about it." She paused. "On second thought, I need more than a few hours, and they can damned well give it to me considering their measly offer. I'll get back to you sometime tomorrow. If they don't like it, they can lump it." She pressed End looking like she might pitch her phone into the river.

"Wow. That's ludicrous," I said.

She crossed her arms, looking grim. "You know what? Edith would kill me if I accepted that insulting offer."

*Oh, crap, crap, crap! Here we go again. I am so sick of this.* I nibbled on a thumbnail.

"Tomorrow, we're gonna go talk to another estate agency over in Downshampton. And don't bite your nails! It's not ladylike."

———

I haven't forgotten what Tessa said at Quentin's funeral. After dinner, I said an early goodnight and went up to my bedroom to do some online research about poison presenting as a heart attack. I don't have a clue where to begin, so I typed: *What poisons cause a fatal heart attack and cannot be detected in blood tests?*

Next thing I know, the internet cops will be knocking on my door wanting to know if I'm planning a murder.

# CHAPTER TWENTY-TWO

**Monday, May 4**

*Posted by Katy McKenna*

We were walking up the street this morning when Ruby froze, pointing at our car. "Don't look now, but I think I see a parking ticket under the windshield wiper."

When we drew closer, we got another nasty surprise. Four flat tires.

"Well, this certainly sucks." I bent to inspect one of the tires. "This one has a hole in it."

Ruby knelt next to me. "Are you sure?"

"Yeah, look." I tapped the puncture in the sidewall. "Who would do that?"

"Looks like someone jammed an icepick into it."

I moved to a back tire. "Look! There's a hole in this one, too. Right next to the valve." I glanced around at the other parked cars. "Ours is the only one. Who would do something like this?"

"It's a rental. Maybe someone hates tourists," said Ruby.

"If we were tourists, we'd be having fun—which we are not." I strode down the lane checking other cars. "This one's a rental." Three cars ahead... "So's this one." I returned to her. "We're being targeted and it's making me really freaking me out. First the vandalism, next the weird fire, and now this."

"Perhaps whoever did this had planned to do all the cars, but then didn't have the chance, for whatever reason." She shrugged. "I'll call the rental agency. Good thing I bought the extra insurance."

I tugged the folded paper from the windshield wiper and read it to Ruby with a sinking heart. "Go home, or you'll be sorry."

My grandmother's eyes widened, mirroring the dread I was feeling. "Just like the message on the living room wall."

———

D.C.I. Jonathan Nelson and Sergeant Anne Caldwell arrived at the cottage about twenty minutes after we called them.

"That was quick." I ushered them through the door. "I know you're understaffed, and this isn't exactly an emergency."

The rumpled, weary-looking inspector looked like he'd slept all night at his desk. "We can't have our visitors being harassed by thugs."

Caldwell, on the other hand, looked fresh, prim, and proper in her navy blue blazer and sharply pressed slacks. She nodded and cracked her thin red lips into more of a weird grimace than a smile.

Nelson glanced around the living room. "We heard about your fire. The fire captain said it appeared to be accidental and was limited to the sofa."

"It really wasn't a fire," I said. "The sofa was smoldering, but that was the extent of it, thank goodness."

"Although, neither one of us recall lighting the candle," said

Ruby. "Let alone setting it on the cushions. You'd have to be an idiot to do that."

"Or have a death wish," said Caldwell. "I assume the sofa out front is yours?"

"Yes." I retrieved the ominous note from the coffee table. "This was left on the car. At first we thought it was a ticket. Now I wish it had been." I handed the note to him and watched his face as he read it.

"This is the same warning that was painted on the wall. Word for word. Let's go look at the tires."

"You people can do that," said Ruby. "I'll wait here and call the rental agency. Katy, better put on a jacket. You sound like you're coming down with a cold."

"It's just hay fever." But even though it was pushing seventy degrees outside, I did as I was told and then led the officers up the lane to where the compact rental car was sitting.

"You said the note was under the windscreen wiper," said Caldwell.

"Yes. The driver's side."

Nelson crouched by a tire, touched the puncture, and then walked around the car.

"What do you think?" I asked.

"Some people don't like tourists, so it could be as simple as that."

"But there are other rentals parked here." I pointed at one just two cars from ours. "And they didn't puncture their tires."

Hands on hips, he glanced around the parking area and pointed up at a camera mounted on a nearby roof. "That CCTV camera should have a video of this."

"What does CCTV mean?" I asked.

"Closed circuit TV used for surveillance. There's approximately five million throughout the UK—most are privately owned. Homes, businesses, schools, hospitals."

"Probably more now, sir," said Caldwell. "That was the estimated number several years ago. No one actually knows how many there are."

"So what you're saying is that practically anywhere I go someone's watching me?"

Caldwell nodded with a pleased expression. "The average person on a typical day is seen by approximately one hundred CCTV cameras. Makes you feel safe, doesn't it?"

"Not really. More like creeped out," I said.

I followed Nelson to the camera mounted on the long golden stone building lining the left side of the narrow road. Upon closer inspection, we saw that the cobwebbed lens was cracked. A faded sign below it said, "These Premises are under CCTV Surveillance."

Nelson harrumphed an exasperated sigh. "Looks like this camera's been broken for a long time."

"So once again, that's that," I said.

"We'll talk to the neighbors. Perhaps someone may have seen or heard something that would help us identify the culprits." He turned to his sidekick. "Get started on that and I'll catch up with you."

She briskly marched toward the first cottage on the lane.

The inspector returned his attention to me. "When are you planning to go home?"

"Hopefully very soon." I lightly touched his arm feeling apprehensive of what I was about to say. "There's something else I'd like to discuss with you." I realized he was gazing off in the distance and not paying attention to me.

He refocused on me. "You were saying?"

In that split second, I decided it was not the right time to get into the Quentin thing again. I needed to give it some more thought. "It can wait."

———

I climbed into our replacement rental car and waited for Ruby. She was leaning on the trunk of the vehicle, or "boot" as they call it here. I checked text messages while I waited for her to have her contemplative moment. It's been a rough couple of weeks, so I figured I should give her some space.

My heart did a nosedive when I saw Josh's name at the top of the messages list. *Things are going pretty good here. Nicole is still responding well to treatment. Miss you. So sorry about all of this. Love you.*

I texted back: *Miss you too. Not your fault. Glad Nicole is doing better.*

Yeah, I know I didn't add *Love you too*. What's the point? That ship has sailed.

Ruby finally opened the passenger door and slid in. "Don't start the car yet."

"We don't have to go to that real estate agency if you don't feel like it." *You could just accept the lousy offer so we can get the hell out of here before someone kills us.*

"No, I want to go. I just need to think," she said in a peevish tone.

"About what?" I asked through tight lips.

She counted on her fingers. "The vandalism, the fire, now the tires, and the frightening note. Not to mention the one on the wall the other night. Who's doing this to us? And why? I tell you, I am really scared."

"The fire may be our fault. I mean, we were both tired, and we'd had a couple glasses of wine."

"More like three," said Ruby. "We finished the bottle as I recall."

"So who knows? Maybe one of us lit the candle."

"And put it on the sofa?" She shrugged. "You'd have to be nuts to do that."

"The door was locked, so it's not like anyone could've sneaked in and done it. Although, I guess they could've done the credit card thing. Maybe it was our vandals again. But why would anyone want us dead? It doesn't make any sense."

"I doubt those vandals would have the nerve to come back again," said Ruby. "Katy." She gazed down at her lap, wringing her hands. "What if I did it and I don't remember? You went to bed before I did. I stayed up to watch another *Whitechapel*. What if I lit the candle and put it on the couch and then went to bed?"

"Why would you do that?"

Her voice dropped to a whisper. "What if I'm getting senile? You know, I've been forgetting a lot of things lately."

My anger instantly evaporated. "Oh, *puh-leeze*. You're not getting senile."

She shook her head. "I'm seventy-five, honey. It could be happening. And if it is, we need to face it."

"You're the sanest person I know. Next, you're going to tell me that you sneaked out last night and punctured the tires."

She cracked a tiny smile. "I'm not that far gone. Yet."

I started the engine and put the car in gear. "Maybe, just maybe, you lit the candle while half-asleep. It's really the only plausible explanation. But let's not make the huge leap to senility."

At the corner, I waited for a tour bus to pass and then pulled onto the main road. "As far as the rest of it—it's probably some local thugs who know we're here to sell the cottage, and they think it's fun to scare the Americans. Heck, they could be watching us right now and having a good laugh."

We subconsciously scrunched down in our seats and glanced around, then peeped at each other and shared a nervous giggle.

About a mile out of Bridleford, I had another thought. "There's one other possibility that comes to mind. Margaret. I don't think she started the fire, but she definitely could've punctured the tires. Just because she said she's sorry, doesn't mean she really is."

I expected an answer to that, but instead I got silence. Finally I said, "Did you hear what I said?"

"Yes, I heard you, and I'm thinking about it."

"Okay, then let me give you something else to think about."

"Watch out for that car!" she screamed, pointing at the windshield.

I swerved to the left, onto the soft shoulder trying to honk the horn, but had no idea where the horn button was.

"The idiot was texting," said Ruby.

I took a moment to figure out where everything was located in the new car. The horn, headlights, windshield wipers.

Back on the road again, Ruby said, "You said you had something else for me to think about."

"I've been thinking about something that Tessa said."

"Who's Tessa?"

*How can she not remember Tessa?* "She's Helen's daughter." I shot her a quick glance and saw the blank look on her face. *Oh, God. Maybe she really is losing it.* "You know. The nice lady who owns the café? Near the Wakeham Coal Mine? Remember her? Red hair? We talked to her at the funeral."

"Oh yes, I remember now. Such a pretty girl. What about her?"

"Do you remember what she yelled at Mathew at the funeral?"

"I haven't got a clue, but then I wasn't paying attention to her. I was keeping an eye on Margaret, who, the more I think about it, the more I'm sure she's the one doing all these nasty things to us."

"You may be right. But back to Tessa. She was talking to Mathew, and it was pretty obvious he didn't want to talk to her. Then she got mad and yelled, 'It was your bloody baby, you twit.' Or maybe it was twat—I dunno—anyway, she finished with 'I hate you, and it should've been you that died.'"

"Oh, yeah. I do remember that. The entire room went silent. So she didn't want to get an abortion, and he didn't want to be a father. Sad, but a pretty common dilemma these days. But why do I need to think about it now?"

"It's the part where she said, 'It should've been you that died.' She's the one who sold the sandwich to Mathew so there's a good chance she made it, too," I said.

"Uh-huh."

"And Quentin said the pickle stuff on the sandwich tasted different."

"Uh-huh. Oh, wait a minute. Are you back to the idea that Quentin was poisoned? The inspector told you it was a heart attack."

"I've been doing some research."

"You mean googling."

"No, I went to Oxford University. Of course, I was googling. I learned there are plant poisons that are hard to detect in the bloodstream, and if they aren't specifically looking for it, they're not going to find it. Usually, the autopsy report will list the death as a heart attack. Plus, some of these poisons grow abundantly in this area."

"My folks grew castor bean plants. They constantly warned us not to touch them—although we did and nothing happened. Very pretty plant, I might add. It's what ricin comes from. The seeds, I think. So, Miss Marple, what kind of poison are you talking about?"

"Monkshood. Also known as wolfsbane. It grows everywhere around here. The flowers are beautiful. Tessa could've mixed a little into the pickle relish, and that's why Quentin said it tasted different."

"But why would she want to kill Quentin?"

*How is she not following this?* "She didn't. The sandwich was supposed to be for Mathew, but he gave it to Quentin." I glanced at her. "So, do you think I'm onto something?"

"I suppose anything's possible. Especially given the stress that poor child is under. Plus, teenagers often do foolish, impulsive things without thinking through the consequences. But do we want to add to her heartache by accusing her of murder just because you found something online that might fit with your (she finger quoted) theory? Let's let the cops do their job. They're the experts, not us."

That annoyed me, so rather than answer, I kept my attention on the road and gave her the silent treatment.

"Now I've made you mad," she said.

"I'm fine."

"No, you're not."

"I'm concentrating on the road, that's all. Not easy driving in a foreign country, you know." Yes, I was annoyed, and at that point I just wanted to drop the subject.

"Look, all I want to do is sign with another agency, book our plane tickets, and go home. Not get further involved in something that doesn't concern us and could very well keep us stuck in England for who knows how long. I for one have had enough." She pointed ahead. "There's the turn."

A couple blocks further I pulled into the Worldwide Estate Agency parking area and killed the engine.

Instead of getting out, we sat silently staring out the window. It's not often that I get aggravated with my grandmother, but I was steaming mad that she wasn't taking me seriously. It was hot and stuffy in the car, so it was either get out or say what I had to say.

"Since we were with Quentin when he died, that makes us involved. And I'm not totally satisfied that it was a heart attack."

And she said, "Well, it's a moot point, anyway, Nancy Drew, because the poor guy has been cremated. End of story."

———

I was still fuming when we stepped through the double doors but was instantly distracted by an anorexic platinum blonde, who pounced on us like a hyena on fresh road kill.

"Hello, I'm Holly. I have some amazing homes that I know you're going to love."

Before we could answer, she rushed us around a pack of caffeine-deficient realtors huddled around a Keurig coffeemaker watching it dribble out one cup at a time, and seated us at her desk.

While Ruby explained the reason for our visit, I marveled at Holly's leathery brown tan, wondering what she'd look like in ten or twenty years. When my grandmother finished her story, the estate agent's initial killer enthusiasm sank to a tepid temperature.

Holly shook her head with a pouty expression. "Unfortunately, there's nothing I can do while you're under contract with another agency. My advice is, go home and read your contract. Normally, there's a notice period anywhere from fourteen days to twelve weeks."

"Twelve weeks? Are you kidding me? I'm too damned old to wait that long," said Ruby. "I could be dead by then."

"No. It's quite common. An agent puts a lot of hard work, time, and money into finding buyers for your property. Let me take a quick look at your listing." Holly pursed her puffy orange lips as she tapped her long snowy white acrylics on her keyboard. "Here it is." She swung the monitor around for Ruby to see an exterior photo taken from across the street. "Is this your cottage?"

"Yes, that's it."

"Here are the interior shots."

The poorly lit photos made the cottage look dismal and depressing.

"No garage or parking area, and the kitchen is very, um… compact, which is typical of these old homes." Holly shook her head with a gloomy expression. "You know, nowadays everyone wants big kitchens with no walls so they can watch their kids every second of the day."

"We can't tear down the walls in a four-hundred-year-old cottage or add more windows, you know," I said.

"True." She shrugged her scrawny shoulders.

"You might be best off taking the cash offer."

Her greedy-beady eyes shifted to the entrance. A young pregnant couple had entered, and Holly stood, beckoning them to her desk before any other agent had a chance. "I'll be right with you," she yelled. And then to us she hurriedly said, "I don't want to keep you. If you decide not to take the offer, I'd love to represent you.

When your contract expires, that is." She smiled. "Mustn't get ahead of myself."

We stood and her attention immediately transferred to the fresh prey lurking behind us.

———

The Harrington Estate Agency agreement says the notice period is thirty days. Tomorrow, I'll take Ruby back to Worldwide to sign a contract with Holly, then she'll tell Mr. Harrington to take a hike—in thirty days. That'll be fun.

# CHAPTER TWENTY-THREE

**Tuesday, May 5**
*Posted by Katy McKenna*

*First, the bad news.*

Someone smashed our car's windshield during the night and left another warning to go home. We reported it to the police (like that will do any good) and the car rental agency sent someone to replace the windshield. I'm surprised they didn't take the car and say they were done with us.

*Now the good news.*

Ruby booked our plane reservations for Saturday. We'll head to Heathrow on Friday and stay at a hotel, have a nice, relaxing dinner, and in the morning, hop on the plane and go home. This time next week, it will all be a memory, and not one of my favorites.

_Harrington Estate Agency_

"I have acted in good faith on your behalf," said Mr. Harrington in a persnickety tone. "And I think you'll come to realize this when those Worldwide people take over. That's a huge corporation with thousands of offices and agents, whereas the Harrington Estate Agency is exclusive to this area. No one cares more about the sale of your sister's home than I do. I considered Edith a dear friend. Can those Worldwide people say that?" He shuffled some papers on his tidy desk. "No, they cannot. But I suppose you must do what you think best."

Ruby tapped a fingernail on his desk. "Listen, Bub. You've been trying to bamboozle me into selling my sister's house at a fraction of its value. How is that caring?"

He tweaked his curled silver mustache. "You have to appreciate how recent events have greatly reduced the value of your home in a buyer's eyes. Vandalism, fire. Your sister slipping on the steps and..."

"Whoa," said Ruby. "What does that have to do with the value of the house?"

"Bad karma, as they say. Your house has a negative reputation now. It's tainted. There are those who may even think it is haunted."

Ruby sat there staring at him coldly for a good thirty seconds. I watched her hands clench and unclench, and I wondered if she might punch him in the nose. Actually, I hoped she'd punch him in the nose. The man was begging for it.

Finally, she spoke in a quiet, measured tone. "Personally, I don't care who sells the house as long as we get a fair price for it. If you can do that, then be my guest. But you better do it before our contract runs out."

"The market is very slow right now, and with all things considered, 125,000 pounds is a fair price."

"Says you. There's something else I'd like to ask you about." She leaned forward in her seat and folded her hands on his desk. "My sister's diamond necklace is missing from the house, and I found out that you gave it to your mother."

Nigel stiffened and nearly yanked his 'stache off. "How do you know that? If I did, that is."

"Never you mind how. Edith's necklace is a pear-shaped diamond with an engraved clasp that has a heart and the number fifty on it. Just like the one you gave your dear old Mummy. My brother-in-law gave it to Edith on their fiftieth anniversary. So how did it wind up in your possession?"

He cast his eyes about the office. "It's a complicated story."

"I've got time. How about you, Katy?"

"Yup. Got all the time in the world."

Harrington looked flushed as he proceeded with his tale. "My mother once owned that necklace. It was stolen from her home many years ago. You can imagine my shock when I saw your sister wearing it."

"If you're suggesting that Arthur stole it, then you've got another think coming, Bub."

He shook his head vehemently. "No, no. I'm most certainly not suggesting that."

"I would be remiss if I didn't mention that you told your mother you bought the necklace at an estate jewelry store," said Grandma.

His eyes bugged out. "How did you know that?"

"Never you mind. I have my ways. Do continue your tale."

"As I was about to say, my mother's eighty-fifth birthday was coming up and I thought about how happy it would make her to have her necklace back again." Harrington paused and reached for a crystal water carafe and poured a glass. "Would either of you care for a water?"

We both said no.

"Tea, perhaps?"

"Just get on with your story," snapped Ruby.

He swallowed half the glass and set it down. "Several months ago, I told your sister that I believed her necklace was the one that had been stolen from my mother. After hearing my story, she agreed to sell it to me. Edith was a very dear, gracious woman and her death was a great loss to our community."

*Oh, brother.*

Ruby crossed her arms, staring at him with narrowed eyes for a long, chilly moment. "Do you have a receipt for the sale?"

He shook his head, looking insulted. "No. Of course not. It was all very amicable. I assure you I paid a fair price for the necklace."

"If you say so." Ruby sighed as she stood. "Thank you for clearing that up."

"I'm glad I could help." He walked us to the door. "I do hope you'll reconsider and accept the offer on the cottage. Wouldn't it be nice to have that burden lifted before you go home?"

"Yes it would—so get me a *fair* offer."

———

Before I revved up our rental car, I said, "Do you find it odd that once again there were no other agents in the office? The last time we were there, he said everyone was out looking at homes. But two times now?"

"Yes, I do think it's odd," Ruby replied.

"There are ten or twelve empty desks. And come to think of it, no clutter on any of them."

"Just because your desk is always a mess doesn't mean everyone else's is, ya know," said Ruby.

"I'll have you know that Albert Einstein's desk was messy, too."

"Yeah. My granddaughter—Katy Einstein."

"We don't have anything good to eat in the house, so why don't we stop at the Mermaid Café?"

"Sounds good to me," she said. "It'll give us a chance to see how our dear friend Margaret is doing."

After we were seated and our dinner order placed, I went to the lobby to inquire about Margaret.

The stout, young man behind the lobby desk said, "We haven't heard from her in days Maybe she's decided she doesn't want to work here anymore. She wouldn't be the first to quit with no notice."

"Has anyone called her?"

He shrugged with a who-gives-a-fig look on his pimply face. "Doubt it. She was not well liked here."

I returned to our table just as the waitress was delivering our white wines.

"Cheers." We clinked glasses, and then I told Ruby what the man had said.

"Maybe she's left town."

"If she's left town, then who's been doing all those awful things to us?" I said.

"Well, I wasn't totally sold on it being Margaret, you know." She sipped her wine and wrinkled her nose. "Too oaky. I'll let it breathe." She set her glass on the table. "Let's go back to her house tomorrow, and this time, we'll really look around. She could be sick or injured, and nobody around here seems to give a hoot."

"Are you sure you want to get involved in something that doesn't concern us?"

"Okay, throw my words back at me. Going to check on a person who may need help is not going to keep us here any longer, unlike your murder investigation. She could be lying on the kitchen floor with a broken leg, or worse, like a stroke. I would hope that if it were me, someone would come and check."

"Someone would come and check because you are loved by many people."

"And Margaret is not. All the more reason for us to go." She sipped her wine again. "Nope. This isn't going to get any better."

"It's only been breathing about a minute." I sipped mine.

"I'll let it continue to catch its breath while you go to the bar and get me something decent to drink."

After dinner, I debated about dessert. Samantha and I always say it's not a good vacation unless you gain at least five pounds. This trip doesn't qualify as a vacation by a long shot, so dessert is therapy for me.

I settled on the bitter chocolate tart with orange sorbet, and Ruby said she'd steal a bite.

"Oh, look. The Mortons just walked in." I stood and waved at them. "Come sit with us."

"It looks like you two have already eaten." Bill glanced at his watch. "It's only seven."

"Us old people eat early," said Ruby. "But Katy ordered dessert so we'll be here for a while still."

They sat, and our waitress gave them menus and took their drink order.

Diane handed her menu back to the server. "I don't need the menu. I'm having the butternut squash risotto."

"It's what she always orders," said Bill.

"Guess I'll have to try that before we leave," I said.

"When is that?" she asked.

"We leave here on Friday and fly out on Saturday."

"I hope that means you got everything sorted with the cottage," said Bill.

"Pretty much," I said. "We'll throw out whatever food is left, and everything else is done. We already shipped several boxes of keepsakes home. And thanks again for taking the sofa to the land-fill, Bill."

"No problem. Glad to do it."

"I think Bill was talking about the sale of the cottage," said Diane. "Have you come to terms on that?"

"More or less," said Ruby. "I signed a contract with Worldwide…"

"But what about your contract with the Harrington Estate Agency?" blurted Diane.

"The new contract won't go into effect until the one with the Harrington Agency runs out. If Mr. Harrington can drum up a better offer than the ridiculous one we have now, I'll take it."

"Tell them about the necklace," I said.

"Oh, this is too funny." She regaled them with the case of the missing necklace.

"It's a rather amazing coincidence," said Diane. "Edith getting his mother's stolen necklace and all, and then being the lovely person she was, selling it to him. It couldn't have been easy for her to part with it."

"I'm sure it wasn't," said Bill. "But that's the kind of lady she was."

The Mortons placed their dinner order, and my dessert arrived, with an extra spoon for Ruby.

"Bill told me someone broke your windshield," said Diane. "This is getting ridiculous."

"Yes, and left another warning to go home," I said. "Believe me, it can't be soon enough. I guess we'll never know who's been harassing us, but it's really got me freaked out."

She shook her head. "I don't know what the world is coming to. This used to be such a safe village. Now I'm locking the doors and windows every night."

# CHAPTER TWENTY-FOUR

**Friday, May 8**
*Posted by Katy McKenna*

*Today was supposed to be the day we put Bridleford behind us and headed for home. But sometimes life (and incredibly bad decisions) can get in the way of your best-laid plans.*

Wednesday
*Part One*

That morning I wasn't feeling as gung-ho about checking in on Margaret as I'd been the night before. It's amazing what a good dinner and couple of glasses of wine can do to boost your bravado. Then in the cold light of morning after a big, steaming cup of Fuzzy Buzzy laced with three heaping teaspoons of sugar, your bravado morphs into: it's none of our business.

If we hadn't told the Mortons our plans, I think we easily could have talked ourselves out of the mission, but we did tell them—

actually, I told them. Me and my big mouth. And they basically had told us we were nuts considering how Margaret had treated Aunt Edith.

---

*Margaret's House*

We parked on the side of the road near the "For Sale" sign, buttoned up our sweaters, locked our purses in the car, and marched up the long gravel driveway. Her old Toyota Corolla was still parked where it had been the other day.

At the front door, I hammered the doorknocker several times, then waited for a response that didn't come. I knocked again while calling her name. Still nothing. "Now what?"

Ruby banged her fist on the door. "Margaret. Are you all right?"

While she assaulted the door, I traipsed through the weedy flower garden searching for a window to peep through. I worked my way around the house and returned to the doorstep. "All the curtains are closed. Try the door handle."

She backed away from the door. "You try it."

"It's probably locked." I pressed the thumb latch. "Or not." I narrowed my eyes at her. "Are we really doing this?"

She nodded and I pushed the door open. From the threshold, we peered into a gloomy living room.

"Helloooo," called Ruby. "Anyone home?"

Silence.

"Margaret?" I yelled. "Are you here?"

Nothing.

We reluctantly stepped inside.

"Everything's pretty tidy," I whispered, running a finger over an end table by the sofa. "Though a tad dusty—not unlike my house."

I screwed up my courage and ventured into the kitchen. There were a few dishes in the sink. I touched the teapot and coffeemaker. Cold.

Ruby joined me. "This kitchen's a lot bigger than Edith's." She opened the refrigerator. "Not much in here. The lettuce has seen better days." She sniffed the milk. "I should throw this out." She set it back in the refrigerator.

"She's obviously not here and hasn't been for a while. She must be on a trip, and we should get out of here," I said.

"Not yet. We need to check the bedrooms and bathrooms in case she's sick and can't call out to us."

I groaned. "Really don't want to go in the bedrooms."

The first room down the narrow, dark hall was an office/sewing room. An ironing board heaped with wrinkled clothes stood in the middle of the cluttered space.

The master bedroom was crammed with massive, ornate, Moroccan-influenced furniture, circa the 1970s. I've seen pieces like these made over on Pinterest boards and still didn't like them. The double bed was neatly made, the dresser top protected by a needlepoint table runner.

I opened both wardrobes. One was empty except for a ratty, leather men's belt hanging on a hook, a few dust bunnies, and a lonely spider residing in the top left corner. The other was jammed with Margaret's dowdy clothes. "It doesn't look like she's packed anything for a trip."

"That's not a good sign." Ruby sighed hard. "I'll check the bathroom." Her tone sounded flat, determined.

"I'll go with you." *Oh God, please don't let Margaret be in there soaking in a bloodbath.*

The tub was empty. The cupboard over the toilet housed the usual essentials, plus a couple of prescriptions. One for blood pressure and the other for depression.

"I don't think she's gone on vacation. Maybe, she went for a walk and tumbled into a ravine."

She shook her head. "Margaret doesn't strike me as the hiking type. I've had enough of snooping around her home. You ready to call it?"

"I'm so ready."

We were closing in on the front door when we heard tires crunching in the gravel driveway. We froze, staring at each other bug-eyed.

"Oh, crap. That could be her," I whispered. "How're we going to explain being in her house?"

"There's gotta be another door out of here. Maybe in the kitchen. I'll check." From the kitchen, she said, "No door."

Panic zapped up my spine. "I'm gonna peek out the front window." I tiptoed to the closest window expecting the door to fling open and come face-to-face with Margaret. How could I explain our presence to her? What if she had a gun and didn't like my explanation? I shifted the white ruffled curtain just enough to get a glimpse of a red sports car using the driveway to do a three-point turn down on the road. "False alarm. It's nobody."

"Let's get out of here before our luck runs out," said Ruby.

We scurried out the front door, and when the door latch dropped into place, I released a lungful of air I hadn't realized I'd been holding.

Halfway down the driveway, Ruby stopped. "We shouldn't leave without checking the barn. She could've fallen while feeding the animals."

"Haven't you had enough anxiety for one day? What if she shows up while we're snooping around?"

"I'm not nearly as nervous about checking the barn as I was traipsing around her house. And if she shows up, we'll tell her the truth."

Before entering the barn, we stopped to gaze at the animals peacefully grazing the lush, green grass in the fenced pasture. I counted four sheep in need of a haircut; three little lambs; two black and white cows; and a grumpy-looking goat perched on a tree stump giving us the stink eye.

Ruby slid back the barn door's steel bolt and opened it. "After you, my dear."

We went inside, and the heavy door slammed behind us.

Ruby glanced around. "Looks just like every big, old barn I've ever been in."

"Like you've been in so many."

"I took riding lessons as a teenager, so I spent my fair share of time in barns. I traded lessons for grooming horses and mucking stalls and loved every single minute of it." She tilted her head with a little laugh. "Well, maybe not the muck so much."

We were in a large open area facing a mammoth stack of baled hay.

I wrinkled my nose. "It smells weird in here. Must be the hay." I narrowed my eyes. "Please tell me that's not smoke I see."

"It's steam. It's pretty warm in here and the hay was probably a little damp when they baled it," said Ruby. "Look at all the loose hay on the floor. I wonder when the last time was that anyone swept."

"Not up to your barn-keeping standards, huh?"

"Ha! Ha! Very funny. And true."

"Margaret?" I hollered at the top of my lungs. "You in here? Margaret!" I glanced at Grandma and shrugged. "Guess not."

"We need to do our due diligence. Just because she didn't answer doesn't mean she's not here."

The scrawny calico cat we'd met the other day ran to greet us, and I scooped him up listening to his little motor purr. "Isn't anyone taking care of you?"

"Katy, he's a barn cat. I'm sure he gets plenty of juicy mice to eat."

"From the looks of him, he—or she—could use a few more." I held him up for a peek. "He's a him." I stroked his soft fur and came away with a handful. "Okay, Barney. Time to put you down so we can do what we came to do." He was not happy with that plan and clung to my navy blue cardigan with his claws. "It's a good thing for you that I'm a cat lover because some people might not appreciate you snagging their sweater."

He leaped out of my arms and beelined to the other side of the barn.

"Let's go check the stalls," said Ruby. "She could've been cleaning them out and fallen."

"Sounds lovely. I'll catch up in a minute. I'm going to check the back of the barn behind the hay."

A moment later, I heard her shout. "Oh, my God. This is disgusting!"

I ran to her. "What? What?"

"This." She was standing in front of the first stall in the aisle pointing at a wet mess of ankle-deep, trampled manure, urine, and straw. "Whatever Margaret's been doing, she sure hasn't been cleaning stalls."

I plugged my nose. "Wow. That really stinks. The ammonia smell is making my eyes water. I can't believe you used to clean stalls like this. Especially as a teenaged girl—I mean I would've had no tolerance for this at all."

"First off, cow manure is a lot sloppier than horse manure, and secondly, we never let the stalls get in this condition. This stall hasn't been cleaned in who-knows-when. Months, probably. Plus, we used sawdust. It absorbs the urine—whereas straw absorbs nothing. This is absolutely revolting. However, I was a horse crazy girl, and would've done anything to be around them—so even if it had been like this, I think I would've done it. Of course, then it wouldn't have been like this."

I followed a few steps behind her while she peeked into the next two equally disgusting stalls. Halfway to the last one, she stopped, wrinkling her nose. "Something's rotten in the state of Denmark."

I sniffed the air. "Oh, geez. I know that smell. Something must've died. Maybe a cow or something."

"Or Margaret," she yelped.

I hung back as Ruby rushed to the stall. "Oh, my God! Oh, my

God!" She clapped her hands over her nose and mouth, spun away from the stall, doubled over, and heaved. She lifted her ashen, terrified face. "Don't look."

Margaret had hanged herself. Late morning sunlight filtering through the grimy stall window illuminated her gruesome face. Beneath her dangling swollen feet lay a tipped over wooden stool. The reality of it was staggering.

It was a lot to take in, and I stood there, transfixed. I wanted to run but it was like I was rooted to the spot. Finally, I found my voice. "Look. There's a piece of paper sticking out of her waistband."

Ruby had propped herself against the wall opposite the stall. "I can't look. It's too much. I knew in the back of my head that we might find her dead. But not like this."

Swatting files away, I took one shaky step into the stall.

"Katy. Stop. Whatever that note says is meant for her family, not us."

"You're right. Let's get out of here and call the police."

I was in the lead as we sprinted to the barn entrance. Without slowing my pace, I rammed my shoulder into the wood door expecting it to swing open. It didn't, and I bounced back. "I think it's locked."

"How the hell could it be locked?"

"I don't know." I squinted through the crack between the door and the frame and saw the slide bolt was locked in place. "Damn it. It must've slid back when the door slammed. I saw another door at the back of the barn. Hopefully, it's not locked."

We rushed to it, and I pressed the rigid rusty latch handle. "No! No! No!" I tried again, pushing with both thumbs. "It's locked, too. Now what?"

"Let me give it a try." She elbowed me aside and tried her luck with the lever. "You're right, it's locked." Mouth pursed in a tight frown, she glanced around. "Let's try to stay calm, okay?"

"Calm? How can I stay calm? I'm freaking out right now."

A car door slammed. "Did you hear that?" Ruby banged on the door. "Hey! We're locked inside!"

I joined her, pounding the door with my fists. "Let us out!"

The car roared into life, and we heard its tires crunch through the gravel and fade away.

I sagged against the wall. "That's just great. Whoever that was must've locked the barn, not realizing we're in here. I wonder who it was?"

"My first guess would be Margaret's husband. Who else would lock up the barn?"

"Oh, my God," I said. "Do you think he murdered her and staged it to look like a suicide?"

She shook her head. "Kind of hard to stage a hanging I would think. Plus, Margaret has been dead for a while. At least a few days. All I know is we need to get the hell out of here and call the police."

"How're we going to do that?"

"It's not like we're locked up in Fort Knox. It's just an old, dilapidated barn. We need to calm down and think." She crossed her arms, frowning for a few seconds, then her eyes widened. "The bars over the stall windows should unlatch and swing out. Then we can climb out. Trouble is, the only clean stall is the one that Margaret's in."

"I'm fine with going through one of the dirty stalls."

We made our way to the stall furthest from the one where Margaret hung, with Barney-the-cat trailing behind us.

"I'll wait here," said Grandma. "When you get out, you can open the door for me."

I rolled up my jeans, dipped one toe in the sludge, and my stomach lurched. Eyes drizzling and holding my breath, I plunked both feet into the cold cow poop stew and sank in up to my ankles. "Oh geez, this is so disgusting."

"I'm so sorry you have to do this, honey. I owe you one. Maybe a really good dinner tonight."

"Not really a good time to be talking about food." I pulled one foot up to take a step and my red canvas slip-on was sucked off with a wet, smoochie sound. Another step and I said goodbye to the other one. No way was I fishing them out of the pungent slop.

Tears drooled down my cheeks as I gagged and sloshed my way across the rank stall. At the window, I gripped the iron bars and gave a hard yank. "Damn it! It's stuck."

"Look for a lever to release it," said Ruby.

I ran my eyes around the entire window frame. "No lever. No lock. No nuthin'. It's screwed into the frame."

"You're kidding me," she said.

*Yeah, like I'm in a kidding mood right now.* "No."

"I know you're not, sweetie." She glanced down the row of stalls with a scowl. "I think I smell something funny."

"Yeah. This disgusting mess reeks of rotten eggs and ammonia, but it's like roses compared to poor Margaret."

"No. Something else." She backed away from the stall entrance and sniffed the air. "It can't be. It's got to be my imagination."

"What?"

"It smells like…" She dashed down the hall toward the front of the barn and yelled, "There's smoke coming from the hay bales!"

In my rush to vacate the stall, I slipped face-first into the slime. I grappled to my feet, spitting putrid gunk out of my mouth, and trying to clear my eyes with my filthy hands as my stomach sent me a tsunami warning.

"Come on, Katy!" screamed Ruby. "Hurry up!"

I took a step and my stomach made good on its warning. Over and over, until I was on my knees, one hand down in the manure, propping me up.

"Please, Katy!" shouted Ruby. "We have to get out of here!"

I crawled to the stall entrance where she reached in to help me up, but I waved her hand away. I didn't want to risk pulling her down with me. I made my way to the dirt floor in the hallway and we ran to the main door, shoving against it and hoping for a different outcome this time. It rattled and heaved, but the bolt wasn't giving up. I spun around and leaned against the door.

The haystack was smoldering in its mid-section and puffing out spirals of smoke, but since I didn't see any actual flames, I tried not to panic. After all, we'd survived our smoldering sofa and there hadn't been flames then, either.

"There's got to be a fire extinguisher somewhere around here," said Ruby.

The walls and dirt floor were cluttered with what you'd expect to find in a barn: a wheel barrow, pitchfork, sawhorse, gas cans, rakes, shovels, a farm utility vehicle. A workbench strewn with rusty tools. But no fire extinguisher. I moved the gas cans further from the hay.

"Katy! Look! There's a sledgehammer leaning against the wall by the workbench. We can use it to break down the door."

I dragged the big hammer to the door. "This thing's a lot heavier than I expected." As I started to lift it to swing at the door, Barney appeared and tried to climb my legs. "Barney! Out of the way!"

The terrified cat ignored my command and Ruby snatched him up, clutching him close to her chest. He struggled and scratched her arms and face. She let go and he darted away.

The hammer was too heavy to lift overhead, so I swung it underhand. My first swing was so feeble that all I managed to do was make a small dent in the wood. I kept at it, and twice slammed it into my shin on the return swing.

A pungent stream of smoke was billowing out of the haystack, filling the barn and choking us. "Grandma, get down low. The air will be better."

She hunkered down. "That utility vehicle over there. See if it has keys. If it does, maybe we can ram it through the door."

I hopped on the seat, cranked the keys dangling in the ignition and got nothing. "The battery must be dead!"

Ruby gestured me to move over and slid in behind the wheel.

She pulled out the choke, turned the key, and after so
complaints, it started. Hunched over the wheel, she move
vehicle a few feet, aiming at the door. "Hang on and cover y
face!"

She stomped on the gas. The tires skittered in the dirt, then
gained traction, and the vehicle jolted forward, slamming into the
barn entrance. The door flew open, and we blew through, skidding
to a dusty halt in the middle of the barnyard. Ruby collapsed over
the steering wheel, not moving.

"Oh, God, oh, God! Please don't be dead." I shook her shoulder. "Grammy, Grammy."

She lifted her head and coughed in my face. "What...(cough-
cough-cough)...a...(cough-cough-cough)...RUSH!"

We whooped for joy, hugging and hacking like we were three-
pack-a-day smokers. When I caught my breath, I said, "I need to
get my purse out of the car and call for help."

She nodded, clearing her throat several times. "Faster to go in
the house and use the phone."

"You're right." I glanced around the barnyard. "I don't see the
cat. Oh, no! What if he's still in the barn?"

"I'm sure he ran out the door. He'll be fine."

"Can you go call while I check around?"

"You're not going back in the barn, right?"

"God, no. I just need to know he's okay. Remember—emergency is 9-9-9, not 9-1-1."

"Got it!" Ruby hit the accelerator, and the back tires spit black
gravel at me as she careened across the yard to the house.

My adrenaline had fizzled, my sledge-hammered shin was
throbbing, and I felt every sharp pebble grind into my bare feet as I
limped toward the barn. "Barney? Here kitty, kitty, kitty."

I surveyed the field where the livestock was grazing, oblivious to
all the drama. "*Baarrnneey*! Where are you?"

"*RRRAAAA*."

The bloodcurdling feline scream had come from the far end of

ed under the ashy smoke spewing through the
ntrance and called out to him.

*wish I knew his name.* "Here, kitty, kitty!"

ed like he was in Margaret's stall. His momma.

"Please come, baby!"

His pitiful shrieks gutted me.

"Oh, God. Please come, kitty! Please!"

Could I just stand there and listen to him die an agonizing
death? What would I do if this were my cat, Tabitha? I'd save her.
No question about it.

A stiff breeze kicked up, blowing the smoke back into the barn
and away from the door, giving me a clear view inside.

Was this a sign from above telling me to do the right thing?

# CHAPTER TWENTY-FIVE

**Friday, May 8**

*Posted by Katy McKenna*

Wednesday

*Part Two*

The hay bales were still just smoldering—no flames—so I figured it was pretty safe to go grab the cat. I sprinted down the stall aisle and found the boney feline clinging to Margaret's shirt, mewling pathetically.

"Come on, baby. Come to Katy."

Of course, he didn't come to me. That meant I had to go to him. Something I really did not want to do. But I was there to save him, not leave him behind to die in a fire.

"I'm getting you outta here." Holding my breath, I edged close to the hanging corpse and on tiptoe, reached up hoping the cat would leap into my arms.

"KATY!" screamed Grandma from the entrance. "God-dammit, get the hell out of there."

"I'm okay! I'll be right there!" I bent over to right the wood stool beneath Margaret's dangling feet, and her work boot clunked my forehead. With a head-to-toe shudder, I jumped back with a shrill squeal.

I perched on the stool and wrapped my hands around Barney's chest, feeling his ribs through the fur, and gingerly drew him toward me. His legs stretched out, but his claws remained pinned to her shirt. With shivering revulsion, I plucked one paw at a time, receiving several ungrateful scratches for my effort.

When the last claw ripped free, he transferred his desperate clutch to me, digging his sharp talons into my soggy clothes. Holding him close, I stepped off the stool. Just as I was leaving the stall, I remembered the note in Margaret's waistband and snatched it.

Outside the stall, smoke was billowing down the aisle toward me. Bending low, I clutched the cat and ran headlong into it. I rounded the corner at the end of the stalls and got another shock. In the few minutes it had taken me to grab the cat, the smoldering haystack had burst into a towering inferno.

"Katy! Katy!" yelled Grandma from outside.

"Grandma!"

"Katy! Are you all right?"

"It's so smoky, I can hardly see!" I could barely make out the entrance—a lighter shade of gray in the murky smoke. As I tried to move toward it, the heat kept beating me back.

"Katy! You have to get out of there now!"

A flying ember hit my shoulder. Another seared my scalp. It was nearly impossible to breathe, and the radiating heat forced me to backtrack.

Suddenly, the top tier of the burning hay bales crashed to the ground, sending blazing rivulets streaming across the dirt floor. If I didn't get out of there immediately, I'd be toast.

With fire literally nipping at my heels, I dashed toward what I hoped was the open door. I staggered out into the barnyard and sank to my knees, still clutching Barney.

My grandmother coaxed me further from the burning barn, then folded her arms around me. "My baby, my baby. What the hell were you thinking? Are you trying to send me to an early grave?"

Fire engines roared up the driveway. Moments later, strong arms settled me on a stretcher and tried to dislodge the cat, but he wasn't having it.

I must've lost a minute or two, because the next thing I knew I was in an ambulance, cat-less, with an oxygen mask strapped on my face. Ruby was lying across from me, also wearing a mask, and glaring at me.

She pulled her mask aside. "Of all the idiotic things you have done in your life—and you have done a lot of idiotic things, my girl—but this one takes the cake. Thank you for aging me about a hundred years today."

"I'm sorry. I just..."

"Your parents never would've forgiven me if you'd died. And for what—a goddamned cat? What the hell were you thinking? Never mind, don't answer that. I already know the answer. You weren't thinking. Sometimes you need to make decisions with your brain, not your heart." She coughed, sounding croupy, and cleared her throat. "What you don't realize is I love you as if I gave birth to you. You are my heart and soul. And furthermore..." She coughed several times, and drew a wheezy breath.

"Ma'am. Please stop talking." The male paramedic attending us repositioned the oxygen mask on her nose and Ruby went back to glaring her grandmotherly love at me.

———

We were in the E.R. hooked up to heart monitors, blood pressure machines, I.V. saline bags, and pulse oximetries to check our oxygen saturation levels. You name it, we were hooked to it. Given my grandmother's age, I'm sure they were concerned about lung damage.

As for me? I was hot. Literally smokin' hot. Breathing was painful. My throat felt raw. I had a killer migraine, my battered shin was throbbing, the top of my head hurt, and my eyes felt deep-fried. Other than that, I was fine.

A matronly nurse named Carol wearing a medical mask and blue latex gloves gently removed my putrid clothes. She snipped my pants leg. "Oh, my. What happened here?"

Talking hurt, but I felt obliged to answer—just like I always do when the dentist asks me a question while drilling a tooth. "I slammed a sledgehammer into it."

"Oh. Of course. We'll need to get a history on you. And an X-ray of that leg. Any drug allergies?"

"She's allergic to penicillin," said Ruby.

The nurse began washing my arms. "We have to get you thoroughly cleansed to avoid infection. The doctor will be in shortly to check your burns and order some antibiotics and pain medication."

———

Because of the severe hoarseness coupled with the length of smoke exposure, and my blood oxygen level, Dr. Sheldon decided to intubate me. That was fine by me until she explained that "intubate" meant a tube would be snaked down my throat to keep my airway from swelling shut.

I protested and was interrupted by Grandma. "You ran into a burning barn to save a damned cat, and you're fussing about this? I've done it, and it's a piece of cake."

They gave me a valium, which always knocks me for a loop, waited a few minutes, then squirted numbing spray in my throat. The next thing I knew, they were done. Piece of cake.

The downside of this was now Ruby could scold me to her heart's content, and I couldn't defend myself. The upside was, I was so groggy, I didn't care.

———

Around midnight, a nurse woke me to see how I was doing. After checking my vitals, she said she was going to remove the endotracheal tube. The thought of snaking that thing out of me scared the bejeebers out of me, and when she saw my terrified expression, she explained why it was time to remove it.

"Prolonged intubation can lead to many complications, including sinusitis, vocal cord injury, laryngeal injury, laryngeal stenosis, tracheal injury, hemoptysis, and pulmonary infection."

That was supposed to make me feel better?

# CHAPTER TWENTY-SIX

**Friday, May 8**
*Posted by Katy McKenna*

*Thursday Morning*

"Wake up, sleepyhead. We have a visitor," said Ruby from her bed.

"What?" I opened my eyes to D.C.I. Nelson's haggard, sympathetic smile.

"You certainly look better than you did yesterday."

I tugged the thin blanket up to my chin wishing I could pull it over my head. "I don't remember seeing you yesterday."

"Sergeant Caldwell and I arrived at the scene shortly before you were taken away in the ambulance. Let's see, you've been in England for about two weeks, give or take, and have been in two fires. Who does that?" He chuckled. "Is this a hobby or are you a pyromaniac wannabe?"

"I was trying to save a cat." I sat up straight. "Oh, my God. I've been so drugged up that I completely forgot about him."

"Not to mention poor dead Margaret," said Ruby.

"We found her body." He tilted his head with furrowed brows. "Why were you two there?"

I had no desire to tell that story. "My throat's sore so I'll let my grandmother explain."

She launched into an animated blow-by-blow monologue of our escapades. I leaned back and listened, thinking about what we'd done and why. It brought to mind some of the shows I watch that make me yell at the TV, *This is so ridiculous. No one would ever do that.* Turns out, they do. Or at least I do.

As Ruby droned on, Nelson asked a few questions and took notes. I tuned out until she got to the part where we found ourselves locked in the barn.

"You're sure the door wasn't stuck rather than locked?" he asked.

"I'm sure. Not only that, there was a car outside of the barn. We heard it start up when we were trying to get out the back door. We screamed and pounded on the door, but either they didn't hear us or didn't care."

"Do you think someone deliberately locked you in the barn?" he said.

"Damned if I know," said Ruby. "But you gotta wonder. Could this have been the same person or persons who've been harassing us and now they've decided to ramp it up to murder? And if so, why?"

"The note!" I blurted, then whispered, "Oh, that hurt!"

"That's right!" said Grammy. "There was a note stuck in Margaret's waistband. Katy was going to grab it, but I said we shouldn't touch any evidence. Dammit. Now we'll never know what it said."

"I did get it."

She sat up in her bed speaking in that soothing tone that people use when talking to a child. Or a lunatic. "No, you didn't, honey. Remember?"

"Yes. I remember. When I went back for the cat..." I paused to cough up a hefty wad of phlegm. The detective handed me a box of tissues. "I found him latched to her chest."

"Oh, geez," said Ruby.

"Anyway, when I pulled him off her." The memory made me quiver. "I took the note, too. I figured it wasn't going to survive the fire."

"Where is it?" asked the inspector.

"I put it in my pants pocket. Oh God, I hope no one threw away my clothes."

"Why would they do that?" he asked.

"You tell him, Ruby."

She did, in graphic detail, and I could tell by his pursed lips that he was having a hard time not snickering. Who could blame him? The scene in the stall sounded like a slapstick comedy.

He went searching for my clothes and returned carrying a clear plastic bag full of my putrid garments—with my bra on the top for all to see. He laid the bag on the bed table, unzipped it, and stepped back, wrinkling his nose. "That's bloody awful."

He pulled latex gloves from his pocket, snapped them on, and in a business-like manner, extracted my slimy padded underwire, then realized he had nowhere to put it. Dangling it between two fingers, he glanced around the room.

"You can put it in the garbage can," I muttered.

Next item into the trash was my sensible beige big girl briefs.

"You say you put the note in one of the pant pockets?"

I answered through clenched teeth. "Yes."

His eyes watered as he wriggled out the smelly pants and plopped them on top of the bag, then gingerly extracted the damp, stained note from the back pocket.

"You can throw everything away."

He did and then spread the note on a paper towel. "Okay. Let's see what we have here." He read it, emitting a few "hmms." When he finished, his face was grave.

"Well? What's it say?" asked Ruby.

"It appears to be a suicide note."

"So that means you're not going to tell us even though my brave granddaughter…"

*Oh, now I'm brave instead of an idiot.*

"…risked her life to get that letter."

"This is a critical piece of evidence, and I'm glad you had the foresight to take it. Had the fire made it to the stall it would have been destroyed." He picked up the note and slipped it into a manila envelope. "Do you have anyone to give you a ride home?"

"Uhhh…" I glanced at Ruby.

"We can call a cab," she said. "Our car is still at Margaret's. Katy, will you be up to driving?"

"If we were in California, yeah. But not here. Not today." I shook my head with a sigh. "I dunno. Maybe I can."

"I'll take you to your car," said Nelson. "When we get there, if you don't feel up to driving, I'll take you home and arrange for your car to be brought to you."

"Oh, thank you. That will give me a chance to check on Barney," I said.

"Are you kidding me?" said Ruby. "You're still worried about him?"

"Who's Barney?" asked Nelson.

"He's the reason Katy ran into the burning barn."

"Oh, yes. The cat. Didn't know his name. No need to worry about that mangy little rascal. He's found a home already."

"Really? Where?" I asked.

"Yesterday, when Caldwell wrestled him off of you, the little tosser attached himself to her. She felt she had no choice but to take him…"

*Oh, no. That cold fish took him to the pound.*

"…home. She told me this morning that he's already taken over the place."

# CHAPTER TWENTY-SEVEN

**Friday, May 8**
*Posted by Katy McKenna*

Thursday
*Part Two*

Dr. Sheldon had good news and bad news. The good news was our blood tests came back and everything was in the normal range, more or less. Ruby more, and me less.

"Your lungs have been compromised. Right now, your resting oxygen saturations are fair and will continue to improve so I don't expect any serious complications. But I'd feel better if you postponed your trip home on Saturday to give your lungs, and body, a few extra days of rest." The doctor brushed a stray curl from her forehead and turned her attention to Ruby. "You amaze me. You must follow a very healthy diet and workout routine."

"My diet is pretty good," said Ruby.

Neither woman noticed my snarky eyeroll. "Pretty good" is a

pretty big stretch. Yeah, she eats her vegetables, usually drowning in cheese sauce or butter. Canned fruit smothered in several squirts of Reddi-wip. Prime rib, steaks, cheeseburgers, bacon.

Ruby continued. "But it could be better. I probably drink too much wine, but I do work out regularly. I'm also blessed with good genes, I think."

"Well, whatever you're doing, keep doing it." Then back to me. "You should take a page out of your grandmother's book."

*It would probably kill me.*

"To be fair," said Ruby. "Katy was in the barn a lot longer than me." She swung her cranky eyes on me. "Even though I begged her not to go back in."

The doctor picked up both my arms and inspected them. "Make sure you keep the antibiotic cream on these burns. Luckily, they're superficial, so no lasting damage. Let me see your scalp."

I tipped my head, and she inspected the spot on top of my head where an ember had landed. "That one will hurt for a while, but the hair should grow back nicely."

*I have a bald spot? Again?* Last year I had to have several stitches in the back of my head, and a big patch of hair was shaved off. Took forever to grow out.

———

At four o'clock, Inspector Nelson returned. "I'm told you're free to go now."

"I just realized I have no clothes," I said.

The big, rumpled man grinned. "No worries. It's a sunny, warm day. You'll be fine."

Ruby stood and grabbed her purse. "All righty, then. Let's vamoose."

"Seriously? You expect me to waltz out of here in a hospital gown?"

"It's not like anyone knows us here," she said. "Besides, they'll be too distracted by your puffy, red eyes and scorched bald spot to notice."

A chipper senior hospital volunteer rolled a wheelchair into the room. "Hello. I'm Lesley. I hear you two are going home. As soon as I have one of you seated and in the hallway, Cyril—" She waved at an elderly man waiting with a wheelchair outside the room —"will come in for the other. Who wants to go first?"

I pointed at Ruby. "She's going. I don't have a thing to wear so I'm staying."

"Oh, my. We can't have that. You've been discharged. Where are your clothes?"

"They're in the garbage."

"I'll go fetch something for you to wear." Lesley scurried out of the room.

"While we wait, are you going to tell us what the note said?" I asked the inspector.

"No. Not just yet. We have a number of inquiries to make so it would be premature to discuss it."

"What's the harm in telling us?" said Ruby. "If it weren't for Katy, you wouldn't even have the thing."

The cheery volunteer trotted back into the room. "Here we go, love. This should do nicely. You can keep on the gown you're wearing and wear this one like a coat." She held up a faded blue hospital gown. "And you can take your disposable slippers."

By the time we were buckled into Nelson's car, I was worn out. I must've looked it because he announced he was taking us straight home. If only straight home meant 539 Sycamore Lane, Santa Lucia, California, USA.

He parked on the sidewalk in front of the cottage and assisted us up the stone steps and into the house, then said someone would be 'round with our car later.

I made it up the first flight of stairs easily enough, but the second set to my bedroom on the third floor did me in. I was puffing, and my lungs felt like they were being crushed in a vise. I perched on the edge of the bed and did a breathing exercise that the pulmonary specialist said helps you retain more oxygen. When I got my breath under control, I slipped on undies, sweats, and socks, then sat again, feeling like I'd just run a marathon.

In the living room, I planted myself on one of the armchairs, and Ruby served me a cup of tea.

"Woo-hoo. Knock-knock," called Diane from the porch.

Ruby opened the door to the Mortons, and Diane rushed to me, clucking like a mother hen. "You poor thing. We heard what happened." She leaned back to take a good look at me. "Oh, my God. You look bloody awful."

"I feel bloody awful, too."

"Maybe you should have a lie-down," she said.

"I've been lying down all day. How did you hear what happened?"

Bill shrugged. "Word travels fast around here. You can't keep anything a secret for long. That's why I don't fool around."

Diane playfully punched his arm. "Is there anything we can get you two?"

"A one-way ticket home sure would be nice," I said.

"Saturday will be here before you know it."

Ruby shook her head still looking none-too-pleased with me. "The doctor wants Katy to rest a few days so Saturday is out. She inhaled a lot of smoke and her lungs need to recuperate. That's what happens when you run into a burning barn to save a cat. My granddaughter will be the death of me yet." She grunted as she got up from her chair. "I don't know about you guys, but I need a glass of wine or several shots of tequila."

Diane waved her back down. "Sit. Let me get it for you." She stepped into the kitchen, then brandished a nearly empty bottle at us. "Bill. Would you run to our house and bring a bottle—and some glasses?"

"Red or white?" he asked, heading out the door.

"I know! Bring that bottle of champagne in the fridge we've been saving for a special occasion," she said.

"Don't waste that on us," said Ruby.

"I think we have something to celebrate," she said. "And that requires champagne."

"Celebrate what?" I probably sounded like a grumpy old man.

"That you're both alive."

Bill returned a few minutes later and busied himself in the kitchen popping the champagne cork and filling glasses. He handed me a glass of golden bubbly. "You look absolutely knackered, so we won't stay long. But first—a toast!"

"To a long healthy, *safe* life," said Diane. "And to going home and putting all of this behind you. Cheers."

Ruby raised her glass higher and gazed heavenward. "And to our guardian angel, whoever he or she may be."

"What're you talking about?" I asked.

"In all the hullabaloo, I completely forgot about this. When I went into Margaret's house to call for help, the phone was dead. But evidently *someone* called because the fire engines and para-medics arrived just as you ran out of the barn."

"Someone in a neighboring house must've seen the smoke," said Diane.

"After everything that's happened, are you still switching to another estate agency?" asked Bill.

"If it were me I would take the offer and be done with it." Diane reached out and patted Ruby's hand. "But that's just me. I'm not good with stress. I always tend to take the path of least resistance."

"That's why she agreed to marry me. She knew I would never give up, so it was easier to give in."

She flashed a coy grin. "Like I said, I take the path of least resistance, and usually never regret it."

After they left, I stood and stretched my achy body, then noticed movement outside the front window and panicked. I checked to ensure the door was locked, and saw it was D.C.I. Nelson standing on the porch.

"I wasn't expecting to see you again today," I said after opening the door.

"Here's your car key." He dropped the fob into my hand. "I parked it up the road. May I come in for a moment?" He waved at a sedan out front, then bent his head to clear the low door frame. "Hello, Mrs. Armstrong. Mind if I sit?"

"Be my guest. Any updates on the barn fire?"

He dragged a dining chair over to the sitting area. "We are investigating."

"What about tire tracks in the back of the barn? You know, from the car we heard?" I said.

"It's a heavy layer of gravel, so no clear tracks." Nelson removed an envelope from his inside breast pocket. "I'd like to tell you what Margaret's note said." He extracted a copy of the original, cleared his throat, and glanced at us.

"Go ahead," said Ruby.

*"I'm sorry for what I did. I never meant to really hurt Dr. Edith. I'd been so upset over everything and I placed the blame on her.*

*It was bitterly cold that night, and the pavement was icy in spots. I was walking to my car after work and slipped and fell.*

*As I drove past Dr. Edith's cottage, I was hurting from the fall and thinking about everything I'd lost. All because she had killed our cow. I knew she walked her dog late every night and I hoped she would slip on an icy patch like I had.*

*Then I noticed the water bottle in my cup holder and without really thinking, I stopped the car and poured the water on her steps, hoping it would freeze in time for her walk.*

*I swear I never meant to kill her. I know now that none of my problems were Dr. Edith's fault. But her death was my fault. I'm so sorry."*

The inspector took in our stunned faces. "I know this must be hard for you."

I perched on the arm of Grandma's chair and put my arms around her trembling shoulders.

"This is too much," she said. "And to think I accepted that woman's apology. Never in my wildest dreams did I suspect she was apologizing for murdering Edith."

"I don't think she meant to kill your sister," said Nelson.

"Just because she only meant to *hurt* Edith doesn't change the fact that it was her fault that my sister died. Simply put—she murdered my sister."

"It may not be as simple as that. After I read Margaret's confession, I spoke to the pathologist who performed the autopsy."

I cringed when he said that last word.

"We knew a bad fall led to your sister's untimely passing. We assumed it was an accident. Case closed. Now, we have a woman who has committed suicide and left a letter confessing to a malicious act. So now I have to ask questions."

"I feel like there's something you're not telling us," I said.

He sighed, looking ten years older. "The pathologist said there were possible signs of asphyxia, though it's hard to pinpoint if that was the actual cause of death."

"Asphyxia is..." I shook my head, thinking I was way off base.

"Suffocation," Ruby said flatly. "How? And why is this the first time I'm hearing about it?"

He seemed reluctant to continue. "The forensic pathologist said there were indicators in your sister's blood levels that raised some questions."

"The neighbor who lives in the back cottage, Bill Morton, was administering CPR when the paramedics arrived," said Ruby. "So how could she have been asphyxiated?"

"Why did you administer CPR to Quentin Wakeham in the coal mine even though you knew he was already gone?" he said.

"That is what I was taught to do. Even when you're sure they have died, there's always a chance they might revive," she whispered, shaking her head. "So that must be what Bill did."

"But if Aunt Edith was suffocated—how could that have happened?" I asked. "I mean, she fell down the steps."

The inspector glanced at my stricken grandmother.

"It's okay," she said. "I can handle it."

"The report said that Bill Morton found Mrs. Halsey facedown with no pulse. He turned her over to administer CPR." He read his notes. *"She was wearing a quilted jacket, a knit hat, and a heavy woolen scarf around her neck. Lying face down and unconscious, she may not have been able to breathe if something were blocking her nose and mouth, such as the scarf."*

Ruby sagged against me, gripping my hand. "So you're saying the fall may not have been the cause of death. It might've been her damned muffler?"

"Yes. However, the pathologist said she most likely would have been unconscious and not aware of what was happening."

"Well, thank you for that small comfort," grumbled Ruby.

"What if Margaret was still there when Aunt Edith fell?" I said. "She could have been hiding in the bushes on the other side of the pathway to see if her plan worked. And when she saw Aunt Edith trying to get up, she rushed out and smothered her."

Ruby stood abruptly. "That's it. I can't listen to any more of this. You two can talk it out without me. I'm going to bed."

We watched her drag herself up the steep stairs before we resumed our conversation.

Keeping my voice low, I asked, "Do you think what I said could've happened?"

"Margaret confessed to killing your aunt, so why wouldn't she have written that in her confession? Since she was about to commit suicide, I don't think she would have left out that pertinent piece of information."

"But could it have happened?"

"Yes. But before we jump ahead of ourselves, please remember what the doctor said. *'There were possible signs of asphyxia.'* The operative word here is *possible*. So it may not have happened, and if it did, without a witness I don't think there's any way to prove anything was done deliberately beyond what Margaret confessed."

# CHAPTER TWENTY-EIGHT

**Friday, May 8**

*Posted by Katy McKenna*

*Without a witness, I don't think there is any way to prove anything was done deliberately beyond what Margaret confessed.*

Inspector Nelson's words woke me up at 5:35 this morning, which I did not appreciate. Just because the sun had already started its day didn't mean I was ready to start mine. I lay there willing the sleep gods to take pity on me, but instead the inspector's words led me to a big question.

*Was there anyone who could have benefited from my aunt's death?*

I tossed back the covers and trudged downstairs to brew a pot of wake up juice. While the coffee percolated, I tidied the little kitchen and took the garbage out. Then I stood at the stove watching the water bubble up through the glass stem in the pot. When it was the color of dark chocolate, I poured a cup and sat at the dining table to contemplate the question that had woke me. I decided to make a list of possible "benefiters." I opened my laptop and started a new document.

Who would have benefited from Aunt Edith's death?

1. Margaret

I guess she would've had the satisfaction of knowing that Aunt Edith had paid for ruining her life. Trouble is, after Ruby set her straight on that, she became so overcome with remorse that she wound up killing herself. So she sure didn't benefit from my aunt's death. But who knows what she was thinking when she killed herself.

I thought about picking Samantha's brains and wondered if it was too late to call. I googled the time in Santa Lucia, CA. 10:07 p.m.—yesterday. Late, but maybe not too late.

I texted, *Got time to talk?*

A few minutes later, she called. "Hey, how're you doing?" She spoke in the motherly tone she uses when her five-year-old, Casey, has a tummy ache.

"I've been better."

"When're you coming home? You've been gone forever."

"Hopefully sometime next week. Did you read my blog post about Aunt Edith possibly being smothered?"

"I did. And I'm so sorry. Do you think it was accidental, or do you think someone did it? I mean, other than what that horrible Margaret person did."

"I don't know what to think. I'm hoping to get a fresh perspective from you."

"I'll try, but I'm really sleepy so I may not get far." Then she yawned. "Okay. Let me think. Why would anyone want your aunt dead? Hmmm. What about that creepy Nigel guy? He really wanted the necklace."

"But he bought it from Aunt Edith. So there goes his motive."

"He *said* he bought it but did he really?"

"Why would he lie?"

"Indeed," she said, sounding mysterious. "And yet, he doesn't have a bill of sale to prove he bought it."

"All right, I'll put him on my list of suspects, although I have no idea how he could have done it. Any other thoughts?"

"How about your neighbors?"

"The Mortons? Seriously? They've been nothing but nice to us."

She yawned again. "Wish I had neighbors like them instead of mean old Mrs. Hooper who won't let Casey have his balls back when they land in her yard."

"She is such a witch."

"I guess every neighborhood has to have one. Oh well, back to your problem."

"Why on earth would the Mortons want Aunt Edith dead?" I said, feeling protective of them. "She was a pleasant, quiet neighbor."

"True. It's a stretch. Last night I was watching a *Midsomer Murders* on Netflix so I could see what it's like where you are, and the grieving widow of the murder victim seemed so nice. But, oh my gosh. She was so not. So I was thinking that it's possible the Mortons aren't all they seem."

"That was a TV show. This is real life. And besides, they don't stand to gain anything by her death, except her dog Charlie."

"That's it! Maybe he's from champion stock and they can sell him for thousands of dollars, or pounds."

"He's a cute corgi, but I don't think he has papers. Aunt Edith got him at the pound, and he's fixed."

"Okay. Moving on. What about Martini Lady?" she said.

"Really? You think a frail, eighty-five-year-old murdered my aunt? She just happened to be toddling by late that night, hanging on for dear life to her walker as it bounced over the cobblestone sidewalk. Then she sees my aunt on the ground and decides to smother her just for the heck of it."

"It was just a thought. But let's get back to her son, Nigel. He's been pushing Ruby to accept that offer on the house, and when it sells, his agency will earn a commission. Maybe he did it so he could get the listing."

"But why not push the potential buyers to up their offer, instead? Then he'd make more money," I said.

She was silent.

"You still there?" I asked.

"Yes. I'm thinking. Or trying to. It was a long day at the hospital. Then I had to take Chelsea shopping for a prom dress—which did not go well, and that's another reason why you need to come home 'cause I need help with my hormonal teen zombie who wants to dress like a slut. Plus Casey needed help with his homework and Spencer's out of town."

"Homework? The kid's in kindergarten."

"Uh, yeah. I know. It's crazy." She yawned. "Okay, how about this? Maybe the *buyer* is actually Nigel, and he plans to fix it up and sell it for a big profit. You know, flip it."

"That's actually not a bad idea," I said.

"Good." She yawned again, which made me yawn. "My work is done here so I'm going to bed. Just one more thing. Please, please, please be careful. You need to come home before anything else happens. And stay out of burning barns! Seriously. Who does that? Oh, yeah. My crazy best friend."

After we hung up, I texted Mom (thinking she was asleep) to assure her we're okay. Moments later she called and gave me a lengthy lecture about me not having the brains I was born with, and pushing her into an early grave. She's beginning to sound a lot like Grandma.

After promising several times never to run into a burning building again, we said goodbye, and I went back to working on my list: Who would benefit from Aunt Edith's death?

1. ~~Margaret~~

2. Nigel Harrington

I envisioned how he would have killed Aunt Edith: He was driving by and heard her pitiful cries for help. He finds her sprawled at the foot of the steps and was about to call 9-9-9 when he realized that this could be the perfect opportunity to get what he wants—the diamond necklace she refused to sell to him.

Harrington waved his phone in her face. "Dr. Halsey! Promise you'll sell the necklace to me or I won't call for help!"

She feebly nodded her head.

Then it dawned on him that if she survived, she'd tell the police what he did. So he smothered Edith with the scarf and turned her over to make it look like an accident.

Next, he realized that this was the perfect opportunity to snatch the necklace. He knew the door would be unlocked since no one in the village locks their doors. He dashed to her bedroom, found the jewelry box on the dresser, grabbed the necklace, and scrammed.

That could work. But what are the odds of Harrington driving by the cottage late at night at the exact moment that Aunt Edith fell, with his car window open so he hears her calling for help? It was an unusually cold night so I doubt he would have had a window down. And if she'd been calling for help, Bill or Diane might have heard her—although Bill said his TV was turned up loud. But he *did* hear Charlie barking and that's why he went out to check on Edith. If Nigel had been smothering her, Bill probably would have caught him.

I thought about it a little more. "No, the Nigel theory definitely doesn't hold up."

1. ~~Margaret~~
2. ~~Nigel Harrington~~
3. The Mortons

The Mortons had absolutely nothing to gain from Aunt Edith's death. I think she would have wound up selling the cottage to them once she realized that owning a vacation rental comes with a lot of difficulties.

*After reading through this post, I have come to the conclusion that I am not cut out to be a detective.*

———

The Mortons came by in the late afternoon bearing a delectable looking homemade veggie pie for our dinner.

"We figured you didn't have much in the pantry since you'd planned on leaving today," said Diane.

"You shouldn't have gone to so much trouble," said Ruby. "But I'm glad you did."

"No worries, love. I made three of these a couple of weeks ago, and popped two in the freezer."

After a bit of chitchat, the talk came around to Margaret's confession letter. After Ruby told them what it said, they were dumbfounded.

"Oh, my God," said Diane. "How much more can you two take?"

"So that's why the steps were icy," said Bill. "We assumed Edith had watered the potted plants on the steps."

"I can't help but feel a little bit sorry for Margaret," said Diane.

Bill looked astounded. I'm sure we did too. "How can you say that?"

"You didn't give me a chance to finish, Bill. Yes, it was a malicious and incredibly stupid, stupid thing she did, but then to realize you're responsible for someone's death. No wonder she couldn't live with herself. Because of her actions, two people died."

"Two people?" asked Bill. "Who else died besides Edith?"

"Margaret. If she hadn't killed Edith, she never would have committed suicide."

"Really makes you think about the repercussions of everything we do," he said.

"Like ripples in a pond, eh, Bill?" said Diane.

"Bill?" I said. "I remember you said you heard Charlie barking the night Aunt Edith died. You said you were watching the playoffs. But I was wondering if you remember how long he barked before you went out to check?"

He frowned, thinking. "I was watching football, so really haven't got a clue. It could have been ten minutes. Maybe more." He scrubbed a hand over his mouth looking close to tears.

"It's no one's fault," said Grandma. "There was no way you could've known she'd fallen, and it wouldn't have made any difference, anyway."

We were quiet for an awkward moment, and then Diane pulled scissors out of her back pocket. "I thought I could trim off the frazzled ends where your hair got singed. I'm no hairdresser, but trimming might help the hair lay flat. I'll be very careful."

"Be my guest." I sat on a dining chair, and while she snipped, I listened to Bill chat with Ruby. As usual, the conversation came round to selling the cottage.

"The offer for the house still stands at 125,000 pounds, so it looks like Worldwide will be our agent as soon as my contract runs out with Mr. Harrington."

"They may not do any better, you know," said Diane.

"At this point, I'm in no hurry," said Ruby. "However, I do have another option I'm seriously considering."

"What's that?" asked Bill.

"As you may know, my sister was planning on turning the cottage into a vacation rental, and I've been thinking that might be a good option for me."

"This is the first I've heard about this idea," I said. "Two minutes ago you said you're going to sign with Worldwide."

"I know. But nothing's set in stone, you know."

"Wouldn't that be a lot of bother?" said Diane. "Especially living so far away?"

"I agree with Diane," I said. "We're like over five thousand miles away. How would you manage it?"

"A vacation rental agency would take care of things for me. Edith had talked about having a positive cash flow after she moved to California, and maybe that's a good idea for me, too. You know, hang onto it for a few years, and then sell it when the market improves, rather than practically giving it away now."

"Sounds like a big fat headache to me," I said.

"Well I can't do anything until my contract with the Harrington Estate Agency runs out," said Ruby. "But the more I think about it, the more I like the idea."

Diane grabbed a shank of my hair and whacked. "Oops. That was a little more than I intended. Sorry, love. I'll even it out, and you'll never notice."

# CHAPTER TWENTY-NINE

**Sunday, May 10**
*Posted by Katy McKenna*

Saturday
*Part One*

I called Inspector Nelson and asked him to drop by if he was in the area. I told him I might have a new angle on Aunt Edith's death—you know, the "who would gain from her death?" angle. I also mentioned that I had some fresh thoughts about Quentin's death. I really don't want to cause trouble for Tessa, but it doesn't seem right to leave the country without mentioning my monkshood theory.

Surprisingly, he genuinely sounded interested. Or he's just a nice guy who feels sorry for me. He said he'd come by in the afternoon when he's off duty.

I heard three sharp raps on the door at half past four and opened it to find prim and proper Sergeant Anne Caldwell standing at attention. I wanted to say "at ease," but I doubt she would've appreciated my humor.

"Hello." She smiled a little too brightly like she'd been studying that old book, *How to Win Friends and Influence People.* "D.C.I. Nelson had a home emergency and asked me to pop by."

"I hope everything is all right."

Caldwell nodded. "His wife was trying a new recipe for her blog and had a little mishap. Flambéed pears over gingersnaps. The kitchen curtains caught fire, but she got the fire put out before it spread. However, she's a bit shook up." She stepped inside.

"Glad she's all right. We can offer you a cup of coffee, but not much else, unless you'd like a slice of veggie pie," said Ruby. "We need to go to the grocery store, but really don't want to."

"I don't want you to go to any trouble. Do you feel like walking down to the pub for a coffee or a pint?" she said.

"Oh, I don't know. I look so awful." I ran my fingers over my bald spot, thinking it felt more exposed since Diane's repairs.

"It looks fine," she said.

We all know that "fine" is the international safe word for "awful."

"You're very kind, but we both know it's a mess."

"You need to get out of this dreary house, Katy," said Ruby. "But I need a nap." At the foot of the stairs, she said, "Sergeant Caldwell? Make her eat something, okay? She's barely eaten in the last two days."

"I promise, Mrs. Armstrong," she said in a dutiful tone.

Even though it was a dreary, overcast day, I slipped on my sunglasses wishing I could put a bag over my head. Halfway down the block I stopped, trying to catch my breath.

"I'm sorry. Am I walking too fast for you?" said Caldwell. "Would you rather drive there?"

"No, I've been sitting too much and need a little exercise. I breathed in too much smoke, that's all, but I'll be fine. The fresh air feels good."

"My boss said you had some questions about your aunt's death."

"I wouldn't call them questions, more like hypothesises?" I shook my head, snickering. "Not sure how to say the plural of hypothesis."

"Hypotheses."

*Of course, she knows how to say it.* "But let's wait until we're sitting before we talk, okay? Walking and talking seems to be beyond my capabilities, right now."

It was stuffy in the pub, so we sat outside at a picnic table. Caldwell cranked up the faded red umbrella and shifted its angle to shade me. "I'll be right back." She returned with two beers and a menu. A few minutes later, a server came out and I ordered the cream of mushroom soup, and Caldwell ordered chips—A.K.A fries.

"How's Barney doing?" I asked.

"Barney?"

I shook my head. "Sorry, not thinking. Margaret Sullivan's cat. I had no idea what his real name was, so I was calling him Barney that day in the barn."

She glanced down at her navy blazer and brushed off a crop of kitty hairs. "I named him Romeo because he's such a love. Thank you for saving him. I've never had a pet before. It's nice having someone waiting for me when I get home." She smiled, and this time instead of looking like a robot, it was warm and genuine.

The moment passed, and she got down to business. "Are you ready to talk about your aunt's death now?"

"Ever since I heard about the asphyxiation possibility, I've been wondering. I get it that Margaret didn't mean to kill her, but did someone else? God, I wish Inspector Nelson hadn't told me about this."

"There were no signs of struggle or bruising which lends

credence to your aunt being unconscious, and therefore, unable to move when her breathing was obstructed. Homicidal smothering is very difficult to detect or prove, but I believe that if your aunt died of asphyxiation, it was accidental."

"So that's that, huh?"

"To be honest, I think it is. Unfortunately, there are no surveillance cameras installed in that area to prove otherwise."

I pondered that a moment, then nodded—feeling a weight lift from my shoulders. "Good. I was beginning to view everyone as a suspect, and it's been making me miserable."

We stopped talking while our server set our food on the table. When he was out of earshot, I asked, "Have you figured out who started the barn fire?"

Caldwell nibbled a fry, then liberally salted the basket. "It has been ruled spontaneous combustion."

"Seriously? How does that happen?"

Sergeant Caldwell wiped her fingers on a napkin and pulled out her phone, typed a few words, scrolled a bit, then read, "If hay is baled while too moist or becomes wet while in storage, there is a significant risk of spontaneous combustion." She showed me the screen. Wikipedia. "It happens at least two or three times a year around here. You'd think people would learn."

"Ruby and I had noticed the hay was steaming and she told me that can happen when hay is baled when it is damp. But she didn't tell me about hay fires. But what if…" I paused, thinking she would laugh at what I was about to say.

"What if what?"

"What if Margaret didn't commit suicide? What if she was murdered and the killer was trying to burn the evidence by deliberately setting the hay on fire?"

She frowned for a split second, and then reset her expression to noncommittal.

"Remember that we heard someone driving away?"

Caldwell nodded.

"So it stands to reason that whoever that was could have started the fire and locked us in."

"You're forgetting that Margaret had been dead for several days, and there's no reason to suggest it was anything other than a suicide. It's more likely that *if* someone locked the barn, they had no idea anyone was inside."

"But surely they would've seen our car."

"Your car was parked down on the road. Why would that make someone think you were in the barn? Also, the fire investigators found no evidence of the hay being deliberately set on fire."

Her cool, dispassionate tone made me want to pull out my hair. "But why would someone just show up and lock the barn? It makes no sense. At least not to me."

"Katy. You told us that the barn door slammed when you entered. You even said that at the time you thought the bolt had slid back into place, remember?"

"Yeah—but that was before I heard a car outside. What about the back door being locked, too?"

"That lock was rusted shut. Probably hadn't been used in years."

"Have you talked to Margaret's husband yet? Maybe he killed her to collect her life insurance. Then for whatever reason, he decided to go back and burn the barn down. When he got there he realized we were in there, so he attempts to kill us so we couldn't tell anyone."

"Tell anyone what? You didn't see him or anyone else there, so you have nothing to tell, other than you *think* you heard a car outside. Have you ever noticed how sometimes, when the air is just right, you hear things and think it's close by when it isn't? There are times I could swear the train is across the street from my flat, when in reality it's several miles away…"

*Dammit, I know we heard a car outside the barn—not several miles away!*

"Plus, Margaret did not have life insurance, so her husband had nothing to gain."

"But have you questioned him?"

She shook her head. "Since this is an ongoing investigation, I cannot say more. How's your soup?"

The sergeant had pretty much shut me down, so it didn't feel like a good time to talk about my Tessa murdering Quentin theory. I'm sure she would have shredded that to bits anyway. Maybe it's time to let that go, too.

———

We were on our way back to the cottage when we saw a crowd gathering further up the street.

"It looks like there's been a car accident," I said.

"I'm going to have to leave you and run up there. We'll talk soon."

I didn't want to be a looky-loo, so I crossed to the other side of the street to walk home. As I neared, my heart dropped when I saw Caldwell bending over a body in the road.

# CHAPTER THIRTY

**Sunday, May 10**

*Guest Posted by Ruby Armstrong*

Saturday
*Part Two*

*Katy asked me to add my two cents worth. With all this typing I'm doing for her blog, maybe I should start my own.*

After Katy and the sergeant left for the pub, I headed up to my bedroom for a lie-down. I was really pooped. Until I lay down. You know how that goes. I counted the cracks in the ceiling a few times, then gave up and got up.

Our cupboards were bare, so I decided to make a run to the little grocery store. I thought it would be fun to cruise there on Edith's three-wheeler.

I wheeled the bike out of the shed, and stopped near the

Morton's six-foot backyard fence to try on the red helmet dangling from the handlebars. It was too snug. No wonder Edith always called me a fat-head when we were kids.

Diane and Bill came out into their yard and I thought about yelling hello but decided to leave them in peace. Instead, I sort of half-listened to them gabbing while I struggled to adjust the bike helmet. As best as I can recollect—here's what I heard.

"Hey, Charlie boy. Want this ball?" said Bill.

*Woof,* said Charlie.

"Go fetch!" yelled Bill.

"And there he goes," hollered Diane, laughing.

Bill chuckled. "And there he stops. Charlie, don't lie on the flowers!"

"Next time, plant roses. Thorny ones."

"He's a good boy," said Bill. "It's nice to have a dog again."

I gave up on the helmet and tossed it in the basket. I was about to climb onto the bike when Diane said something that grabbed my attention.

"I'm glad Ruby is willing to leave him with us," she said. "Edith was a lovely lady, and I miss her so much."

"Me too," said Bill.

"But that doesn't change the fact that when Edith told us she was going to turn her home into a vacation rental, I felt so betrayed. She literally killed me when she squashed our dream of running a bed and breakfast."

"And now Ruby is thinking about doing the same thing," said Bill. "Can you believe it?"

"When she told us, I was absolutely gutted. Can you imagine how awful it will be? People coming and going at all hours. All night parties, family reunions, drunken bachelor parties. The mere thought of unsupervised vacationers keeping us up all night, seven days a week, chills me to the bone. At least with our B and B, we would've been onsite and had strict house rules."

"How late they can come in, how many in a room," said Bill.

"No pets, no loud music. Definitely not a party house. And we would have had that indoor passage between our kitchen and the B and B."

*When Bill said that, I realized he was talking about that section in the kitchen they said is going to be a bookshelf.*

"This will destroy our home's value," said Diane. "Who in their right mind would ever want to buy a cottage that has an adjoining wall to a party house?"

"We'll be the worst hit, but it will impact the surrounding neighbors, too," said Bill. "Back when Edith was talking about it, I told Old Man Collins, and he said she should be shot."

"He's never been one to mince his words," said Diane. "Everyone else on the street was upset, too. We've all heard about the difficulties other villages are experiencing with vacation rentals. You know, the Taylors wanted to start a petition to stop her."

"And yet, everyone was fine with our bed and breakfast plan."

"Not quite everyone."

"Everyone except Collins. He doesn't like change," said Bill. "He always was a curmudgeon, but he's gotten a lot nastier since his wife died. Now he doesn't even take care of his yard. Rose Cottage had the prettiest yard on the street before Martha passed. No wonder his kids moved so far away."

"Australia is about as far as you can get."

"Just wait till Collins hears about this newest development," said Bill. "Charlie! Quit digging under the fence! I've never seen him do that before."

"I still think we should've made a direct offer to Ruby before she signed with an agent. Before Edith got the vacation rental idea, she'd been willing to be the banker. Who knows, maybe Ruby would've too," she said.

"I know. I know. But catching that obnoxious bloke in the act like that, I couldn't pass up the opportunity to make him give us what we want," said Bill.

*At this point, I was really confused. Were they still talking about Mr. Collins?*

"Well, that plan certainly hasn't worked out, has it? I guess he doesn't believe you'll really go through with it now," said Diane. "If you were to show that video to the police now, after so much time has passed, the first thing they're going to ask is why you didn't show them immediately. The next thing you know, you're in prison."

"I've really made a dog's dinner of it, haven't I? I should've gone straight to the police, but it's too late now."

"We never should have remodeled the kitchen until the bed and breakfast was open and making money," said Diane. "I don't know how we'll ever pay off that loan."

"We'll figure out a way to pay it, love," said Bill.

"With what, Bill?" Diane's tone had become heated. "You lost your pension."

"And you'll never let me forget my lapse in judgment, will you? I was drunk, and I made a terrible mistake. I promised you I would never let you down again and I will keep that promise, no matter what it takes."

*I stood there, hands frozen on the handlebars, afraid to move. I couldn't tiptoe away and leave the bike where it was because then they'd know I'd been there, and realize I heard them.*

"Why don't you ring Collins and tell him about Ruby's vacation rental plan. For some odd reason, knowing how furious that crotchety old man will be actually makes me feel a bit better," said Diane. "I need to go see what's upsetting Charlie. Maybe there's a gopher on the other side of the fence."

*In a panic, I rolled the bike back into the shed, closed the door, and held my breath, praying she wouldn't find me. The yard gate creaked open.*

"Charlie, stay in the yard," ordered Diane.

The gate clanked shut.

"See anything?" called Bill.

"No. I wonder what was upsetting him so much."

"Whatever it is, he's still worried," he answered. "I'll let him out, and maybe he'll show you."

The gate opened again, and I heard the dog's paws scrambling through the gravel.

"He's heading to the garden shed. Maybe there's a raccoon or a squirrel in there," said Diane.

Before Charlie reached the shed, I pushed open the door with a big, goofy grin on my face. "Hi there! I thought it would be fun to take the bike for a spin." I scratched the dog's head. "Hey, Charlie. Whatcha doin'?"

Diane shouted to her husband. "It's Ruby. She's going to ride the bike."

"Have fun, Ruby," he said. "Diane? I'm going inside to make that call."

"Say, I was thinking. Would you like to keep the bike?" I yammered, praying she wouldn't realize I'd been eavesdropping. "I don't want to ship it home, but I also don't want it cluttering up the shed if you don't want it or you need the room."

"I'd love to have the bike. That's very generous. Thank you." She glanced pointedly at the helmet I was fidgeting with. "Wouldn't be easier to do that out in the daylight? Not much light coming through the dusty shed window."

"Ha. I wasn't thinking. You're right. Senior moment!" I tapped my head, then wheeled the bike out and went back to work on the helmet.

"Let me try. I'm pretty good at those things."

I handed the helmet to her. "It's too tight."

"How long have you been out here?"

"Oh, a minute or two." Averting my lying eyes, I petted Charlie.

She pushed and pulled the straps then handed the helmet to me. "Now try it."

I slipped it on. "Perfect."

"Let me see if the chin strap is okay." Diane snapped it closed under my chin and gave it a little tug. "I think that'll do."

"Thank you. Now my noggin will be safe from injuries, though I doubt I'm going to fall off a three-wheeler." I climbed aboard the bike. The handlebars and seat were a little too high, and it was a stretch to reach the pedals in their lowest position. Luckily she didn't notice and want to adjust them, too.

"Where are you going?" she asked pleasantly.

"To the grocery store to get some things to tide us over for a few days. I hope they have some of those delicious Bakewell Tarts. I've been dreaming about them. Do you need anything?"

"No. Please be careful. We have a lot of tourists drive through here, and they can be terrible drivers. You know, not used to the roads and all."

"Will do." I jingled the bike bell. "Bye-bye!"

I leaned forward on the seat, pumped the pedals a few turns, then freewheeled down the path to the street and nearly careened into a passing car. Skidding to a stop, I waved and yelled, "Sorry!" to the driver who gave me a nasty scowl in return.

I wanted to think about the bizarre conversation I'd overheard, so I rode up the street to the church courtyard and found a sprawling old oak to sit under. It was my first time away from the house all by myself. I don't know why, but it felt strange and a little unnerving. I guess it was because I'm so far from home.

A gentle breeze rustled the oak's leaves, and I caught a hint of honeysuckle in the air. A little gray squirrel scampered by and zipped up a nearby tree. In the distance, noisy crows were yakking at each other. Suddenly I didn't feel so disconnected from my Santa Lucia life. I plucked a clover flower from the grass and twiddled it between my fingers as I thought through everything I'd overheard back at the cottage.

I was flabbergasted that a nice man like Bill could blackmail someone. And what had that person done? Obviously, something illegal. But who was it? And why didn't Bill go to the police? And why did he lose his pension? Surely, it wasn't just because he got drunk.

———

At the shop, I loaded up with enough provisions to get us through the next few days and set the cloth bags into the basket. Back on the bike, I pedaled past the shops, the post office, and the library on the main street.

A grumpy looking old man stood in the Rose Cottage's over-grown yard scowling at me as I drew near. I figured it was Mr. Collins, and I debated whether to wave or not, and decided to take the high road.

"Hello," I called. "Lovely day, isn't it?"

"Bloody Americans," he bellowed. "Think you own the world and can do whatever you want."

I slowed down thinking I should stop to assure him I had no intention of harming the village, when he flung a rock at me, hitting my anklebone. The sudden sharp pain made my foot lurch off the pedal, causing the bike to tip over and land in the path of an oncoming car. The vehicle screeched to a stop just inches short of my front tire. The driver jumped out screaming, "Bloody hell! I could've killed you!"

I lay sprawled under the heavy three-wheeler. My cheek ground into the pavement, giving me a ground-level view of the woman's red stilettos. I tried to get a glimpse of her face, but her kneecaps were blocking the view.

"Are you all right?" she asked, sounding panicky.

I really had no clue if I was or wasn't. "Need to catch my breath."

"Maybe I should call an ambulance." She moved, giving me a clear shot of Collins.

"Watch out! He's going to throw another rock."

"What the bloody hell?" She spun around to face him, hands

on hips. "Chucking stones at nice old ladies? Aren't you the big man?"

Collins stomped to the low stone wall bordering his property, bearing chunky rocks in both bony fists. "She's a bloody American —comin' here—tryin' to ruin our peaceful village. Just like her daft sister was gonna do. Well, I'm not havin' it."

The woman reached in the car window and grabbed her phone. "Throw another rock and you'll wish you hadn't."

"Oh? Are you gonna hit me with your mobile?" he sneered. "Oooo, I'm afraid."

"No, I'm going to report you to the police."

Sergeant Caldwell appeared out of nowhere, yelling, "I'm a police officer." She flashed her I.D. at Mr. Collins. "Drop those rocks and stay where I can see you."

He lowered his hands but did not release his weapons.

"I said drop them. Now. And don't move."

Clearly, he did not like taking orders from a woman, but he let go of the rocks.

Caldwell crouched next to me and touched my shoulder. "Mrs. Armstrong, are you all right?"

"I'm fine. Just a bit rattled."

The sergeant dragged the bike out of the way and helped me sit up.

"Grandma!" screamed Katy from across the street.

"Katy?"

I struggled to get up and felt Caldwell's firm hand on my shoulder. "Maybe you should stay down," she said. "You know, in case anything's broken."

"I'm sure nothing's broken." I glanced at the crowd that had gathered around us. "I feel like such a dope. Who falls off a three-wheeler?"

Katy hunkered down beside me. "What happened, Grammy?"

The pretty blonde driver stepped up to Katy and the police officer. "I'm Georgiana Winston. I was driving by and saw that tosser," she pointed at Collins, "pitch a stone at her. He literally knocked her off the bike, and I'll be happy to say it in court."

Georgiana yelled at Collins, "I could've hit her with my car, you know, and it would've been your fault."

Caldwell went to the stone wall and confronted the nasty man. "Why were you throwing rocks at people?"

"I wasn't throwing rocks at people. I was throwin' 'em at her." He pointed at me. "And it was just one."

"Do you realize you could have killed Mrs. Armstrong?"

"What? With a bloody rock? Are you daft? I was just tryin' to scare her so she'll go home and leave us alone."

"I'm arresting you for assault with a deadly weapon." Caldwell pulled out handcuffs. "Hands behind your back, please. You do not have to say anything, but it may harm your defense if you do not mention when questioned something which you later rely on in court. Anything you do say may be given in evidence."

"What the bloody hell? You can't arrest me for protecting my property," Collins screamed.

"I wasn't even on your damned property," I yelled. "I was just riding by on my bicycle, minding my own business."

"You're out to spoil our peaceful village," Collins yelled back.

"No, I'm not, but you sure are." I glanced up the street and saw the Mortons fast approaching.

Collins saw them too. "Ask them. They'll tell ya."

"I have no intention of ruining your village," I hollered loud enough for everyone to hear.

"I heard what you're going to do," said Collins. "You think just because you won the war you can walk all over us."

"What war is he talking about?" asked Katy.

A skinny mohawked boy in the crowd spoke up. "He's talking about the revolution. The American Revolution. He talks about it all the time. He's obsessed with it."

"Are you kidding me? You're still mad about that?" said Katy.

"What if I am? You Yanks think you own the world and can

push everyone around. Well, you don't own Bridleford, and you don't own me, and I'm not going down without a fight."

Bill said, "This is all my fault, Ruby. I should've realized he'd do something daft."

"I'm really confused here," said Katy. "Would someone please clue me in?"

"Collins is upset that Ruby is going to make the house a vacation rental," said Diane. "So are we, and a lot of other people." She gazed down at me—still sitting on my rump. "But it's your house..." she ended with a defeated shrug.

"I've changed my mind, and I'm not going to do that. We need to talk, but not here."

As Caldwell led Collins up the lane to her car, the old man yelled, "You won't get away with this. I'm not the only one who wants you gone. You'll see."

# CHAPTER THIRTY-ONE

**Sunday, May 10**
*Posted by Katy McKenna*

Saturday
*Part Three*

The Mortons helped me walk my wobbly grandma home. In the living room, they got her situated on an armchair. Diane fussed over her, clucking with concern as she tucked a wool blanket around her.

"This is all our fault," she said, sounding near tears.

"How could this possibly be your fault?" I dragged a dining chair over to Ruby. "You want to put your legs up?"

She shook her head. "No. You sit."

Bill settled in the other armchair, hanging his head. "It's our fault. I was angry and called Collins and told him you were turning the cottage into a vacation rental." He faded off, looking forlorn, then sighed. "I don't know if Edith told you about our dream to buy this cottage and make it into a bed and breakfast."

"She did mention it when she visited us last December," I said. "She said you asked if she would be the banker. But since you never said anything to us about it, we assumed you didn't want to do it anymore."

"I have a confession to make," said Ruby. "When I was getting the bike out, I overheard you talking in the yard."

Diane hauled a chair over and sat by Bill. "Is that why you were in the garden shed? I did wonder."

"Yes. I was hiding. I didn't want you to know I'd eavesdropped. Unintentionally, that is."

"You must think we're awful people," she said.

"I really don't know what to think," said Ruby.

"Well, folks. I for one am completely clueless," I said. "Does anyone want to fill me in?"

Diane sighed, glancing at her husband with a sick expression.

"We've been less than honest with you." He shook his head, looking chagrined. "The low offer for the cottage? That's us."

"Are you kidding me?" screeched Ruby.

"Ooooh," I said. "No wonder you kept asking."

Ruby crossed her arms. "I don't know what to say. This is too much."

"There's a lot more," said Bill. "Ruby, I don't know what you heard."

"I heard a helluva lot more than I wanted to, that's for damned sure. Like the fact that you're blackmailing someone."

"Whoa. Blackmailing? Are you serious?" I felt like I'd stepped into *The Twilight Zone*.

Ruby nodded. "Bill saw *someone*—I have no idea who—doing something illegal and has tried to take advantage of it rather than report it to the police. Sure sounds like blackmail to me."

"I think you should hear all of it." He pulled a deep breath. "The truth is, I'm an alcoholic. Not the drunk in the gutter type, but what you would call a social alcoholic. I rarely drank at home, but most evenings I'd meet some mates at one of the local pubs and drink until I was pissed, then walk home. One night, three years ago, I drove to Downshampton and met up with some retired army blokes at the Golden Lamb. On the way home, I swerved to avoid a man lying in the road and crashed into a stone wall. I spent a week in the hospital and then six months in jail for drunk driving."

"He was also fined twenty-five hundred pounds and not allowed to drive for a year," said Diane, flatly.

"Thank God you didn't kill yourself," I said.

"Sometimes, I wish I had died. Then Diane would have collected my life insurance and been financially set."

She reached out and took his hand. "You know that's not what I would've wanted. Not then and not now."

"I had a few broken ribs, a collapsed lung, broken collarbone, and," he tapped his nose, "a broken nose. But the worst thing was —I lost my military pension. I'm surprised Edith didn't tell you."

"She never was much of a gossip," said Ruby. "The man in the road. Was he dead?"

"You'll love this. He was dead-drunk."

"I'm so sorry this happened to you," I said.

"It's Diane that you should be sorry for, being married to a nob like me."

"At first my anger almost pushed me to divorce," said Diane. "But Bill has worked so hard to make it up to me. Sometimes it flares up though, and that's what you heard today."

"The thing is, none of this is really any of our business, so why are you telling us?" said Ruby.

"What we just told you is the reason why we asked Edith to be the banker," said Diane. "We can't qualify for another house loan on top of the one we already have, even though my virtual book-keeping keeps me busy and Bill paints houses and does handyman work. We both have a few years before we can collect our state pension. It's not much, but it will help, and I know the bed and breakfast would be a financial success—so we wouldn't have a problem paying another loan. I feel so terrible about everything. If only we'd been honest with you instead of all the bloody lies. This isn't who we really are. You have to believe me. We've always tried to be good people, and now we've ruined everything."

"Well, you've certainly made a mess of it, I'll give you that." Ruby shifted on the chair with a groan. "Ooo-boy. I'm gonna be hurting tomorrow."

"I think you need to see a doctor," I said.

"Nothing's broken, so there's nothing a doctor could do for me, except tell me what I already know: that I'm going to be stiff and sore."

"Do you want a cup of tea?" I asked.

"Hell, no. I want a glass of wine. Diane, you want one, too? You may need it because I have a few more questions."

"I'll take a cuppa, please," said Bill.

———

After guzzling half a glass of red wine, Ruby said, "Now I want to know who you're blackmailing and why."

The Mortons glanced at each other a long moment, looking loath to talk.

Finally, Bill said, "The day you went on the coal mine tour—"

"Oh, God. Don't remind us about that day," I said. "We should've gone back to California the very next day."

Bill gave me a soft smile, and I could see the goodness in his deep blue eyes. "It certainly would have saved you a lot of grief. That day, I was walking back from parking the car when I saw Nigel Harrington enter your cottage."

"Well, he did have a key since he was the listing agent," said Ruby.

"Was he showing the house to someone?" I asked.

Bill set his cup on the coffee table, shaking his head. "No, he was alone. But before he stepped inside, he glanced around as if looking to see if anyone was watching him. That odd behavior made me instinctively step behind a tree—without even thinking. I felt like something was off about his behavior.

I've never thought much of the bloke, so I decided to see what he was up to. I found him upstairs going through a jewelry box. His back was to me and he had no idea I was standing in the doorway. My first impulse was to ask him what he was doing, but then I saw him remove Edith's diamond necklace from the box. Clearly he was up to no good so I videoed him. He spent a minute examining the necklace under a lamp, then wrapped it in a handkerchief and put it in his pocket.

As he turned around, I slipped down the hall to the bathroom and hid until he left. I watched him through the front window, and when he was out of sight I went home and showed the video to Diane. She wanted me to go to the police straightaway, but oh, no. I had a better idea. I thought that I could use the video to force him to buy the house for us." He scrubbed his face with a beleaguered sigh. "Of course, Diane was against that idea, but I talked her into waiting a few days before we made a final decision."

Diane picked up the narrative. "Then we found out he'd given the necklace to his mother for her eighty-fifth birthday. How could we report him to the police and ruin that? It isn't her fault her son is a crook."

"And is that when you decided to blackmail him?" I couldn't believe I was talking about blackmail so nonchalantly.

Bill nodded.

"I would've loved to have seen his face when you showed him the video," said Grandma.

"Actually, you can," said Diane. "I went with Bill because I thought we should have a recording of the meeting. Do you want to see it?"

"Not yet. I need to digest what you've told me. It's been a long and very upsetting day and I need a clear head before I decide what I'm going to do." She saw the sudden panic on their faces. "Don't worry. I'm not going to call the police."

After they left, I asked Grandma if she really wasn't going to report the theft to the police.

"I'd love to, but then the Mortons will go down with him, and I don't want to do that to them, even though they have been lying through their teeth to us the whole time."

"And pushing the price of this house way down, don't forget," I said. "If they were trying to make Harrington buy the cottage for them, why do that?"

"That was probably all Harrington, not them." She sipped her wine. "No, I don't want to go to the police. Bill and Diane have been through enough. They made terrible mistakes and I don't want to compound them. They could both wind up in prison, and as far as I'm concerned the only one who belongs there is dear Nigel." She handed her empty glass to me.

"More?"

"Half a glass."

I brought back a full glass. "You've only had one, so try to relax and enjoy it."

"Thank you, honey." She swirled the glass a moment. "Harrington needs to pay for what he did. Just how that will be, I have no idea. Yet. But believe you me, that contemptible S.O.B. is gonna be sorry he tangled with Ruby Armstrong."

# CHAPTER THIRTY-TWO

**Sunday, May 10**
*Posted by Katy McKenna*

We were sitting at the dining table sharing the last cherry Bakewell Tart. Like a greedy little kid I kept a vigilant eye on Ruby to make sure she didn't take more forkfuls than me. Of course, I wouldn't have said anything, but I probably would've glared at her.

"Have you decided what you want to do about Nigel Harrington and the Mortons?"

"I think I have," said Ruby. "You know what they say about when life hands you a bunch of lemons?"

"Make lemonade."

"Exactly. We're going to have a little fun with Mr. Harrington. He doesn't know it yet, but he's going to pay me my original asking price, and the Mortons will have their bed and breakfast. A happy ending for almost everyone." Ruby pushed the plate to me. "Here. You take the last couple bites."

I dragged the plate closer. "Are you sure?"

"Since I've been off my regular exercise routine, I've gained a couple pounds, so I don't need any more calories. Plus, I saw you glaring at me."

*Three p.m.*

I opened the front door, beaming my most charming smile. "Mr. Harrington. How delightful to see you." I stepped aside and grandly waved him through the entrance. "Do come in."

Grammy was sitting at the dining table looking like the queen of everything. Perfect makeup, hair artfully fluffed, and dressed to the nines.

"Mrs. Armstrong. I was pleased to hear from you," he said.

She held out her hand like she expected him to kiss her ring. Instead, he limply shook it. "I take it you've decided to accept the offer?"

I butted in before she could answer. "How about a cuppa?"

"No, no. I'm fine." He turned back to Ruby, looking expectant.

"Cookies?" I asked.

"No, thank you."

"I'll have a cookie," said Grandma. "Oh, and tea would be lovely. You sure you don't want tea, Mr. Harrington? It's no trouble. And we do have something to celebrate, don't we, Katy darling?"

"We sure do."

His grumpy countenance instantly bloomed into a greedy grin, like a kid eyeing a bowl of soft-serve covered in sprinkles. "Well, then tea would be very nice."

A few minutes later, the Mortons arrived. I'd invited them earlier when I borrowed their china teapot and cups. But they had no idea that Harrington would be there.

"Come in," I chirped brightly. "I'm making tea. Please make yourself comfortable at the table."

Diane and Bill stood in the doorway looking like they'd rather crawl under a rock. But what choice did they have?

"Mr. Harrington," I said. "Do you mind scooching your chair over a bit so Bill can sit next to you?"

Casting a surly glare at the Mortons, he moved with a harrumph. "Will somebody please tell me what is going on?"

"In due time, Mr. Harrington," said Ruby. "In due time."

I set the tea service on the dining table, and then in my bad version of an English accent, I said, "Grandmother? Shall I be mother?" I've seen this many times in British movies and have always wanted to do it.

"Yes, dear. By all means," she said.

"Do you care for milk, Mr. Harrington?" I asked.

"No."

"Sugar?"

"Two, please."

After I stirred his tea and handed it to him, I served the miserable Mortons. Grandma looked like she was going to bust a gut, but we both managed to stay in character. With her pinky finger up, she declared the tea delicious, and everyone agreed. She set her cup on the saucer with a little wince.

"Sorry. I'm a bit achy."

Diane looked like she might cry. "I must apologize again for our part in your accident."

"I'm fine. Actually, better than I've been since I first got here. You know what they say about the truth." She let that hang like a lead balloon over our festivities.

Finally, Harrington said, "What do they say about the truth?"

"Three things cannot be hidden. The sun, the moon, and the truth."

My turn. "A quote I like is—the truth will set you free, but first it will make you miserable."

"Well done, Katy. Now, I'm sure you're all wondering why

221

we've asked you here." Ruby swung her gaze to Mr. Harrington. "I'm ready to make a deal."

Harrington sneaked a side-glance at the Mortons, who were staring intently at Ruby. "That's good to hear. I'm glad you've finally come to your senses."

"Oh, I have indeed. I want full price."

Harrington coughed a few times, and his face flushed an alarming crimson.

"Something stuck in your craw?" Ruby asked with a wicked grin.

"No." He cleared his throat, glancing at Bill and Diane again. "It's just that you led me to believe we had come to an agreement. The, um, buyer cannot possibly meet your demand. And have you forgotten that this property now has a bad reputation?"

She lightly slapped his arm and snickered. "I'm just kidding."

"Oh, well, then." He looked relieved as he stole yet another furtive peep at the Mortons, who were perched like stone statues on the edge of their straight-backed dining chairs.

Ruby continued. "Tell your buyer that I want ten percent above the market value of the house."

He raised half out of his seat bellowing, "What?"

"Oh, give it up, Nigel. I know you're the buyer. You're going to do what I ask because I know you filched my sister's diamond necklace while Katy and I were on that ridiculous coal mine tour that you arranged to get us out of the way."

The man slapped the table looking gobsmacked. "I have no idea what you're talking about."

Ruby patted his sunspotted hand. "Nigel. Do you mean to tell me that you've forgotten that Bill videoed you in the act? I must say you looked very distinguished as you pocketed the necklace and sneaked out."

Grandma hadn't watched the video yet, but he didn't know that.

"And then Diane recorded Bill showing you the video of you

stealing my sister's necklace. My, that's a bit confusing, isn't it? So, we have you for grand theft, or whatever you call it here in England, plus breaking and entering. Because you sure as hell weren't invited in. The more I think about it, the more I think you're the one who vandalized the house and car, too. You know, to push us into accepting your paltry offer."

"Maybe he even started the fire in the barn that could've killed us," I added.

"I may have taken the necklace." He huffed and puffed. "But I most certainly did not vandalize your property or try to kill you. What kind of a man do you think I am?"

"When I turn you in to the police, they can decide what kind of man you are."

He jabbed a manicured stubby finger toward the Mortons. "They did it."

They both shook their heads, waving their hands in denial. "How dare you accuse us," said Bill. "Why would we do that?"

"To force her to accept the offer, just like she said."

"Ruby," said Bill. "I swear to you, we did not do any of those things. Yes, we're guilty of blackmailing this tosser, and yes, we weren't honest with you. But we would *never* do anything to frighten or endanger you."

A tear trickled down Diane's cheek and she grabbed a paper napkin to wipe it away. "Please believe we are utterly sick about everything that's happened, and our part in it."

"They loathed your sister because she was going to turn this cottage into a vacation rental," sputtered Nigel. "The whole town detested her."

"It's true that we hated the vacation rental idea," said Diane. "But we loved Edith. The only people who were angry were the nearby neighbors who would have been directly affected by it. Everyone else wouldn't have given a toss. Especially the merchants. More tourists are good for the village economy so they would have loved it."

"Everyone knows that Margaret Sullivan committed suicide because of what your sister…" Harrington stabbed his index finger at Ruby, "…did to her."

"Now you've gone too far." Bill flung his eyeglasses on the table and leaped up looking like he was going to punch Harrington in the nose.

"That's outrageous," blurted Diane. "Margaret was her own worst enemy. That's why she killed herself."

Ruby held up a hand. "While I'd love to see you deck this weasel, Bill, I'd rather not have you brought up on assault charges." She paused, then grinned, arching a brow slyly. "Oh, wait. He can't report this to the police because he'll wind up in prison. So go ahead. Flatten his snotty aristocratic nose."

Bill balled his fists and puffed his chest. Harrington flinched, covering his face and whimpering like a toddler. "Please don't hurt me."

"You're not worth it." Bill shook his head with contempt and sat down.

"That's too bad." Ruby sipped her tea, then set her cup on its delicate saucer. "Here's what's going to happen, Mr. Harrington."

At that point, it dawned on me that I should be recording the meeting. "Hold on. I think I'm getting a text." I retrieved my phone from the kitchen counter, sat back down, and held my phone at an angle to record without Harrington realizing it. "Sorry, don't mean to be rude, but my friend Samantha needs an answer right away. Please don't let me stop you. You were saying, Grandmother?" I pressed video on my phone and twiddled my fingers like I was texting.

If looks could kill, I'd be dead from the one Harrington was shooting at me. "Bloody Americans and their bloody obsession with social media," he muttered.

I peeped at the Mortons and could tell they knew what I was doing. It had to be pretty obvious, but Harrington seemed oblivious.

Ruby patted her hair and smiled for the camera. "Here's what's going to happen. As I said, you're going to give me the market value plus ten percent. Then, I'll sign the house over to the Mortons so they can open their bed and breakfast. To make you feel better about all this, Mr. Harrington, the extra ten percent will go to a local charity of their choice."

I panned over to catch the Morton's stunned reaction. Priceless. Then back to Nigel who looked close to going into cardiac arrest. Again, priceless.

"Well, I can't possibly do that. Business has been in a slump. Adding ten percent is pure extortion."

"Maybe your business is in a slump because you haven't been paying enough attention to it," said Ruby. "I've a feeling your pretty, young cockney wife did not come cheap—eh, Professor Higgins?" She paused, tapping her chin, looking deep in thought. "I certainly don't want to be accused of shaking down a jewel thief, so I'll go ahead and report you to the police. I wonder how many years you'll spend in prison?"

She shifted her gaze to the Mortons. "I'm sorry. I know this means trouble for you, but what can I do? Nigel leaves me no choice." Then to me: "Katy, call our good friend, Chief Inspector Nelson. We'll let him sort it all out." She chuckled. "Those horny convicts are certainly gonna love getting a piece of your uppity ass, Nigel."

"No!" he yelped in a girly voice. "I mean, there's no need to do that. I can borrow the money from my mother."

"And in exchange..." Ruby narrowed her eyes and wagged her finger at him like she was scolding a child. "I won't tell your mummy what you did. It would break her heart, and she doesn't deserve that. However, when she passes, the necklace will be returned to me."

"But I'm giving you far more than the house is worth, and that necklace isn't worth more than fifteen thousand pounds. That's what the insurance company paid when I took—" He abruptly stopped with a queasy look on his face.

"Uh-oh," said Ruby in an ominous tone. "Do you mean that you were the one who stole the necklace from your mother's apartment all those years ago? Shame on you, Mr. Harrington."

"How do you know about that?"

"I have my ways, Mr. Harrington."

*Yeah, we eavesdropped on you.*

His padded shoulders sagged. "I will send you the necklace."

Ruby continued. "My brother-in-law said he bought the necklace at an estate jewelry shop. Is that true?"

Nigel gazed at his shiny nails and sighed. "I overheard him talking about his fiftieth anniversary coming up and told him about the necklace."

"So he bought it from you," said Ruby.

"Yes. And I gave him a very fair price, I might add."

"Let me see if I have this straight. You stole it, got the insurance company to pay out on it, then sold it, then stole it again. Brilliant." She shook her head. "Here's the thing. I want to go home as soon as possible so I want this deal done within, hmmm...three days. That means all the paperwork is done and filed. If I don't hear from you by five o'clock tomorrow—telling me you have the money, then your mummy will be hearing from me. You may go now, Mr. Harrington."

After the weasel scuttled out the door, Ruby and I burst into giggles like a couple of seventh graders.

"Oh, it hurts like hell to laugh," she said, holding her ribs. "But it feels so damned good!"

"I almost felt sorry for him," I said. "Almost. We are so bad."

"I can't believe what just happened." Diane got up and hugged Ruby. "I'm simply gobsmacked."

"Neither can I," said Bill. "After what we've done, you're really going to give us the house?"

"Technically, Mr. Harrington, or rather his mother, Mrs.

Harrington, is giving you the house because I'm walking away with fair market value in my pocket. I do feel sorry for his mother, though. You would think that at eighty-five she wouldn't still be dealing with a rotten son."

"Hopefully, she won't ever find out," I said.

"Trust me, honey, she is very aware," said Ruby. "Maybe not about the necklace, but she knows she raised a rat."

"Sometimes, I think we were lucky not to have kids," said Diane. "When you think of all the grief they can give you."

"Or we could have had a lovely daughter like Katy," said Bill.

Diane burst into tears, and Bill embraced her. "I can't believe what you're doing for us. I feel like it's a dream, and I'm going to wake up any minute. I'm so relieved."

"You're not dreaming, Diane," said Ruby. "But there is one stipulation."

"Name it," said Bill.

"We have a free place to stay whenever we come to England."

# CHAPTER THIRTY-THREE

**Monday, May 11**
*Posted by Katy McKenna*

*5:10 p.m.*

Grandma called Harrington and wound up leaving a voice mail. "Either you've dropped dead and that's why I haven't heard from you, or you don't believe I'll tell your mummy what you did. But, you know what, bub? I think I'll leave your mother out of it and go straight to the police. The poor woman will find out soon enough." She hung up with a sigh. "Now what do I do?"

"If you go to the police, then the Mortons will be in trouble. Harrington knows you don't want to implicate them so I think he's going to call your bluff."

"You're probably right." She fell silent, staring out the window.

"You okay?"

"I'm thinking."

At 5:20, her phone rang, and she glanced at the screen. "It's him."

"Put it on speaker," I said.

"Hello, Mr. Harrington. Have we got a deal?"

"After much thought, I've decided you can transfer the deed to the Mortons since you seem to care so much about them, or you can list it with the other agency. But as of now, I am done with the lot of you."

"Then you leave me no choice but to go to the police, Mr. Harrington."

"If you go to the police, I will say you tried to extort me. Who are they going to believe? You? An American who threatened to blackmail me? Or me. A wealthy, successful businessman with distant connections to the throne."

Rolling my eyes, I whispered, "What a pompous ass."

"Mr. Harrington—you do remember we have videos of you stealing the necklace from our cottage, and admitting to stealing it from your mother several years ago. That adds up to two thefts and insurance fraud."

"While it's true, if you show the police those videos it will cause me a lot of legal problems; but as you well know, the videos also prove the Mortons were complicit by not reporting the theft. Let me remind you again, you tried to extort me instead of going straight to the police. So, the way I see it, we're all in this together. If I go down, we all go down."

"Wow. You are really something, you know that?" said Ruby.

"You underestimated me, Mrs. Armstrong."

"No, sir, I did not. But I know for a fact you have underestimated me."

He hung up.

She set her phone on the side table by the chair. "Well, that was interesting."

"Now what do we do?" I asked.

"We take a walk," she said.

"*O-kay*. Are you sure you're up to it?"

She started to rise from her chair and then held up her hands for me to haul her to her feet.

"I'm pretty darn stiff so a walk will do me good. The fresh air and warm weather will loosen up my aching joints and clear my head."

We set out toward the church, strolling in silence. I tried to concentrate on the peaceful sounds of the birds twittering in the swaying trees, the lazy river lapping against the grassy shore, and the rapturous guttural calls of swans in love. I tried, but I was too wound up.

"Isn't it lovely out here?" Ruby stretched her arms wide and inhaled deeply. "Is that honeysuckle I smell?"

"Clearly, you are up to something. Mind cluing me in?"

"You'll see."

We strode through the gate that leads to the Manor House Hotel.

"Why are we going here?" I closed the gate.

She set her hands on my tense shoulders, massaging them. "Don't be so uptight, dear. Just relax, and go with the flow."

Inside the manor, we headed to the bar. Gerard looked like he'd been expecting us and pointed at the patio. "She arrived at her usual time—5:45."

"I don't suppose she's alone, is she?" asked Ruby.

He shook his perfect pompadoured head. "Sorry, love."

"What's going on?" I was feeling very uneasy.

"I had a feeling Nigel wasn't going to be cooperative, so I made a little arrangement with my friend, Gerard."

"May I get you lovely ladies something to drink?" he asked with a cute wink.

"I think a martini would be appropriate."

He raised his eyebrows and smiled. "And you?"

"She'll have one, too," said Ruby.

I started to protest, and she shut me up with, "I know you don't like martinis, Katy. But it's symbolic. You'll see."

We watched Gerard mix our cocktails. After he plopped two ripe, green olives in each chilled stemmed glass, he said, "I'll carry these out and get you settled. I made sure they were seated at a table that would accommodate all of you."

We followed him through the French doors where our unsuspecting quarry waited at a large, round table. As soon as I saw them I wanted to bolt. Ruby must have felt my panic and grabbed my arm.

"Oh, God. What are you planning to do?" I hissed.

Gerard set our drinks on Martini Lady's table, pulled out chairs · for us, and boisterously announced, "The rest of your party has arrived."

"What's the meaning of this?" blustered Nigel, rising from his seat.

"Blinkin' heck! It's our friends from Cali-*fawnia*." Daphne appeared genuinely pleased to see us. "Wha' a lovely surprise. I didn' know you were joinin' us."

"They're not." Nigel stepped away from the wrought iron table, motioning us to follow him. "I'd like a word if you don't mind."

"Nigel? Why're these people sitting with us?" asked his mother in a flustered, feeble tone. "Are they friends of yours?"

"Yeah," said Daphne.

"No, they certainly are not," barked Nigel.

Grammy was seated next to Mrs. Harrington. She leaned close to her and said, "Don't you just love a good martini? It's so hard to find a bartender these days who can make a decent one." She held her glass out over the table to me on the other side. We clinked and sipped. And I tried not to gag.

Nigel hovered behind his mother looking like he might have a stroke.

"Please sit down, Nigel," said Mrs. Harrington. "You're making me nervous."

He grabbed his drink off the table and chugged it before obeying.

"Will someone please tell me what is going on?" said Mrs. Harrington.

"Allow me to explain," said Grandma. "My name is Ruby Armstrong, and this is my granddaughter, Katy McKenna."

I smiled at Martini Lady. "Pleased to meet you." I dug an olive out of my drink, popped it in my mouth, and settled back in my seat to watch the scene unfold.

Mrs. Harrington's watery, blood-speckled eyes lit up. "I've seen you somewhere before, haven't I, Mrs. Armstrong?"

"You must be thinking of someone else. But you may have heard of my sister, Dr. Edith Halsey."

She shook her head. "Is that supposed to mean something to me?"

"It will very soon. By the way, that's a gorgeous necklace you have on."

The elderly lady beamed, touching the sparkling pendant. "Thank you. It was a gift from my son."

"My goodness, how thoughtful and generous. You know, my sister, Edith, had one just like it. And then it disappeared."

"Oh, that's awful," said Daphne. "What do you reckon 'appened to it?"

"Until recently it was a mystery to us, but now we know, and I'd love to share the story with you."

Daphne leaned forward, propping her chin on her hand. "Oh, I do love a good mystery. Go on."

"Maybe some other time," said Nigel bluntly. "I think our table's ready, Mummy." He stood and plunked her red walker next to her chair. "Let me help you up."

Mrs. Harrington waved his hand away. "Nigel, sit down. You're being rude. I'd like to hear Mrs. Armstrong's story."

"Please call me Ruby."

"And you may call me Lily."

"Before I begin..." Ruby caught the eye of a waiter who hurried to our table. "Lily, I'm ordering another martini, how about you?"

"Yes, thank you."

"Daphne, Katy? Another martini?" said Ruby.

"Oh, I'd love one," said Daphne.

"I'll pass." I plucked the other olive out of my cocktail, and then slid the glass over to Grammy. "I'll have a white wine."

"Sir, would you care for another scotch and soda?" asked the waiter.

"Make it a double scotch, neat," Nigel snapped, glaring daggers at my grandmother.

Mrs. Harrington flashed her boy a stern "no-no" look. "He's driving, so please make it a tall scotch and soda, heavy on the soda. And that's his last one."

"Good thing we're walking." Ruby drained her glass and reached for mine. "I'm sure I'll pay dearly for this in the morning, but I've had a rough couple of days—no, make that weeks—so I need it." She sampled the martini. "I'd forgotten how much I like these. I quit drinking them years ago because they don't like me." She set the drink down. "Now I'll tell you our mystery story."

"All right, that's quite enough," said Harrington.

"Nigel! Where are your manners?" said Lily. "Don't interrupt."

Daphne laid a hand on her husband's arm. "Darling, you're bein' rude to your mum."

He crossed his arms, glaring at Grandma. "All right. You can have what you want if you stop this damned charade right now. You're upsetting my mother."

"I think it's too late, Nigel," said Lily, suddenly sounding strong and forceful. "Ruby, please tell your story."

"No. *I* will tell it," said Harrington.

"Oh, this should be good," said Ruby. "If you get confused about any of the facts, I'll be glad to set you straight. And remember, Katy has her phone if you need your memory refreshed."

He tugged his stiff, white collar, tweaked his mustache, and cleared his throat. "A few years ago, I attended a dinner at the club. It was a fundraiser for homeless, abused dogs. The guest of honor was Dr. Halsey. She was a local veterinarian, Mummy."

"Was? Did she die?" asked Lily.

Ruby held up a hand. "Allow me to color in the storylines a bit. Recently, my sister died after slipping on icy steps."

"I'm so sorry for your loss," said Lily, sounding sincere.

"What makes it so much worse is someone deliberately watered down the steps so they would be slippery," said Ruby, staring straight at Nigel.

"Dreadful," said Daphne.

Ruby continued, speaking louder. "Furthermore, there's evidence that she may have been suffocated."

"Why are you looking at me like that?" said Nigel.

She ended with, "The police are still investigating."

I don't think they are, but it was fun seeing the squirmy look on his face.

"May I continue now?" he asked.

Ruby waved her martini. "Yes, by all means, do continue."

"At some point during the evening at that fundraiser, I introduced myself to Dr. Halsey with the intention of asking how I might further help the cause. Perhaps something through my estate agency. You know, a sizeable donation to help the poor unfortunate dogs. However, I never actually asked my question because when I got close to her, I noticed the necklace she was wearing was the same necklace that was stolen from your apartment. Well, you can imagine how stunned I was. Dr. Halsey was a highly regarded member of our community, and here she was wearing stolen property."

"Hold on there, bub," I said. "You know perfectly well that—"

Ruby held her hand up. "Don't interrupt, dear. Let the man finish his tale."

He continued. "Well, of course, I had to ask where she got the necklace. She told me it had been a gift from her husband on their fiftieth anniversary. I knew that Mr. Halsey had passed so I couldn't say anything."

"Why not?" asked Daphne.

"It would have been bad form."

The waiter set our beverages on the table, and Lily said, "Please put the drinks on my bill." She swallowed a few sips, leaving a dark red lipstick print on her glass, then nodded at her son to continue his fable.

"Several months ago, I asked Dr. Halsey if she would consider selling the necklace to me. I told her the history and felt sure she'd want it to be back in the possession of the rightful owner. But she wasn't having it. I don't think she believed me."

"I wonder why," muttered Ruby.

"If she refused to sell it, then how did you get it?" asked Lily.

"I'm not proud of what I did. After Dr. Halsey died so tragically…" He paused to shake his head, looking grieved and oh-so contrite. "I realized the necklace was still in the house and knew no one would miss it. I mean, it's not as though she still had need of it. So I—"

"Oh, my God!" blurted Daphne. "You nicked it?"

His eyes flitted about like a nervous tic, not making contact with his mum's glare. "I knew how happy it would make you to have the necklace back, Mummy, and I wanted to do something really special for your eighty-fifth birthday."

"I've heard quite enough," said Lily. "I would like everyone to leave. Except Ruby."

"It's not what you think," said Nigel.

"It's not what I think?" she said. "It's what I know. Now I need time to think."

"Are you sure you want me to stay?" asked Ruby.

"I do."

"I'll wait in the lobby," I said.

"Honey, go on home," said Ruby. "I'll call a taxi."

Nigel started to protest, and Lily said, "Daphne, please take this necklace off of me and then take your husband home."

"Yes, Mum." Daphne unclasped the diamond pendant and set it on a cocktail napkin on the table, then slung her huge rhinestone bedazzled purse over her shoulder, and tugged her old man's arm.

"I'm not going anywhere," he shouted, yanking his arm out of his wife's grasp. "I need to explain the rest."

Lily's eyes bored into her senior son. "You need to leave, bub. Now."

# CHAPTER THIRTY-FOUR

**Tuesday, May 12**

*Guest Posted by Ruby Armstrong*

*Katy asked me to write about what happened after she left me at the Bridleford Manor. Boy, do I have an excruciating headache today.*

Last evening, after Nigel, Daphne, and Katy departed, I said to Lily, "I think we're going to need another martini. But I have to order some food, or I'll be drunk."

"Pissed sounds good to me right about now," said Lily, gesturing a nearby waiter to our table. "Two more martinis, and some cheese and crackers, please. Oh! And chips. I haven't had chips in years. I'm supposed to watch my cholesterol." Her rheumy eyes widened as her accent took on a less snooty tone. "Hell, I'm bloody eighty-five, and I'm bloody sick and tired of not enjoying anything. Forget the cheese and crackers. I'll have fish and chips and mushy peas."

"Same for me," I said.

After the waiter left, Lily fingered the sparkling necklace, looking weary. "We've both raised children. I have a feeling yours turned out better than mine. You seem to have a close relationship with your granddaughter. You're very fortunate, you know. How many kids do you have?"

"I have one daughter, Mary Beth. She's fifty-three now. She's a good girl. Bit of a hellion as a teenager, but weren't we all?"

"As long as we're not breaking laws, it should be a time of growth and discovery. Heartache, disappointments, failures, learning from our mistakes and hopefully growing into

good, upstanding adults."

"I used to say I was raising my daughter to be a good citizen," I said.

"I like that. That's what we are supposed to do. Perhaps I was too hard on Nigel." Lily hesitated, shaking her silver head. "Or too lenient. I don't know anymore." She sipped her cocktail. "I came from a wealthy family. And I married into a wealthy family, as was expected. But it was a good, loving match. So where did we go wrong with Nigel?"

"That, my dear, is the sixty-four-thousand-dollar question that parents all over the world have been wondering since time began."

Our drinks arrived and a few minutes later, the food. After several delicious bites, and a few complaints about the younger generation, we returned to the Nigel and the necklace topic.

"I've got a feeling that I haven't heard everything yet," said Lily, as she ran a chip through a bowl of aioli. "What did Nigel mean about explaining the rest?"

Feeling like a schmuck, I told her about him taking the necklace from her apartment long ago, then eventually selling it to my brother-in-law. She didn't ask questions, just listened with a grim expression. Once I got through all of that, I explained the deal that I'd made with Nigel the day before, including the ten-percent above market price, and finished with, "Although, after meeting you, I will forgo that. That was just my anger spilling over."

"The Mortons. They're good people?" asked Lily.

"In general, I think they are. The blackmail thing? I don't really know what to think about that, so I guess I'd rather not think about it at all, and just move on." I sighed. "Especially since I was willing to do it to your son. Probably not my finest hour."

"He deserved it. I would've considered it, too—given the circumstances. Now I fully understand why Nigel has been hounding me to sell my apartment and move in with him. He's not worried about my wellbeing. He wants my money. Which I'd suspected all along, although I had no idea that his agency is failing."

"Thank God, I don't have enough money for my family to get greedy about. I plan to die one dollar short of broke. Or as my husband used to say: Live long, party hard, die in debt. That was his high school yearbook motto."

"That sounds like a great plan." Lily raised her hand and hollered, "Party on!" She emitted a hearty, rumbling belch, and clasped her hand over her mouth. "Oops! Excuse me!" Then she tittered, giving me a glimpse of the young girl that lurks within all of us old ladies. "I think I've had a wee bit too much to drink, and yet I feel very clear-headed. But just in case I forget, do you have a mobile? I'd like you to record what I'm about to say."

I plucked my phone from the side pocket of my handbag. "Give me a sec. Okay, ready."

"I am Lily Beatrice Harrington. I will purchase Edith—what was her last name?"

"Halsey."

She nodded. "Edith Halsey's home at fair market value and put the deed into the name of…?"

"Morton. Bill and Diane," I said.

She nodded again. "Bill and Diane Morton's name so they can

fulfill their dream to own a bed and breakfast in the town of Drith-folth, I mean *Bri-dle-ford*."

At that point, she broke into a giggle fit.

"Are you sure about this?" I asked.

"I may be a bit bladdered, but yes, I'm very sure. And when I die, one hundred pounds will go to my son, Nigel Eldridge Harrington. My remaining assets will go to that homeless dog fund that my son seems to love so much."

"I don't think he actually loved it."

"Well *I* do," she said. "You always know where you stand with a dog. They love you unconditionally."

"Nigel is going to hate this, you know."

"If he doesn't like it, he can go to bloody hell."

"Is there anything else you'd like to say?"

She scrunched her brows in thought, then grinned. "Yes, as a matter of fact, there is. When Daphne divorces my son, and she will because she's too good for him, I will help her get that little dress shop business going that she's always talked about. All right then, I'm done now."

I stopped recording and was about to put my phone away, when she said, "Wait. I'd like you to send me the video so I can share it with Nigel and Daphne."

"Oh, he'll love that.

Lily gave me her cell number, and I sent the testimonial video to her.

"Make sure you keep your copy," said Lily. "Just in case."

"You bet I will." I slipped the phone back into my purse. "Are you all right?"

She sighed, dabbing tears away. "No. But I will be."

I picked up the necklace and held the engraved clasp toward Lily. "This beautiful necklace has been cherished by two good women. Thirty-five years ago, it was a loving gift to you from your husband. And then a few years ago, a precious gift from a dear man to my sister. Its recent history may be unpleasant, but maybe you can cherish it once again for what it was meant to be—a token of love."

I stood behind her and fastened the necklace around her neck. As I moved away, she reached for my hand with tears in her eyes.

"When I'm done wearing it," she said. "I'll make sure it passes to you, Ruby. In the meantime, I will remember your wise words and cherish it."

# CHAPTER THIRTY-FIVE

**Tuesday, May 12**
*Posted by Katy McKenna*

I read Ruby's guest post and asked her about the phrase, "the $64,000 question." She told me it was a game show that she used to watch with her family in the 1950s. That amount of money today would be close to $600,000, clearly making it a very important question. Over the years, the phrase has become an idiom. You know, like don't beat around the bush, get down to brass tacks, back in the day.

*Private*

The doctor has approved me for flight. As soon as the legal matters are settled, we'll be jetting home. Not a day too soon for me!

What a relief it is to have the cottage sold and the diamond necklace mystery solved. But there are still a few $64,000 questions that will haunt me forever if I don't get them answered before we leave.

1. Was Quentin poisoned?
2. Did someone lock us in the barn, and if so—who?
3. Who's been terrorizing us?

A little after two p.m., I pulled into the parking lot at Helen's Café. There were only two cars in the lot, so I wouldn't be stepping into a lunch rush.

Tessa was leaning against the counter twiddling on her phone when I walked in. I caught a glimpse of a game on her screen, and after waiting a while to be noticed, I said, "Hi. Remember me?"

She glanced up a split second, and quickly averted her gaze, mumbling, "No."

"The last time you saw me was at Quentin's funeral, and the time before that I was standing right here covered in coal dust and screaming for help." I beamed my sunniest smile trying to keep it light. "Ring any bells?"

She gave me another glance. "Oh, yeah. I remember you now." Then her demeanor sagged, and she cast her eyes down at the counter. "The day Quentin died. Bloody awful day."

"Yes, it was. Is your mother here?"

"No. It's just me and Wendy—the cook. Care for some lunch?"

I wasn't hungry, but it gave me a reason to hang around and maybe get an opportunity to coax some answers out of the reluctant girl. "Sure. Why not?"

Tessa led me to a table, plunked a menu in front of me, and said she'd be right back to take my order. I glanced over the menu and settled on the baked brie and grape sandwich on a ciabatta roll.

After Tessa took my order, I followed her to the counter and asked if she would sit and chat a minute with me. "I have a few questions about Quentin that I desperately need answers to so I can return home with a clear mind. If any customers come in, I promise I won't keep you."

She scrunched her face looking like she'd rather slash her wrists than talk to me.

I decided to go for pity. "Please? It would mean so much. It's really been a rough time. First, losing my dear aunt. That was a huge blow."

"What happened to her?"

"She died."

"Oh. Sorry."

"Thanks. And you know, being trapped in a burning barn wasn't any fun."

"That sounds awful."

"Plus my disastrous coal mine experience. All in all, it's been a horrible trip." I sniffed a few times for effect. "So please will you talk to me?"

"All right. I will when I bring your lunch."

Ten minutes later, Tessa set my meal on the table, then sat across from me. Before launching into what was sure to be an uncomfortable conversation, I took a bite. The melted cheese burned the roof of my mouth. I dropped the sandwich on the plate and doused the fire with a swig of ice water. "Guess I better let that cool down a minute."

"What do you want to ask me?"

"It's about that day, mostly. You know—at the coal mine office. When Quentin was eating his sandwich, he said it tasted different. Bitter. He thought the pickle brand wasn't the same as usual. He said it didn't taste like Cranston Pickle. Was it a different brand?"

Her eyes widened. Was it fear? Guilt? Or was she clueless?

She picked at a hangnail on her pinky. "I don't know."

"The sandwich was meant for Mathew, right?"

She shrugged. "I guess so."

"But instead, he gave it to Quentin, and he died shortly after eating it. Like half-an-hour, or forty-minutes later."

She nodded slowly. "He had a heart attack."

"Are you sure that's what he died of—a heart attack?" I felt like a jerk doing this to her, but that wouldn't stop me from pursuing the truth. "So, help me get this straight, Tessa. If Mathew had eaten the sandwich, Quentin wouldn't have died, right?"

Tessa glanced over her shoulder. "I don't know."

"Are you expecting someone? Your mother?"

"No. She's visiting her sister in Bath."

I inhaled a lungful, letting it release slowly. "Tessa? I heard you scream at Mathew at Quentin's funeral. Actually, everyone heard you. The gist of it was, 'It was your bloody baby, and I didn't want to abort it. It should've been you that died.'"

Tessa hung her head, thin shoulders trembling, tears dropping onto the red laminate tabletop. "Mathew paid for the abortion. I didn't want to do it, but how was I going to raise a baby all by myself? He wouldn't marry me, didn't want anything to do with me, so..." She shrugged, looking dejected and terribly young. "He was my first, and I loved him, and he said he loved me. I'm so bloody stupid."

I reached across the table, taking her hand, and feeling like a jerk for pushing her so hard. "I'm sorry, Tessa."

"I only wanted to make him feel sick, you know? Like I did. Morning sickness, puking all day long for nearly three months. For nothing." She swiped her forearm under her drippy nose. "I loved my baby. I shouldn't have done what I did. I know I'm going to go to hell. Oh God, I wish I were dead."

"What shouldn't you have done—the abortion?"

"Yeah. And the other thing." She lifted her head, looking me in the eye for the first time. "Quentin didn't have a heart attack, did he? I think I killed him. Me. He was a good guy. A nice man. A really, really nice man and I killed him. Oh, God, I didn't mean to. What have I done?"

"Tessa. What did you put in the sandwich?"

She pulled her hand from mine and whispered, "Monkshood. It grows wild everywhere around here."

*So I was right. God, how I wish I'd been wrong.*

"The flowers are such a pretty purple color. When I was little, my mother told me never to touch them because it would give me an awful stomachache. But I swear I didn't know it could kill you. I really didn't. How can something so pretty kill someone?" Her mouth puckered, and the tears flowed again.

Her anguished sobs became so loud that Wendy ran out from the kitchen to check on her. I waved her away, shaking my head and mouthing, *She's okay.*

She wasn't, but at least I now had my truth.

I picked up my purse, patted the girl's trembling shoulder, and left. As I was unlocking my car, Wendy hurried to me, looking distressed.

"What're you going to do?" she asked.

"I honestly don't know."

"Tessa is a really good kid and doesn't deserve any more heartache." Her chin quivered and a tear slid down her flushed cheek. "If you go to the police, I swear I'll tell them that I was the one who did it."

"But we both know you didn't. It'll be easy for the cops to prove that you're lying to protect your friend."

"Maybe Tessa said she did it to protect me." She jutted her chin out, trying to look tough and failing miserably. "I bet you hadn't thought of that."

That's when I realized the girl was in love with Tessa.

"No matter what, they won't be able to prove which one of us did it." Her momentary bravado sagged and she hung her head. "The whole thing was a bloody awful mistake." She lifted her heartbroken eyes to me. "Please let it be."

"I hope Tessa realizes what a good…*friend* she has in you."

———

It's late, and I'm wide awake, debating over what to do. One minute I'm absolutely sure I should tell D.C.I. Nelson what Tessa did. And in the next minute, I'm not.

She had no intention of murdering anyone; she just wanted to make Mathew sick to his stomach. Quentin was an innocent bystander, and telling the police wouldn't bring him back. Right now his family is mourning his untimely death from a heart attack. But how will they feel if they find out that he died because of a stupid, impulsive choice made by a miserable, hurt young girl who'd been sorely mistreated by one of their close family members?

I can't begin to imagine what the depth of their misery, anger, and sorrow would be. No doubt there would be a lengthy trial and the media would be all over it, dragging out the pain, dissecting it, exploiting everyone.

Destroying everyone.

Especially if Wendy were to make good on her promise to confess to save her friend. A lie detector test would clear it up quickly, but she would still be in hot water for lying to the police. What a tragic mess.

Do I have the right to make this decision? Some will say no, that the law is the law. But I don't see everything as black and white. There are a lot of gray areas in life. Given her age and the circumstances, it's very doubtful she would serve any prison time, but I know that Tessa will suffer all the days of her life for what she did. So I guess my final decision is: Let it be.

# CHAPTER THIRTY-SIX

**Wednesday, May 13**
*Posted by Katy McKenna*

*Private*

Last night, after finally deciding I wouldn't report Tessa to the police, I turned out the light, and then lay in the dark second-guessing my decision. Over and over. One minute I was perfectly fine with not reporting the crime, and the next, I was not.

Finally, I gave up on sleep and read my emails, paid a couple of bills, then checked Facebook.

- My bio-dad, Bert, is at a plastic surgeon's convention in Las Vegas and wishes everyone was with him. Yeah, count me in on that.
- My friend, Jeri, was having another political meltdown and I had to put her on "snooze" for thirty days. Three

things I don't share on social media: religion, my weight, and politics.

- My elderly neighbor Nina is interested in going to a feline nutrition event.
- Mom shared an "I Luv Dachshunds" video. I guess Francine has captured her heart.
- My old college friend from Tel Aviv, Nili, liked my comment about her anniversary party: "What a wonderful day and what a wonderful hubby."
- Samantha wants to plan a family trip to Yellowstone, but her daughter Chelsea just got hired for a summer job at our favorite pizza place, Klondike Pizza, and says she's staying home. No way will Sam allow that.

Got a friend request from Chet, a good-looking divorced older man who lives on Cape Cod with his teacup pink poodle and pet raccoon. Denied. Marked as spam.

Josh was tagged in a photo posted by his ex-wife Nicole. I shouldn't have looked, but I did. They were sitting next to each other on a sofa under a pergola. She was leaning into him, beaming brightly for the photo. Her hand on his knee like she owned him. Josh wasn't smiling. It looked like he was talking to someone off camera.

Nicole didn't look well, but she'd taken pains to look nice. Her bald head was covered with a flattering pink chin-length wig; she had makeup on, gold hoop earrings, and a cute floral summer dress. The photo was hard enough for me to look at, but the comments did me in.

"You two look so cute together."

"True love always wins the day."

"So happy you guys are back together."

"Did I hear you're getting remarried?"

"It's about time you two got back together!"

"Love birds!"

What was I supposed to do? Post a comment? Text him about it? Give him my blessing for a happy life? Fighting back my tears, I slammed down the lid on my laptop.

I went downstairs for a glass of wine and found Ruby nursing a glass of her own and watching a shopping channel.

"Can't sleep either?" I said.

"I can't get the Tessa thing out of my head. Sit with me."

"Let me get a glass, first. Hopefully, it'll knock me out." Glass in hand, I settled in the chair next to her. "So, what're we buying?"

"A full-length mirror that makes you look a stone thinner. I googled it, and that would be fourteen pounds thinner."

"Sign me up for that."

"You going to tell the police about Tessa?" she asked.

I sipped my wine a moment wondering if she would approve of my decision. "I don't think so. Why cause more pain for everyone?"

"Sweetheart?" She patted my knee. "I was hoping you would come to this conclusion. Especially after what her friend Wendy said to you. Absolutely nothing good can come from sharing what you know—only more pain and heartache—and it won't bring Quentin back. You should call Tessa first thing in the morning and tell her you're not going to inform the police. The poor thing is suffering enough, as it is."

"I think I'll call her now. No point in making her agonize anymore than she already has."

What I didn't say is I was fearful she might make another reckless, impulsive, life-ending decision. Like Margaret did.

———

We watched T.V. for a while. The next item for sale was hunting boots that make bear paw prints as you walk through the forest. Doesn't seem like a brilliant idea to me, but what do I know about hunting?

"You know that in the last couple days we've opted to cover up three crimes?" said Ruby, holding out her glass for a refill. "Would you get me a little more?"

I retrieved the bottle from the kitchen and poured about an inch into her glass.

"Nigel—the jewel thief," she said. "The Morton blackmailers, and now Tessa. Murder definitely tops the cover-up list."

"And yet, Tessa is the most innocent of the bunch," I said.

What Grandmother does not know is this is not the first time I've kept a secret about murder. But that's another story.

# CHAPTER THIRTY-SEVEN

**Saturday, May 16**

*Posted by Katy McKenna*

Thursday

*Part One*

I still had a couple of questions that needed answering before we left for home. But time was running out, and I wasn't feeling hopeful about getting them answered.

1. ~~Was Quentin poisoned?~~
2. *Did someone lock us in the barn, and if so—who?*
3. *Who's been terrorizing us?*

Sergeant Caldwell had made it pretty clear to me that she didn't believe anyone had locked us in the barn. But thinking there may have been some new developments in the case since we talked, I fished my phone out of my purse to call Inspector Nelson, then thought about how busy he must be, so I called Caldwell. Not that she'd be less busy, but I preferred to bug her instead of him. I was told that neither of them was in and my message would be relayed.

*3. Who's been terrorizing us?*

Someone's vandalized our house twice (not counting Nigel's theft). After much deep thought, I know for a fact that we didn't start the fire in the living room. Ruby is worried that she may have started it because she's getting senile, but I don't believe it. I'm guessing that whoever vandalized our house is also the one (or ones) who damaged our rental cars. Only makes sense.

I decided to take a walk. Sometimes that helps when I'm grappling with a problem. Just set one foot in front of the other and let my mind drift. Every so often, an answer will hit me. If not at least I burned off some calories.

I meandered up the street toward the church. As I strolled through the parking area for the neighboring homes, Bill drove in. He stopped by me and rolled down his window to ask how my day was going.

"I've wanted to take a leisurely walk on the Manor House grounds, and if I don't do it now, I may never do it."

"That's right. You'll be going home in a couple of days."

"That's the plan. Sunday."

"You must be relieved to finally see the end in sight," he said.

"I am. The next time I come here, I will get to see your beautiful bed and breakfast and have some fun like a real tourist."

"When that happens, we'll set you up with a good sightseeing itinerary that does not include a coal mine. Or barns."

"Can't wait." I chuckled. "Actually, I can wait. No traveling for me for a while."

"I don't blame you. Enjoy your walk."

His silver sedan moved, and I heard a clicking sound.

"Bill! I think you might have a nail in one of your rear tires. Better check."

"Thanks. I'd hate to come out later to a flat." He started to roll up the window, then stopped. "Make sure to walk along the river and over the bridge. There's an old grist mill on the other side that I think you'll like."

"Will do."

He parked in an empty spot up the lane. Before he was out of the car, I'd caught up and squatted to inspect his back tires.

"Aha!" I dug four little sharp rocks from his left tire treads and showed him after he locked the vehicle. "These must have been making the sound."

"That's a relief. Thank you."

"My pleasure, sir." Without thinking, I slipped the pebbles into my back pocket. A habit that I've picked up from my walks with Samantha's little boy, Casey. I swear there's not a rock on this planet that he doesn't think is special. Usually, after a stroll with the little cutie, my pockets are stuffed with all sorts of exotic gems that he has gallantly presented to me.

I passed through the graveyard and into the English rose garden, stopping to admire the profusion of flowers. I plucked a few weeds as I walked under the arbor of climbing roses that ran through the middle of the garden.

Continuing across the sprawling green lawn, I wondered what lucky person got to mow the acres of grass. I followed the path along the lazy river heading toward the arched stone bridge that Bill had told me about. I passed by a bench, then turned back and sat to watch the billowy white clouds drifting by. When you live in a drought, you don't often see clouds like that. A soft breeze ruffled the leaves of the shady trees, and a funny flock of nattering ducks waddled by.

My stomach grumbled. Instead of continuing to the bridge I cut across the lawn to the Manor House thinking it would be nice to have lunch on the patio. As I crossed the parking area, a car was driving in. Its tires crunched through the sand-colored gravel triggering the chilling memory of hearing the car outside the burning barn. I don't care what Caldwell says. There was a car there—not miles away, but I guess there's no way to prove it, so I need to let it go.

The hostess seated me in a sunny spot on the patio, but after a few minutes, I asked to move to a table with an umbrella. I glanced around at my luncheon buddies. A young couple in the far corner were giggling and cooing to each other—definitely newlyweds and kind of annoying. Their behavior made me want to scream, "Hey! Get a room!"

An elderly lady wearing a red straw hat had her nose buried in a book—James Michener's *Chesapeake*. At another table sat a good-looking man who reminded me of a brawnier Clive Owen.

The waitress brought ice water and then recited the lunch specials. Fish pie with crushed peas and dill or a tomato, basil, and mozzarella bruschetta with parmesan French fries. The latter sounded good, and I ordered it without looking at the menu.

The little rocks from Bill's tire were digging into my rear, so I set them on the table intending to toss them when I left. While I waited for my meal, I texted Ruby to let her know where I was. I'm sure she was glad to have some alone time, too. A minute later, she responded that she was in the gift shop in the village.

Lunch arrived. While I noshed, my mind wandered to the photo of Josh and Nicole on Facebook, and I felt a sharp stab of despair. I tried to shake it off, but my appetite was gone. I paid the bill, started across the patio to the exit, then returned to the table to retrieve my doggy bag and rock collection.

Back out on the lawn, I decided to forego the gristmill and head home. As I walked down the street, I passed by the Mortons' parked Ford Focus. Curiosity made me halt to check the front tires treads, and I was rewarded with a few more tiny stones to add to my collection.

At the cottage steps, I was about to fling the black stones

toward the street when an odd thought struck me. Practically every gravel driveway or parking area I'd seen in England was either pea gravel, gray gravel, or that decomposed granite that's become so popular where I live.

There was only one place I'd seen gravel like this: Margaret's.

I went inside and found Ruby napping in her room. I left a note on the bed telling her I was going for a drive to clear my head.

––––––––

I turned up Margaret's driveway and parked near the pasture fence, noting the ominous neon yellow crime scene tape posted around the burned-out barn. The left side of the barn where the stalls are located remained mostly intact while the middle and right side were a charred skeleton. Margaret's dusty sedan was still parked near the pasture fence. The critters that had been grazing in the field were gone. Hopefully to a better place, and I do not mean a slaughterhouse.

I spread my blue cardigan on the hood of the car, then scooped up a handful of gravel and dumped it on the sweater, and set my pocket rocks next to the pile. They were identical. The question was: Why was this gravel stuck in Bill's tires?

And then I had a crazy thought. Did he murder Margaret and then come back to set the barn on fire to destroy the evidence? I told you it was a crazy thought. I mean, why on earth would he do that? Could he have been having an affair with Margaret and she threatened to tell Diane?

I laughed at that idea. "Yeah, right. Bill is married to an adorable, sweet woman. There's no way he would cheat on her with the likes of Margaret. I mean, if you're going to cheat, wouldn't you at least pick someone semi-attractive? Or semi-nice?"

Then I recalled a friend from middle school whose dad broke up his marriage for an older woman who looked a lot like Margaret. Kailyn's mother was really cute and always seemed so nice. So what was it about the other woman that drove him to destroy his family? Chemistry? Maybe she was giving off sexy pheromones that he couldn't resist.

But Bill and Margaret? No way.

I looked at the gravel again. Just because Margaret's farm was the only place I'd seen black gravel like this probably meant nothing. It's not like I'd seen that much in the weeks I'd been in England. Maybe lots of houses have black gravel driveways.

I was about to toss the stones, then hesitated thinking I might want to show them to Ruby when I tell her my hilarious suspicions about Bill and Margaret. Chuckling to myself, I shoved Bill's rocks back in my pocket and set Margaret's gravel in the cup holder.

Before leaving, I wanted to take a quick peek inside the barn. My memory of finding Margaret's body is crystal clear, unfortunately, but everything after that is a little hazy, and I've had some pretty weird, freaky-frightening dreams about it. Who wouldn't? I thought that seeing the barn one more time would help get it all straight in my head.

I pulled on my sweater, grabbed my purse, locked the car, and strode toward the barn thinking, *Just one little look and then I'm outta here.*

The barn smelled like a campfire. A fragrance that until that moment has always been like a calming aromatherapy for me, reminding me of camping trips with my folks. Sitting on logs around the snapping fire, listening to Pop tell spooky ghost stories in the dark. Singing camp songs like, *The Ants Go Marching.*

But I wasn't thinking about those happy memories as I approached the stall where Margaret had hung. I stood in the aisle outside the stall, looking in. It was eerily empty, devoid of anything that would suggest that a suicide had taken place there. But in my mind's eye, I still saw her hanging in the cold gray light. Margaret had been in her late forties. That means she still had the other half of her life to live. Surely, there would have been good times ahead. But sadly, she was not able to ride out the bad times to get to them.

"Rest in peace, Margaret." I was so intent on her wretched ending that I had become unaware of my surroundings. Until I turned to leave.

"Aghh! Oh, my God! You scared the you-know-what out of me! I didn't hear you come in."

"Sorry! Sorry! I was trying not to frighten you. I should have called out when I first came into—" she glanced around—"what's left of this old barn. And then when I got close, I heard you telling Margaret to rest in peace and didn't want to disturb your moment. I didn't mean to scare you."

"That's okay. I'm easily startled. What're you doing here?"

"I was returning from Downshampton and saw you turn in to Margaret's. There's not that many yellow Mini Coopers around here so I figured it had to be you. It surprised me, and I wanted to make sure you're all right." She peered into the stall. "Is this where you found her?"

I nodded, feeling a lump clog my throat. I pointed to the beam over the stall. "She was hanging from there." I sighed heavily and shivered. "I think it's all catching up to me now."

Diane hugged me, patting my back like a mama. "You poor thing. This has all been so dreadful, hasn't it? But why are you here now? If I were you, this would be the last place I'd want to be."

I choked back my threatening tears and pulled away. "You're probably going to laugh at this." I took the tiny rocks from my pocket and told her about removing them from Bill's tire treads. Of course, I didn't tell her about my silly fleeting suspicions about her husband. "These stones led me back here and will hopefully give me closure."

"Yes, Bill told me about you finding the rocks in his tire." She plucked one from my hand. "You know, this is very common around here, Katy."

"I figured that, but it reminded me of here...and her. Anyway, I guess I was curious about what was left of the barn, especially after what happened to Ruby and me. I've been having horrible nightmares, and I thought if I saw the place one more time now that everything is over and done with and I know I'm safe, I might be able to lay it to rest in my head—you know, the closure thing."

"Are you sure that's all, Katy?" She held the stone in front of her face between her index finger and thumb, gazing over it at me with a quizzical look. "Or were you thinking that Bill may have had..." She shrugged with a frown. "Something to do with Margaret's death?"

"No, no." I shook my head vehemently. "Nothing could have been further from my mind. Oh, my God. I hate that you would think that."

"I might have thought it, too, if I were you." She gently pressed the rock back into my palm. "I'm sorry. That was a terrible thing to say to you. Especially after everything you've done for us. Please forgive me."

I set my hand on her shoulder and gave her an affectionate squeeze. "There's nothing to forgive." I shoved the hateful rocks back in my pocket.

Diane stepped inside the stall. "It's hard to believe she's gone. I mean, we weren't close friends or anything. Just long time passing acquaintances, but still." She glanced up at the rafters. "I better get going," she said in a hushed voice. "Bill's going to wonder what's keeping me. You sure we're all right?"

"Of course." I nodded with a toothy smile. "One hundred percent."

"And you're okay if I leave you here alone?"

"I promise. I'm okay. And I'm not staying long, believe me. Just hoping to exorcise the darned nightmares."

"I think it will take some time, Katy." She smiled, looking impish. "Time and a lot of chocolate and melatonin, too."

I laughed, feeling relieved that the tone had lightened. "Works for me as long as it's dark chocolate."

"All right, then." She started to walk away and then stopped. "What day are you going back to California?"

"Sunday. Ruby is making the reservations today. All the paper-work is filed on the house, so there's nothing left to keep us here. We'll leave Bridleford on Saturday and spend the night in an airport hotel. And this time—we really will. No more delays."

"How about I cook dinner for you two tomorrow night? A dinner to celebrate the end of an arduous journey."

"And a new exciting beginning for you and Bill. Sounds lovely."

As she walked away, I yelled, "I'm gonna want lots of pictures of the B and B. I know it's going to be lovely!"

I waited inside the barn until I heard her car fade away before returning to my rental. It was a sunny afternoon, and the hot leather seat felt good against my chilled bones. I let the warmth seep through my skin like a comforting heating pad before starting the engine.

One final glance out the open window at the charred barn, and I put the car in gear, rolled down the driveway, and turned right. Squirrels and chipmunks darted back and forth across the road so I drove at a snail's pace. The last thing I needed was to run over one of the cute little critters. My phone chirped a text alert, and when I found a good place to stop, I read the message. It was Ruby wondering when I'd be home. I answered that I was on my way and then continued inching down the road.

I spotted a silver sedan coming up fast in my rearview mirror, so I sped up a little planning to pull over when I found a good spot and let them pass. Next thing I knew, the car was riding my tail. Through the tinted windows, I couldn't make out if it was a man or woman, so I decided it was a teenaged boy driving the family car like a maniac. I increased my speed praying I wouldn't hit a squirrel. Still, the damned car stayed glued to my butt.

"Oh, come on!" I lowered my window wanting to flip them the bird but instead waved them to pass. I guess they weren't in that much of a hurry because they stayed behind me.

And then the idiot tapped my bumper. Now I was scared.

I sped up and so did he. A gray squirrel dashed in front of my vehicle and there was no way I could avoid hitting him. I've never hit an animal before. I felt the tires thump over his little body, and thought I would throw up.

Up ahead, a green tractor—taking up most of the road—was heading in my direction. I slowed to a crawl and so did my pursuer, and as we inched by the tractor, the farmer waved like nothing was amiss.

When I cleared the wide tractor tires, I stomped on the gas. A quick glance in the mirror showed the vehicle catching up to me. Gripping the wheel, I accelerated, but the car kept coming. I didn't look at the speedometer, but I was probably pushing seventy-five on that narrow country lane. The road curved and as I careened around the hairpin turn, I saw a black Labrador sitting in the middle of the asphalt gazing in my direction with a dopey grin.

"Oh, no! No! No!" I honked and hit the brakes, screaming, "Get out of the way!" Then wrenched the wheel to avoid killing him.

My car hurtled off the road and bumped its way down the rocky slope. I hung onto the wheel for dear life, brake pedal flat on the floor, trying to navigate the rough terrain. The brakes weren't slowing my momentum as I skidded through the rocky dirt and grass, but up ahead, a mighty oak was waiting to stop me in my tracks. A moment before I crashed into it, my thought was, *Oh shit, so this is how I die*—making it the second time this year, that I have had that ominous epiphany. Last time a gun was aimed point blank at my forehead, and this time a gnarly old tree was about to call me home.

# CHAPTER THIRTY-EIGHT

**Saturday, May 16**
*Posted by Katy McKenna*

Thursday
*Part Two*

It took a few seconds to connect the dots. Like, where was I? And why was the steering wheel airbag hanging like a limp blood-splattered pillowcase. And how come a tree limb was in the car?

I reached to unfasten my seatbelt and saw blood dribbling from deep lacerations in my hands and wrists. That's when the shakes slammed me so hard that I couldn't muster the coordination or strength to push down on the red release button on the buckle.

Right then, the driver's side door was wrenched open. Startled, I gazed up into Diane Morton's anxious face.

"Oh, thank God, you're alive. Are you all right, love?" She shook her head. "Stupid question. Of course, you're not all right. Look at you. You poor thing. I saw a car like yours run off the road up ahead of me and I prayed it wasn't you." She reached in and touched my face. "You're bleeding, but it doesn't look too bad. I called for help before I ran down here, but I think I should stand up on the road since I could only give them a general idea of where we are. It would be terrible if they drove past without seeing us down here."

"What happened?"

"You crashed into a tree, Katy. Don't you remember?"

I shook my head. "All I remember is a dog. A big, black dog."

"I don't know about a dog, but maybe that's why you ran off the road. I don't want to leave you, but I'd better get up to the road."

"Before you go, please help me get out. I can't undo the seat belt."

"I don't think that's a good idea. You might've broken a bone or have internal injuries." She gently stroked my hair away from my face. "I'm so sorry this happened. What a terrifying experience."

"I really want to get out of the car, Diane."

She shook her head. "No, Katy. The best thing to do, is stay perfectly still until help arrives."

I watched her leave, then fumbled for the belt release again but could not muster the strength to press down on the button. I needed to get out of the car. What if there was a gas leak? I'd seen too many TV shows and movies where a car crashes and then within seconds, it explodes. I sniffed for gas fumes and couldn't detect any so I slumped back in the seat to wait for help.

I didn't think I had any serious injuries but knew that Diane was right. "God, I do not want to go to the hospital again. I just want to go home. How could this have happened?"

I heard a rustling sound in the branch next to me, and a lizard poked his head out from behind a twig full of leaves. He reminded me of the alligator lizards in my yard.

"Hey, buddy. Sorry about this. Didn't mean to crash your pad."

He blinked and flicked his tongue.

"My door is open. Why don't you scamper out of here and go home?"

As I reached over to give the little guy a gentle nudge, cold hands clamped around my neck from behind. I grabbed the wrists, trying to wrench them away from my throat, while twisting to see who was strangling me and went limp with astonishment. She took the advantage and straddled me, wedging her backside against the steering wheel as she bore down on her death grip.

"Why couldn't you just die?" she snarled.

Time did that weird thing it does when you're fighting for your life. Each second slowed to nanoseconds as we struggled. I was frantic for air and growing faint, feeling hopeless as I realized that this was it. The end.

*Oh, hell NO!* A furious surge of high-octane adrenaline gushed through me, giving me a fighting chance. Letting go of her wrists, I slammed her hard on the bridge of her nose and punched her throat.

She tumbled out of the car landing on her butt. Blood drooled from her nose and dribbled off her chin. I unsnapped the seatbelt and slid out of the vehicle touching down on all fours in the tall weeds, just as she started back toward me.

"Can't. Let. You. Tell," she sputtered, hands outstretched like a zombie with a bad nose-bleed.

"Tell what?" I reared up on my knees and shoved her away.

Diane toppled backward losing her footing as I grappled to my feet. A wave of dizziness overpowered me. My knees buckled and I went down again.

The tenacious bitch was struggling to get up for another go at me. I was too weak to elude her, so I took the offense and rolled toward her and kicked out, aiming for her stomach. But connecting with her thigh. I went for it again, landing my shot in her soft belly. One more hard punch with the rubber toe of my sneaker and she lay writhing in pain, moaning and gasping.

Exhausted and woozy, I kept my eyes on her while I crawled through the grass, putting distance between us. Diane didn't look like she was ready to go for round three anytime soon, so I lay down to gather my strength before attempting to climb the hill for help.

———

"Daisy, stop licking me." I pushed away her slobbery muzzle and opened my eyes to a grinning black Labrador. I flashed on the dog lounging in the road. "Go away. Haven't you done enough damage for one day?"

That got me more kisses. Then she (could have been a he) hunkered down beside me and lay her head on my stomach with a long sigh.

From my prone position, I gazed up the slope wondering how I'd ever have the strength to climb what looked like Mount Everest to me. A quick glance at Diane who was lying in a fetal position groaning and clutching her abdomen reassured me she wasn't going anywhere just yet, so I relaxed a moment longer.

"Okay, Blackie, I gotta get up."

A low, menacing growl erupted in the big dog's saggy throat. She leaped to her feet, barking furiously and snapping at the air, spraying long tendrils of slimy spit on me. Not knowing the dog, I instinctively curled up to protect my innards.

I risked a glance at her and realized she was barking at Diane who had managed to get back on her feet when I wasn't paying attention. Good thing Blackie was on duty.

I sat up. "Stop, Diane! I think this dog means business."

"Oh, please. It's a bloody, stupid Labrador." She took a wobbly step and Blackie stiffened her stance, baring her teeth in a terri-fying grimace.

"It was you in the car behind me, wasn't it? You were trying to run me off the road. Why are you trying to kill me?"

"I don't want to, Katy. I really don't. But if I let you live, you're going to tell the police and ruin everything that Bill and I have worked so hard for."

"What're you're talking about?"

"Oh, please. You know damned well I killed Margaret."

"I do?"

"You don't?" she said.

"I didn't."

"And now you do."

"Why'd you kill her?"

"I had no choice. She was going to tell Bill everything." Diane doubled over, pressing her forearms against her stomach. "Oh, God. You really hurt me." She wiped her mouth on her sleeve. "I think I'm hemorrhaging." She plunked her rear in the grass with a loud moan.

"But the police said Margaret committed suicide," I said.

"That's what they were supposed to think. And it worked. Until you mucked it all up." She rocked back and forth. "God, I'm really hurt."

Blackie sat down, pressing her side against me, reassuring me that she was ready for action at a moment's notice.

I asked again, "Why'd you kill Margaret?"

"I had an affair with her husband."

"I thought he ran off with his girlfriend."

"He did. Me." She shifted her position trying to stand up, which instantly had Blackie on her feet, stiffly stepping toward her like she was about to flush a bird out of the grass. Diane doubled over and vomited. "Need a doctor." She sank back down and lay on her side hugging her knees.

"So do I, thanks to you. I really liked you, you know."

"I like you, too."

"And yet you tried to kill me," I said.

"I didn't want to, but you left me with no choice," she whimpered.

"Oh, you had a choice, Diane. A lot of choices, and you made all the wrong ones. Where's your phone?"

Mine was in my purse in the backseat trapped under the tree limb.

"Car. Up on the road."

"I'm have to climb the hill to get help, and I don't know if I can make it." I felt like I could, but I wasn't going to tell her that.

She broke into gut-wrenching sobs. "I ruined everything."

# CHAPTER THIRTY-NINE

Thursday
*Part Three*

The sun rode low in the sky, and I needed to get up to the road. But I wasn't attempting the trek until I had the full story. Who knew what tale Diane would tell once she felt better?

———

*Here it is in a nutshell:*

When Bill was dishonorably discharged, he lost his military pension and had to do jail time. While he was serving his time, Diane began an affair with Margaret's husband, Mark, who asked her to run away with him and start a new life in Spain. That

sounded good to her. No more gossiping villagers giving her side-
long glances everywhere she went, making her feel like she was the
criminal. No more long dreary winters. And no more dishonorable
Bill.

But Diane didn't have the courage to tell her husband she was
running off with another man. Instead, she said she was visiting
her sister in Leeds while he served his time.

After two weeks on the sunny beaches of Majorca, she realized
she'd made a colossal mistake. Bill had always been a loving, loyal,
supportive husband; his only crime had been a stupid lapse in judgment. He hadn't done it to deliberately hurt her. But she'd run off
with a man she barely knew to hurt Bill. She didn't love Mark, and
in fact, didn't even like him that much. Her heart belonged to Bill,
so Diane packed her bags and left the man sipping sangria under
an umbrella on the beach.

Months later, Mark got drunk one night and called Margaret
and told her about the affair. Margaret was close to losing the farm,
so she went to Diane and threatened to tell Bill about the affair if
Diane didn't pay her to keep quiet.

*Have you noticed that blackmail seems to be a favorite pastime in Bridleford?*

Diane is a clever bookkeeper and for a long time managed to
keep their dwindling savings a secret from Bill. However, Margaret
kept demanding more and more money until Diane finally told her
she couldn't pay her anymore.

Her blackmailer gave her two choices:

1. Diane could sell her home and give Margaret the
   money and she'd go away forever, never to bother her
   again.
2. Margaret would tell Bill about the affair.

Obviously, Diane couldn't sell their home out from under her husband. So, she came up with a third option. Margaret had to go away. Forever.

Everyone in town knew about the Sullivans' financial losses, and that her husband had run off with a mystery girlfriend, so Margaret committing suicide wouldn't be a shock to anyone. Plus, she had no friends, so it wasn't like she'd be missed.

Diane used Bill's hunting rifle to force Margaret to write the suicide note and then to slip the noose around her neck and stand on the milking stool. At the last moment, Diane realized she couldn't murder someone in cold blood. Just as she was about to tell Margaret to remove the rope, a cat shot out of nowhere and attacked Diane, burrowing its claws into her leg, causing her to stumble and fall against Margaret. The stool tipped over, and that was that.

———

"Now you know everything, Katy. Will you please get help now?" said Diane. "I think you ruptured something. The pain is bloody awful."

I pushed to my feet. A fresh whoosh of wooziness made me stagger, bringing me back to my knees. I started to stand again and stopped. "Oh, my God."

"What?" she gasped.

I moved closer to her. "In Margaret's phony suicide note, she confessed to being responsible for my aunt's death, but it was *you*, wasn't it? You poured water on the steps to make Aunt Edith fall."

Diane lay there panting and clutching her abdomen.

"Answer me or I swear to God, I'll kick you so hard you'll wish *you* were dead!"

"All right," she groaned. "God, you're so mean. Someone had to stop her from turning the cottage into a bloody vacation rental. But I certainly didn't mean to kill her. I thought that if she were injured, you know, like a twisted ankle, we could take care of her, and then she'd want to sell the house to us because we're caring people."

"Did you suffocate her, too?"

"God, no. What do you take me for? We tried to save her."

My mind was reeling. Diane—dear sweet loveable Diane—was psychotic. "You set the barn on fire, right?"

"Oh, that."

"Yeah, that."

Diane had watched a forensics show on TV and become worried that she may have left some damning evidence in the barn that could link her to Margaret's death—like a hair or a fiber from her clothes. So she'd gone back to burn it down along with Margaret's body.

"As it turned out, the haystack was steaming hot and I knew it wouldn't be long before it caught fire, so I didn't have to do a thing. I was about to leave when I heard people walking up the driveway. I nearly died when I saw it was you."

"But where was your car? I didn't see it."

"I'd parked behind the barn in case anyone came. And sure enough, someone did. You. I prayed you'd leave when you didn't find Margaret in the house, but no, you both had to keep snooping around. When you discovered her body, that's when I knew what I had to do."

"You locked us in the barn and left us to die."

"I knew I couldn't get away without you seeing me, so I didn't have a choice. But I had no intention of letting you die in the barn —you have to believe that. As soon as I got back to the village, I reported the fire."

"Why'd you wait until you were back in town?"

"I needed to use a payphone. Obviously, I couldn't make that call on my mobile."

*So Diane was the guardian angel that Ruby had mentioned when Bill brought champagne over to celebrate our survival. How ironic.*

"Everything would have worked if you'd just quit meddling.

271

Who do you think you are—Nancy Drew?" She winced, looking a sickly gray in the pink-gold late afternoon light. A fresh dribble of blood leaked from her nose. "Now you know everything."

"Well, the joke's on you, Diane. I never suspected you for a moment." I remembered number three on my question list: *Who's been terrorizing us?* "One more thing. The vandalisms. I assume that was you."

"Just the little sofa fire. I had no intention of anything happening to you or damaging the cottage. I only wanted to scare you into taking the low offer. Nigel said it was all he could afford, and we didn't have the money. I've no idea about the rest."

"How'd you get in?" Sergeant Caldwell had suggested that the vandals had used a credit card to unlock the door, so I figured that's what Diane had done, too.

"Edith gave us a key when she went to California," said Diane. "We took care of Charlie and watered her plants."

"How neighborly of you. All right. I'm going to the road now." I stood, still feeling dizzy. I leaned over, head to knees, willing it to pass.

"I'm sorry, Katy. Truly. Please believe me."

"Uh-huh."

I took a few steps, and she called, "Wait. Will you let me turn myself in? I need to tell Bill first. This is going to destroy him, but maybe if he hears it from me first, I can make him understand why I did what I did."

"Premeditated murder might be a little hard for him to swallow."

"I told you I'd changed my mind, and then the cat—"

"Oh, yeah. That's right. The cat made you do it."

# CHAPTER FORTY

**Sunday, May 17**
*Posted by Katy McKenna*

*Today we were supposed to be flying home. And once again, things beyond our control delayed our plans. But as soon as the police tell us we can go—we are gone! In the meantime, I will continue bringing my blog up to date.*

Thursday
*Part Four*

The hill up to the road felt more like a mountain as I clawed my way up the rocky slope. When I crested the peak, I was drenched in sweat and nauseated. As I hobbled toward Diane's car, a tour bus rumbled round the bend. I waved praying I wouldn't get snubbed like the last time I waved at motorists for help. The big green bus squealed to a stop, the door opened, and the driver hopped down the steps.

Her eyes narrowed as she took in my appearance. "Are you all right?" The short rosy-cheeked redhead reminded me of a roly-poly Christmas elf in her green jumpsuit.

"I think so." I pointed at the edge of the road. "Car crash."

"Oh, dear!" She tapped her name tag. "I'm Betsey. Come sit on the bus step whilst I call for help."

"I'm Katy. Katy McKenna." I sat on the bottom step, hearing windows slide open above me. I was no doubt, an exciting bonus attraction for the tourists onboard.

Betsey peered down the hill as she called for help. When she returned to me, she squatted to my level. "I see there's another woman down there lying on the ground. Is she?"

"Dead? No."

"I should go check on her."

I put my hand on her arm, shaking my head. "No, don't. She'll be all right. She tried to strangle me."

That's not something you hear every day, and Betsey's kind expression turned dubious until she saw the blooming bruises on my neck.

"She did that?"

"Yes, and she ran me off the road. And that's not the half of it. She killed my aunt, and trapped me in a burning barn." I shook my head realizing how nuts that must've sounded. "Long story."

She patted my knee, then stepped around me and climbed the bus steps, and picked up a microphone. "Is there a doctor on board?" She waited. "Nurse?"

"I'm a holistic therapist," said a woman in the back.

"Thank you, anyway, dear." Betsey told the passengers to remain seated, then said to me, "It shouldn't be long, Katy. Need water?"

I nodded, and she fetched a bottle from a cooler. The trembles had set in again, and I couldn't grip the plastic container to unscrew the top.

She opened it for me. "I wish I had a nice cup of tea to offer you, love."

It was going to take a lot more than tea to comfort me.

All the usual emergency people soon arrived on the scene. A fire truck, the paramedics, and the police. Before the crew scrambled down the hill to rescue Diane, I told them what had happened, and they gawked at me like I was bonkers.

"Look at her neck," said Betsey. "The woman tried to strangle her."

A few minutes later, they hauled whimpering Diane to the road on a stretcher. The moment she saw me, she said, "I saw that woman's car go over the edge, and when I risked my life to help her, she tried to kill me."

"Give it up, Diane. They know what happened." I rubbed my sore neck for effect.

"I need to call my husband," hollered Diane, as they stowed her in the ambulance. "He'll be worried about me."

"I need to call D.C.I. Jonathan Nelson to tell him what you did, Diane."

One of the officers on the scene, Constable Brown, crinkled his furry unibrow. "How do you know the inspector?"

"We've been working together on some, um…cases."

"You can both make your calls at the hospital." He tugged down his neon green vest and mumbled something into the radio microphone attached to his shoulder. All I caught was, "Nelson." I bet he was surprised when he found out I'd told the truth—sort of.

———

Diane was convinced that I'd ruptured her spleen when I "viciously" attacked her and made sure everyone in the E.R. heard her sad tale. But no such luck; her spleen is fine. I did manage to break her nose, though. Hooray for the good guys!

Inspector Nelson brought Ruby to the hospital, and I spent a good thirty minutes apologizing to her for almost getting killed. Again. Once she was pacified, I relayed the entire crazy story to

Nelson. Of course, at that point, it was my word against Diane's. According to the inspector, she denied everything, although I'm pretty sure Nelson believed me.

Our vehicles had been towed to the police station, and after Nelson conferred with Sergeant Caldwell over the phone, she confirmed that Diane's front bumper was crumpled and bore traces of paint from my rental. That and the purple fingerprints around my neck were enough to arrest Diane.

# CHAPTER FORTY-ONE

**Monday, May 18**

*Posted by Katy McKenna*

Diane Morton confessed to everything, and her crimes have made a huge splash in the news. We've been featured on all the big UK online gossip sites like Daily Mail and The Sun. Turns out several people on that tourist bus were taking videos of Diane and me, and they are not flattering.

I still don't know who vandalized the cottage or the car(s). Speaking of the car, the rental agency made it very clear that they would no longer be doing business with us. Ever. Anywhere. In the entire world. In other words, if we travel to Timbuktu, and they are the only car rental agency in the area, we will have to rent donkeys.

———

This afternoon, we invited Bill over for coffee. The dear man is utterly devastated and looks dreadful. Unshaven. Dark circles under his puffy, bloodshot eyes. He asked me to tell the story of Diane's confession three times. My story was a little different from the one Diane had told him, and I guess he was having trouble processing it. Who wouldn't? I did soften it as much as possible.

"I know she really loves you, Bill."

Ruby nodded her agreement. "Goes without saying."

"But if she loves me, why did she run off with Mark Sullivan?"

"Anger can make us do crazy things," said Ruby. "But she quickly realized what a terrible mistake she'd made."

"She was desperately trying to make it up to you, Bill," I said.

He rested his elbows on his open knees, hanging his head, staring at the rug that still smells smoky. "By killing Edith?"

"She didn't intend to kill Edith."

"But she did. And she murdered Margaret, too."

"Well, Margaret wasn't exactly innocent in all this. Remember, she was blackmailing Diane," I said.

"On top of that, she started the fire on your sofa while I was closed up in my bloody man-cave watching bloody TV. I feel like such a fool. Then she locked you two in a burning barn. Who does that? And I know for a fact that she likes you both."

"Well she's got a funny way of showing it, that's for damned sure. However, she did call the fire department, so she did not intend to let us die in that barn." Ruby pushed a plate of cheese and crackers on the coffee table closer to Bill. "You need to get some food in your stomach. I wish we could offer you something more substantial."

"Can't eat." He shook his head. "You're very kind. Both of you. My wife murdered Edith and nearly killed Katy, and here you are trying to make everything she did sound not quite so appalling." He ran his calloused hand over his gray stubble. "I understand she was angry about my dishonorable discharge and going to prison and everything. But I never realized just how angry she really was." His voice caught on a sob. "This is all my fault. All of it. I got drunk, crashed the car, and ruined our lives."

"Bill, your only crime was drinking and driving. You didn't hurt anyone and you've paid your debt. You are not responsible for the choices that Diane made," said Ruby.

"If she'd told me about the affair, I swear I would've forgiven her," he said. "I would've understood. Now, Diane will probably spend the rest of her life in prison."

# CHAPTER FORTY-TWO

**Tuesday, May 19**
*Posted by Katy McKenna*

We can go home! Inspector Nelson called this morning and said there is nothing more they need from us and if they have further questions, it can be handled over the phone.

We're hopping on a shuttle bus this afternoon to Heathrow where we'll spend the night in a hotel and fly out tomorrow.

Nothing can stop us now!

Hallelujah!

# CHAPTER FORTY-THREE

**Saturday, May 23**
*Posted by Katy McKenna*

*Wednesday*

We had one delay at Heathrow. A faulty light in the cockpit instrument panel. After several mechanics couldn't fix it we had to change planes. That put us several hours behind schedule, but we were fine about it. Compared to everything we'd been through we weren't about to fuss about a little ol' blinking light. Better safe than sorry, I always say.

Ruby's friend, Betty, picked us up at the airport and dropped me off at my house. It was a little past seven p.m., Pacific Time. I was still on UK time, so make that three a.m. Thursday. I think.

The sun was still shining, but I was too exhausted to pick up Daisy and Francine. Let alone spend time visiting with Mom and Pop. I had a snack and got ready for bed while Tabitha gave me heck the entire time for leaving her alone.

*Thursday*

Daisy was over the moon when I walked into my parents' house. She pinned me down on the floor for a good old doggy love-fest. Yelping, crying, ecstatic. Her too.

Mom took one look at the bald spot on the back of my head and sighed, shaking her head. "It seems like every time I fix your latest hair catastrophe, you wind up having another. And your *friend* Diane sure didn't do you any favors when she gave you a trim. She should've left it alone until I could fix it. Oh, well. I've always thought you would look cute in a layered bob, and tomorrow morning, you're getting one."

*Great.*

Francine was happy to see me, but not so happy to leave Mom and Pop. As I write this post, my old dachshund is snuggled up to me in my bed. Every few minutes she exhales a long shuddering sigh. Thinking back on it now, I saw a tear in Pop's eyes when we left. At the time I assumed it was all about me, but now I'm not so sure.

*Friday*

Samantha was seated on the patio when I arrived at one of our favorite restaurants, Suzy Q's Cafe. A cozy place with a Boho vibe and incredible vegetarian fare. She stood with open arms as I threaded my way through the crowded courtyard. After a big bear hug, we sat at our table under the shady magenta bougainvillea draped on the overhead arbor.

"I took the liberty of ordering lunch because I knew we'd keep talking and never get around to looking at the menu." She glanced up. "Here comes a glass of wine for you, and sparkling water for me. I know you usually don't drink wine during the daytime, but this is a celebration and I'm so happy to see you."

The waiter set our drinks on the table without interrupting our conversation.

"But no wine for you, poor kid, because no doubt you have to pick up Chelsea from whatever after school thing she has going on, and Casey, of course."

"Not today. Spencer has kid duty. So I'm all yours." She reached out and fluffed my hair. "Tell your mom I love your layered bob. I've always thought that would be a good look on you. I like the highlights and beachy waves, too."

"You're just saying that because you love short hair and you know I hate short hair. Except on you, of course. Or anyone other than me."

Sam has a flattering platinum blonde pixie that makes her blue eyes look huge.

"I'm saying it because it's very cute on you. It's chin-length, so in my world it doesn't exactly qualify as short. I know you'll grow it out again, but I think you should keep the bangs."

"Bangs bug me, but maybe I'll try to get used to them this time."

Our food arrived along with two empty plates so we could share.

"We have a teriyaki quinoa bowl, a chopped salad, and garlic truffle fries," said the waiter.

Samantha moved the centerpiece to an empty chair. "Just set it all in the middle, please."

After we had piled our plates, I said, "So. No wine, huh? The last time you opted not to have wine with me was because Casey was on the way. Anything you want to tell Aunt Katy?"

Her neck flushed and I detected a little lip tremble.

I took her hand. "Everything okay?"

She nodded, and a tear leaked down her cheek. "Mmm, mm."

"I'm right, huh?"

"Mmm, mm."

"How far along?"

She swallowed hard and sipped her water. "Just over two months, give or take."

"And why I didn't know about this?"

"I didn't tell you because I didn't know before you went to England, and then with everything that was going on there I wanted to wait and share the news in person. Although, I was beginning to wonder if you were going to take up residence over there. I'm amazed you don't have an accent."

"Okay, you're forgiven. And we're...happy? Right?"

She sighed, looking blissful. "We're happy. Over the moon happy."

"Well, I gotta say I am very surprised. I didn't think you were going to have another kid."

She laughed. "Neither did we!"

"Do you have an official due date?" I started counting on my fingers. "June, July, August…"

She put her hand over mine and squeezed it. "December 25th."

# CHAPTER FORTY-FOUR

**Sunday, May 24**

*Posted by Katy McKenna*

I'm so thankful for the money I have in my savings account from selling some of the rare gold coins I found in my attic a few months ago. The rest are locked away safe and sound for a rainy day. However, I'm bored out of my mind and need to get back to work.

A wise man once said: You need three things in your life to be happy: someone to love, something to do, and something to look forward to.

It sounds like an Aristotle quote, but in fact it was Kenny Rogers.

Right now I have one out of three. Yes, I love Josh, even though he is not in my life now. I have my family, my best friend, and my pets. The point is—I have several someones to love, and I'm grateful for that.

Nevertheless, I do not have something to do or something to look forward to. True, I have my whole life to look forward to, but

I'm talking about something that'll get me out of bed in the morning. Like a job.

As far as my graphic arts career—I think that's hit a dead-end. The industry has changed a lot over the last several years, and I feel like the only way I could ever make a decent living at it would be to move to Los Angeles, or some other big metropolis, and work at an advertising agency—where I would probably be considered a relic of bygone days. I feel like a dinosaur at the ripe old age of thirty-two.

Ruby will be back to work next week at the temp agency, so I gave her a call this morning and said I'm available for a new adventure. Make that a boring adventure. I've had enough excitement for a while.

In the meantime, I'm going to work on doing some updates in the house. Some fun stuff—like a new couch. Some not so fun—like an outdoor surveillance camera system. Why? Porch pirates. Someone stole my vitamin order from Amazon yesterday. Seriously! Too bad it wasn't a laxative.

———

Ruby called a little while ago and said she has signed us up for "Goat Yoga" at the senior center next Saturday. I resisted the urge to make a joke about a bunch of "old goats" doing goat yoga. Don't think she would've appreciated it.

# CHAPTER FORTY-FIVE

**Saturday, May 30**

*Posted by Katy McKenna*

I don't own any cute yoga ensembles, so I dug out my trusty old gray sweats from the back of the closet. I should've thrown them out long ago, but every time I put them in the Goodwill bag, I wind up dragging them back out again. You never know when you might need raggedy old sweats. Painting the house, working in the yard. Going to goat yoga with your granny.

I picked up Mom first and then we headed over to Shady Acres to get Ruby. I turned into the complex and stopped at the security station to receive my usual grilling from George, the skinny, middle-aged gatekeeper. He stood at attention with one hand clutching a clipboard and the other resting on the pepper spray canister attached to his leather belt.

With a snort, he stepped to my open car window. "Name please."

I closed my eyes a second to gather my patience. "Same as it was the last hundred times I've come through, George. Katy-with-a-k McKenna. Why do we always have to do this? You know who I am." *And why do I always ask the same question?*

"My job requires me to follow strict protocol. If I do not, next thing you know it'll be chaos. *Utter* chaos."

Mom leaned close to me and chirped, "Hi, George. Mary Beth Melby—Ruby Armstrong's daughter. Glad to see you finally got over that nasty cold you had the last time I saw you."

He mumbled an embarrassed "thank you," and then barked, "State your business, please."

"I'm picking up my grandmother." I held up my hand. "And before you ask. It's Ruby Armstrong."

"Is she aware of your impending visit?"

I rested my forehead on the steering wheel. "Yes. We're picking her up to go to goat yoga."

George paused a sec, obviously dying to ask about that, but stuck with his security guard protocol. "Please wait while I verify."

He snorted again and took two long strides backwards into his domain to make the call. My backseat passenger door opened, and Ruby slipped in and slouched down low, her index finger over her lips to keep us quiet.

Her cell phone rang. "Hello?"

George: "Mrs. Armstrong?"

Ruby: "What? I can't hear you. Please speak up."

George (louder): "Mrs. Armstrong? Mrs. Ruby Armstrong? Can you hear me now?"

Ruby: "What, dear? My hearing ain't so good, ya know."

George: "CAN YOU HEAR ME NOW?"

Ruby: "What?"

Ruby switched her phone to speaker and handed it to me. "Point it out the window at him."

George: "CAN. YOU. HEAR. ME. NOW?"

You should have seen his face. Priceless.

———

*Goat Yoga*

I'd had visions of big nanny goats with long, pointy horns head-butting me into proper alignment while trying to nibble my clothes. The reality was goofy, adorable little kid goats frolicking around the room. We laid our mats out, sat down, and immediately a kid scampered over to check us out.

The yoga teacher seemed to think he was actually going to get some serious yoga work done, but instead he had a room full of giggling ladies and bleating babies. I need to post the photo of me in downward facing dog position with a goat perched on my rear-end.

After yoga class, the three of us drove ten minutes to Pajaro Beach for lunch at the Clamshell Café. We sat outside on the deck overlooking the Pacific Ocean and watched a group of sea otters bobbing on the gentle swells while we waited for our fish tacos to arrive.

"Good to be home, huh, kiddo?" said Ruby.

"Boy, I'll say."

"Have you spoken to Josh?" asked Mom.

I shook my head. "We've texted a few times. Nothing's changed. Nicole's cancer is stable at the moment."

"So that's a good thing, right?"

"I would think so. But he didn't mention coming home. He did say, again, that he'll understand if I want to date. In fact, he encouraged me to."

"How do you feel about that?" asked Ruby.

"I dunno. Maybe what Josh is really saying is he's never coming back so get on with your life. But I don't feel ready to do that. I mean, I fell in love with him and I just can't turn that off. Besides, it's hard to meet nice guys."

"Especially when you don't go anywhere where you might meet nice guys," said Mom.

"I don't do bars."

"I meant like if you worked in an office. Or were taking classes. Or belonged to some clubs. You know. Places where you can meet like-minded people," she said.

"Oh, good grief. What century are you in, Marybeth?" said Ruby. "Katy? Have you considered online dating?"

"Oh, I don't know about that," said Mom. "It doesn't sound safe to me."

"That's how people hook up these days," said Ruby. "Several of my friends have met nice guys that way."

"They've also met some big time losers, according to the stories you've told me." I sipped my iced tea and added more sugar.

"I can feel this iced tea going right through me." Ruby scooted her chair back. "I'm going to run to the potty before our lunch arrives."

"Me too," said Mom. "Do you need to go, Katy?"

"No, Mommy, I'm fine."

After they left, I thought about what Josh had said about me dating other men, but the idea of seeing anyone but him makes my heart hurt. Then I thought about Sam and her joy about the little one on the way. Which brought me back to Kenny Rogers' quote.

You need three things in your life to be happy: someone to love, something to do, and something to look forward to.

*I need a good man to love. I thought I had one, but maybe I don't now.* I remembered the photo of them on Facebook. Nicole leaning into him looking possessive. She wants to remarry. She told me so, and why wouldn't she? He's a wonderful, kind, thoughtful man and they probably never should have gotten divorced. They should have worked through their troubles. This is her last chance at happiness, and she needs to grab it before it's too late.

And I want a family. "Now that's something to look forward to," I mumbled.

"What is?" asked Ruby as she sat down.

"Oh, nothing. Just talking to myself. Where's Mom?" I glanced up and saw lunch coming our way.

"She ran into a friend and stopped to chat." She glanced up. "Here comes our food."

After our waitress made sure we had everything we needed, she departed, and we enjoyed a bite of our tasty ahi tacos.

Ruby set her dripping taco down and dabbed her mouth with a napkin. "I have a little confession to make."

"Oh, God. What did you do?"

She pulled her cell phone out of the side pocket of her red organizer bag. "I need to show you something, and I want you to keep an open mind." She scrolled through the umpteen apps on her phone. "Here it is." She held the screen in front of my face, looking guilty as hell.

It was a dating app called "30-Something."

"Oh, God, what did you do?"

She winced, reminding me of Daisy when she knows she's done something wrong. "I may have signed you up."

I guess my new adventure is about to begin.

# EPILOGUE

## Updates

*Tessa*

A few days before we left England, I joined a Facebook group. The Cotswolds News. After everything that happened in the so-called peaceful village of Bridleford, I was curious about the rest of the region. What little I saw of the Cotswolds was breathtakingly beautiful, and I shouldn't judge the entire area on my own negative experience. No matter where you are on this earth, there will be a few horrible people who do terrible things. Luckily, most people are good.

That brings me to Tessa. She's a good girl who did a bad thing. A rash, stupid, impulsive decision that had a terrible consequence. As it turns out, she could not live with her guilt, and she turned herself into the police.

Wendy made good on her promise and also confessed to the police.

Now, the media is having a heyday with the story, just as I predicted. My heart goes out to all the victims of this tragedy.

*Vandalisms*

Ruby got an email from D.C.I. Nelson. It turns out that crotchety old Mr. Collins was the mastermind of the vandalisms. He had hired a few teenage boys to do his dirty work. All the rowdies have been rounded up and are doing one hundred hours of community cleanup. Collins had to pay a hefty fine, and (I love this) he must do two hundred hours of community service at the visitor's center—welcoming tourists and answering questions.

Who knows? Maybe getting out of the house and talking to friendly people may be just the right medicine for him. Or it'll kill him.

*Francine*

Since I've been back she has been spending her days by the front door whining and sighing dramatically. She's an old girl who lost her longtime daddy, and just because I was the one who rescued her from the dog pound doesn't mean she has to stay with me. The heart wants what the heart wants, and she wants my father. So, tonight I'm taking her home.

I don't know who's going to cry the most. Me or Pop.

# AFTERWORD

Dear Readers,

Like most authors, much of what I write comes from my life. Like Katy's horrible drive into London on a rainy Saturday night.

I was traveling with my husband, Mike, and our plane had arrived a few hours late at Heathrow. We had rented an ancient stone cottage in the Cotswolds, located in the rural area of south central England. But like Katy and Ruby, we wound up on the road leading into downtown London.

In the dark. On a Saturday night. In the rain.

And I was driving—on the wrong side of the road, on the wrong side of the car.

At one point, we got stuck on the inside lane of a busy five or six lane roundabout. Everyone was zooming past me, and it took forever to work my way out to the outer lane. Once there, Mike kept yelling, "Take that exit! Take the next exit!" Finally, I mustered up my courage and took an exit, but we were hopelessly lost, and I was a frazzled mess. I ended up parking on a side street sidewalk, crying, "I can't drive anymore. I'm done." I still have bad dreams about it.

*The Coal Mine Tour*

Our friendly neighbors in the cottage behind us invited us on the tour. It was just as I described right down to the one key to the rusty padlock. Once we were deep in the bowels of the mine crawling on our hands and knees, I began to wonder what we were doing in this scary place. It was just my husband, the neighbors, the guide, and me.

Then it dawned on me that no one else on earth knew we were in there, and we barely knew the people who'd invited us. What if they were in cahoots with the tour guide to rob us and then abandon us in the mine? What if this was something they did to all the people who rented our cottage? Like their own little "cottage industry."

We all went for lunch after and had a good laugh over my fearful thoughts. But our neighbors did think it was a pretty good idea. They were also thrilled when I told them they would be the bad guys in my fourth book.

Respectfully yours,
Pamela

*P.S.: When we got home from England, I received a seventy-five-pound ticket in the mail for driving in London without a permit!*

———

Did you know that Indie writers live for your kind reviews?
In fact, a good review is like a double shot of espresso for us.
It keeps us going for days!
So, if you enjoyed this book,
please leave a short review on Amazon.
*Thank you!*

# ABOUT THE AUTHOR

I live on the California Central Coast with my husband, Mike, and our furry canine kids. I enjoy gardening, reading, yoga, riding my bike, playing guitar, binge-watching TV shows (especially British crime dramas and period pieces), and goofing around with our three awesome grandkids.

## Pamelafrostdennis.com

---

### Recipes from the books
are available on my website
Try the Peanut Butter Cookies.
I never was a fan until I tried this recipe.
Incredible.

*Our newest family member.*

**Learn about my other books
on the next page.**

*The Fifth Book
in the Murder Blog Mysteries
will be out in 2020*

# ALSO BY PAMELA FROST DENNIS

## The Murder Blog Mysteries

### DEAD GIRLS DON'T BLOG
*Book #1 in the Murder Blog Mysteries*

Katy McKenna's life takes a dramatic turn when she stumbles upon a newspaper story about the upcoming parole hearing for one of the men who raped and murdered her high school friend, sixteen years ago. Fearing he could soon be set free to prey on other innocent young girls, Katy sets out to make sure this doesn't happen, not realizing she might not survive to blog about it.

––––––

### BETTER DEAD THAN WED
*Book #2 in the Murder Blog Mysteries*

Katy McKenna has had enough near-death experiences and heartache to last a lifetime. Now all she wants to do is get her career back on track, find a nice guy, and live happily-ever-after. But when she hears about a man maliciously exposing innocent young women to HIV, she is compelled to put her plans on hold to stop him.

Meanwhile, Katy's mother is forced to reveal a shattering childhood trauma that has come back to haunt her; her obnoxious baby sister is moving in, and her scuzzy was-band is stalking her.

And she's beginning to wonder why every rotten person she has recently heard about has suddenly dropped dead. Is it divine providence? Or is it murder?

———

## COINS AND CADAVERS
*Book #3 in the Murder Blog Mysteries*

While battling a furry vermin invasion in the spooky attic of her old house, Katy discovers a vintage wooden chest hidden behind a wall. Although everyone assures her the box is legally hers, its incredible contents compel Katy to search for the rightful owner. Meanwhile, she takes a temp job assisting her hunky P.I. neighbor, Josh Draper. The assignment: Trap a sleazy wife-cheater. Something Katy knows about all too well from personal experience. During a cozy stakeout in Draper's two-seater, things get awkward as the sizzling tension builds. Who will make the first move?

Since she's already been searching online for past owners of her home, Grandma Ruby asks Katy to use her sleuthing skills to discover what happened to her bigamist great-great grandfather. Katy's quest leads her to find an extended family she never knew existed.

Family secrets are revealed, for better or worse....
Romance blossoms, for better or worse....

And Katy's good intentions lead her into
a terrifying dilemma she may not survive.

Made in the USA
San Bernardino, CA
20 April 2020

68705249R00188